"I intend to see, kiss and lick every glorious inch of you between now and morning," Josh said

Mandy felt a blush burning her skin. "It's already morning, if you haven't noticed."

He smiled, crinkle lines appearing in the corners of his bedroom blue eyes. "In that case, I'd better get busy unwrapping my present." He dipped his head to kiss her throat, and at the same time reached behind to unhook her bra. Moments later he had her breasts in his hands. "So soft, so beautiful," he whispered reverently. Then he bent his head to her breast and took the tip between his lips.

Oh-my-God. Tipping her head back, Mandy desperately tried to gather her thoughts. She knew Josh was safe for the time being. After the holiday she would put her police training to work and root out the mafia hit man before he could hurt Josh again. In the meantime, all she had to do was keep Josh with her at all times. Not exactly a hardship...

"Is that a pistol in your pocket, Officer, or are you just happy to see me?"

She followed his gaze down to her gun belt and blushed. For the first time in five years on the job, she'd forgotten she was wearing her weapon. She must really be far gone....

She tweaked the front of his pants. "I thought that was my line...."

Blaze™

Dear Reader,

Sometimes, as the saying goes, Christmas comes early. For me, I'm feeling so absolutely blessed to be a member of the Harlequin Blaze family. *It's a Wonderfully Sexy Life*, my Blaze debut, is also my very first contemporary romance and my very first holiday theme book.

When Baltimore police officer Mandy Delinski finds herself saddled with an unwanted overtime assignment on Christmas Eve, she soon learns that sometimes the universe drops gifts into our path at the most unexpected times. In Mandy's case, the early Christmas gift is a six-foot-four bartender who happens to be a thirtysomething dead ringer for England's Prince William.

Only, Josh is no bartender. Technology mogul turned federally protected witness, Josh Thornton knows the very last thing he should do is get involved with a feisty, red-haired lady cop the week before he's to go back to his native Boston to testify at his mafia brother-in-law's trial. But that doesn't stop him....

When Josh and Mandy's Christmas Eve date takes an unexpected turn, it takes a wish made on the New Year's new moon to turn the situation around—and the clock back one week. Against all logic, Mandy now has the chance to track down a mafia hit man and save the life of her dream man. But then like George Bailey in *It's a Wonderful Life*, sometimes the very best gift we can give ourselves at Christmas is the permission to close our eyes and dare to believe.

Here's wishing you a wonderful holiday season.

Hope Tarr

IT'S A WONDERFULLY SEXY LIFE
Hope Tarr

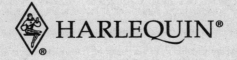

HARLEQUIN®

TORONTO • NEW YORK • LONDON
AMSTERDAM • PARIS • SYDNEY • HAMBURG
STOCKHOLM • ATHENS • TOKYO • MILAN • MADRID
PRAGUE • WARSAW • BUDAPEST • AUCKLAND

ISBN-13: 978-0-373-79297-9
ISBN-10:   0-373-79297-2

IT'S A WONDERFULLY SEXY LIFE

This edition published by arrangement with Harlequin Books S.A.

® and TM are trademarks of the publisher. Trademarks indicated with
® are registered in the United States Patent and Trademark Office, the
Canadian Trade Marks Office and in other countries.

www.eHarlequin.com

Printed in U.S.A.

ABOUT THE AUTHOR

Hope Tarr is the award-winning author of several romance novels. *It's a Wonderfully Sexy Life* is her first contemporary romance novel and her debut with the Harlequin Blaze line. When not writing, Hope indulges her passions for feline rescue and historic preservation. Look for her next Extreme Blaze novel, *The Haunting,* in bookstores next April. And while you're waiting, don't forget to enter Hope's monthly contest. Visit her online at www.hopetarr.com.

For my friend, Susan Shaver; just...well, because.

Acknowledgments

My sincere thanks to Detective Donny Moses of the Baltimore Police Department's Public Information Office, Larry Harmel of the Maryland Chiefs of Police Association, and Anne Mannix, Director of Public Relations, Baltimore Museum of Art, for so patiently putting up with my many questions. Any errors, including those willfully committed in the service of "artistic license" are, of course, entirely my own.

Prologue

January 2007

Dear Diary: (pretty hokey, I know, but since it's a brand-new year with a brand-new diary, I figured I might as well get with the program—or in this case, the format—straight from the start, instead of what I used to do, which was carry it around with me and scribble messy notes while on break in the car).

The thing is, every time I sit down to write about the here and now it gets all jumbled up with the past, the past month that is. I've finally come to grips with the fact that before I can turn over that proverbial "new leaf" on my life, I'm going to have to get the whole crazy story out of my system, and down on paper, so here goes….

The saying that "hindsight is twenty-twenty" holds true for good reason. Looking back a month to Christmas Eve 2006, I can see I'd lost my fa la la vibe along with my groove thing. In fairness, it wasn't the holiday season getting me down so much as where my life was going—make that, not going. The friggin' 2006 diary I'd gotten as a thirtieth birthday present from my best friend, Suz, wasn't exactly a mood elevator, either. I didn't need a nearly empty journal to tell me I was a big fat failure (literally!). Still single, still overweight, and still living with my mom and pop in their Highland Town row house in East Baltimore City, I felt like a female Drew Carey, one of those puffy, pathetic adults I used to secretly make fun of as a kid and swear, absolutely swear, I'd never become.

And then there was my so-called "career." Though I'd joined the city police force five years ago, it was starting to look like my dream of making detective was destined to stay just that—a dream. Whether it was falling one push-up short on the PT or freezing on the written exam, I just couldn't seem to make the grade. On Christmas Eve as I crossed the squad house's cement floor to sign out for the night, I could almost believe the ticking of the wall clock was meant personally for me.

Thing is, holiday humbug was a new experience for me. Before I'd always gone nuts over anything to do with Christmas, from the stale store-bought fruit cake to the burned sugar cookies to the quirky (okay, totally humiliating) holiday sweaters my mom buys me every year to wear on Christmas Day. (Just how sexy can a girl feel with friggin' Santa Claus or a blinking Christmas tree riding her turkey and mashed potato stuffed gut?) Okay, so maybe the sweaters aren't so great, but I love everything else about the season, especially the holiday-themed cartoons and movies. My hands-down favorite Christmas flick has always been It's a Wonderful Life. When Jimmy Stewart's George Bailey stands ready to jump off that bridge on Christmas Eve, who can't help getting a tear in their eye? For me, the scene stealer in that film is the guardian angel sent down to earth to earn his wings by helping poor, down-on-his-luck George see how terrible life would turn out for his loved ones if he'd never been born.

My own personal guardian angel announced himself not with the tinkling of an angel's bell but with a very earthy belting out of, "Yo, Delinski, not so fast."

I love almost everything that goes along with the job from the sacred mission to protect and preserve citizens' lives and property to the fact that Baltimore being the friendly neighborhood town it is, a cop hardly ever has to buy her own cup of coffee. Still, sometimes I miss the little social niceties you give up when you sign on to work in a macho profession like law enforcement, such as being called by my first name, Amanda, or better yet, my nickname, Mandy.

Biting back an "Oh, shit," I turned around to see the overtime supervisor, Sergeant Bob Boblitz, bearing down on me, piggy-eyed gaze honing in on me like I was a target at firearms practice.

"Somethin's come up, special detail at the BMA. I need you there pronto. There was a bomb threat earlier this week, totally bogus but the museum director, who is stuck way up the mayor's ass, is pissing in his pants to make sure nothing goes wrong tonight."

Emotional blackmail or outright bribery, either way I knew my goose, make that my Christmas goose, was cooked. Teeth gritted, I still couldn't keep from asking, "But what could be going on tonight? It's Christmas Eve."

He shrugged, which did scary things to the brass buttons straining the front of his blue uniform. No sylph myself, I ordinarily overlook that sort of figure flaw in my fellow humans, but then again in our five years working cheek-to-jowl in the city's southeastern precinct, Sergeant Boblitz hadn't exactly shown himself to be an angel of mercy where I was concerned.

"I dunno, one of those artsy fartsy shindigs, and seeing as the museum is among the city's leading cultural attractions et cetera et cetera, the department has a vested interest in making sure tonight goes off without a hitch—make that a boom." He exploded with laughter, bulldog face lighting up the Day-Glo red of Rudolph's nose. "Seeing as you're so gung-ho on making detective, I know you won't want to pass up this opportunity to distinguish yourself."

Opportunity, my ass. Standing guard over a bunch of stuck-up blue hairs noshing on crab croquettes and slugging back plastic cups of chardonnay was hardly a résumé booster. On the other hand, the extra money would definitely come in handy when those Christmas-related credit-card charges rolled in. Beyond that, I just had this crazy gut sense I was meant to go.

Giving in to it, I said, "Okay, I'll do it."

Even now I can't say how or why, but walking out the squad house door to the freezing parking lot that night, somehow I knew, just *knew*, I was charting a new course, taking a step toward a life I couldn't yet begin to imagine. But then that's what second chances are, a leap of faith, a shot in the dark. Rare as four-leaf clovers or shooting stars, when one comes your way you can stubbornly stay on the path to Planet Nowhere or stop, change direction and forge ahead into the unknown.

It all boils down to faith, blind faith. Like George Bailey standing on that bridge or Dorothy clicking the heels of those ruby slippers, sometimes you have to close your eyes and just believe.

1

Sunday, December 24
Baltimore Museum of Art
5:45 p.m.

Hours to Christmas: approximately six, oh, joy! Countdown to New Year's Eve, the hands-down worst night of the year to be thirty and single: exactly one week. Calories consumed: 8,000 give or take. (It's only 5:30 p.m.—crap!) Evil bosses on list for strangling: one, but could never get hands around thick, bulldog neck. Yet another dream dies on the vine. (Sigh). Times so far today mother looked up at velvet painting of Virgin Mary and Baby Jesus and asked when am I going to settle down and start having babies like a good Catholic girl: only five so far but haven't been home since breakfast.

THE MUSEUM'S VISITOR PARKING AREA was filling up with BMWs and Porsches when Officer Mandy Delinski turned off Art Museum Drive and pulled into the lot. Bypassing the valet parking guys, she swung her squad car into one of the staff only spaces next to the catering truck, stole a quick glance in the rearview mirror, and then reached across the passenger's side to the glove compartment where she'd stashed her diary and, most importantly, her lipstick. *Why I bother I don't know,* she thought, and then rolled the lipstick on anyway. She didn't usually wear bright colors, let alone red, but somehow the name, Blaze, seemed to promise all sorts of wonderful, sexy fantasies come true, including a much thinner version of herself decked out in Santa cap, fur-lined red minidress, and black fishnet stockings crooning the lyrics to "Santa Baby" to an as yet faceless, nameless hunk.

Mandy, you've got to get a hold on your libido. Better yet, you've got to get a hold on your life. Your love *life, specifically. Actually, first you'd better get a love life, and preferably before your head blows off your damned shoulders.*

Capping the tube, she tucked a curly red strand of hair behind her ear and stepped outside to join the glitterati of Baltimore society filing up the steps to the columned entrance. Inside, she moved through the marbled foyer, following the crowd toward the bank of elevators. Before she'd left the precinct, Boblitz had filled her in on the details, including the event location—the museum's West Wing, which housed its collection of contemporary art. Accordingly, she stepped off the elevator onto the second floor and followed the signage to the stark concrete-and-aluminum foyer. Aside from a few stragglers, the West Wing was deserted; certainly no one from museum security was in sight. She was just about to turn back when a cut-paper silhouette woman caught her eye, the projected image taking up an entire stand-alone wall. Drawing closer, she read the caption card, "Salvation" by Kara Walker. Framed beneath a tree's sheltering bow, the woman waded through a pool of still water, the bend of her naked body and outstretched hands suggesting she was almost to her destination, perhaps hailing something or someone waiting for her within the near reach of shoreline.

Mandy's shadow joined that of the cut-out woman and a lump settled into her throat. *Where are you headed, Delinski? To something or someone good or are you just spending your life wading through one day to the next?*

"There you are."

Mandy swung away from the artwork to see a tall, leggy twentysomething in a red silk suit and John Lennon wire-framed glasses clicking across the tiled floor toward her. Glancing down at the shoes, Mandy mentally calculated the heels at close to four inches. Impressive. Just looking at them made her arches ache.

The woman hauled up in front of her, and Mandy spotted the museum badge announcing her position as event coordinator. Feeling foolish for having gotten sidetracked, she admitted, "I, uh…didn't know museum collections included slides."

Clipboard clutched between perfectly manicured hands, the girl rolled her eyes. "Ms. Walker's work is a transparency projection installation, actually. It's the newest medium in contemporary art, very hip, very hot," she added, appraising Mandy with a head-to-toe look that as good as said the artwork was everything she was not. "The event is in our atrium court, actually, and ends at eight. Come with me, and I'll hook you up with our security manager." With a swish of her shoulder-length bob, she turned and walked off, leaving Mandy to follow.

Geez, is it my day to be ragged on or what? Reaching for her patience, Mandy listened with half an ear to the girl yammering on about the current economic downturn, and the subsequent reduction in charitable giving in general and to the arts in particular, explaining how the museum couldn't afford to lose any of its existing patrons, which was why the recent bomb threat, any threat, was so deeply disturbing, yada, yada, *yada*.

They emerged into an atrium, large-scale mosaics gracing the walls between the glass-paned windows. A tall, dark-suited African-American man stood at the entrance, checking IDs against what must be the guest list. They drew up, and the event coordinator introduced the gentleman as the museum security manager, Mr. O'Brien. Leaning in to Mandy, she added in a whisper, "Because so many of our guests tonight are older ladies, all top-tier supporters of the museum, we thought a female would be better received, especially if any purses need checking."

"Good thinking," Mandy murmured, wishing it was eight o'clock already.

Apparently mollified, the girl excused herself and walked off. O'Brien signed Mandy's time slip, and they spent the next few minutes reviewing the security protocol. It was meat-and-potatoes stuff—check to make sure the photo ID matched the guest and of course, the name on the list, then issue one of the peel-off adhesive name tags that nearly everyone ripped off the moment they crossed over inside but what the hell.

He'd just wrapped up the short orientation when his walkie-talkie went off, spewing out a stream of static and coded radio chatter that Mandy had grown used to deciphering over the years. In this case, a woman had wandered into the roped-off area into the American Decorative Arts exhibit.

Signing off, he turned to Mandy with a look of apology. "Gotta go. You okay here on your own?"

"I've got it covered. Thanks."

Looking relieved, he nodded. "The event wraps up at eight. Things should slow down here in the next hour or so. Keep an eye on the door for any latecomers, but otherwise feel free to walk around, stretch your legs."

"Thanks, I will."

For the next hour, Mandy kept busy checking in the steady stream of guests filing through. A few put up a fuss about having to produce ID but most seemed to appreciate the museum's extra attention to their safety. Around seven o'clock, the volume of passers-through slowed to a trickle and then a stop.

Smothering a yawn, she turned to survey the festivities. From what she could see, the artwork was the liveliest thing about the event. Even with a function in full swing, the atrium vibrated with a tomblike dullness, the formally attired guests speaking in the hushed tones usually reserved for libraries and funerals, the professionally decorated Christmas trees occupying each of the room's four corners done up in monochromatic silver and gold. Even the thready notes struck up by the classical quartet from the city's renowned Peabody Institute seemed a sad substitute for the classic Christmas carols her pop would have blaring from the old hi-fi turntable as he and her mom decorated the tree with the hodgepodge of ornaments amassed over the years.

Her gaze landed on the white-skirted bar set up for the event, conspicuously devoid of any server but with a line of thirsty-looking patrons queuing up in front. *Too bad I'm on duty because a cosmo would go down really good just about now.* She was about to turn away when a blond head popped up from behind the bar, joined in short order by a set of broad shoulders, leanly muscled torso and narrow waist. *Oh my God.* Her brain froze and her breath stuck in her lungs. Talk about drop-dead gorgeous. The bartender who'd just surfaced with a magnum bottle of champagne and an easy smile looked like he was poured into that tuxedo, not to mention being a thirtysomething dead ringer for England's Prince William. Certainly he was the hands-down most amazing hunk of male she'd clapped eyes on in a long time—make that, ever.

And amazingly, he seemed to be looking her way. *Nice fantasy, Delinski, but it's time to get real.* With a sigh, she turned to greet the gorgeous model-type woman who surely must be approaching check-in only to find the alcove empty. *Oh my God.* She whipped around. He was still staring at her, his hot-eyed gaze shooting across the room like flame from a blowtorch. Mesmerized, she watched him pour a glass of champagne and then raise it to her in a mock toast. She thought his lips—his amazingly sensuous lips—mouthed, "Merry Christmas" but couldn't be sure.

My God, he's flirting with me. Me, of all people! She felt her face heat along with other more southern portions of her anatomy that had lain fallow for far too long.

Keep an eye on the door for any latecomers, but otherwise feel free to walk around, stretch your legs.

Maybe it was the whole turning thirty thing or the yet-another-Christmas-alone thing or a bit of both, but for whatever reason, Mandy found herself moving across the room toward the bar as if drawn there by an invisible cord. She walked up just as the last patron moved away, affording her an unobstructed view of her "target."

The target's cobalt-blue gaze settled on her face, making her glad she'd remembered that lipstick, and then slid lower, pausing perceptibly on her breasts before traveling back upward. "Can I get you something to drink...*officer?*" The slow, lazy smile accompanying the question and the close-up look of open appreciation had her heart slamming into her chest.

"Can't...I'm on duty." *Jesus Christ, Mandy, that was smooth—not! What next, recite a line from Dragnet?*

"Coke, then?" One side of his sexy mouth kicked up into an even sexier grin, and suddenly Mandy felt as if the room was spinning around her like a carousel.

She managed a reasonably steady "N-no thanks, I'm good" and then added, "You're not...you're not from around here."

He hesitated. Smile slipping, he asked, "What makes you say that?"

"Your accent, it sounds kind of New England."

The smile made a comeback only this time it didn't quite reach his eyes. "Oh, it's *my* accent, is it?"

Mandy felt a telltale tickle at the corners of her own mouth, and realized she must be smiling back—and damn, it felt good. "If you're saying I have a *Bawlmer* accent, then I'm guilty as charged. I can't help it. I grew up in the city."

"I like your accent. It's distinctive...like you."

Distinctive, huh. Distinctive could be good or bad depend-

ing on the circumstances. Given the sultry looks he was
sending her, she decided she could safely take it as a compliment, or better yet, a gift—the best Christmas gift she'd gotten
in a long, *long* time.

"Thanks, *hon*," she said with a wink, deliberately exaggerating the infamous truncated Baltimore *O*.

He threw back his head and laughed, a deep baritone that
had her thinking of her favorite Godiva dark chocolate—rich,
complex and full of sensual promise. Suddenly the hunk in her
"Santa Baby" fantasy had a face, and it was staring back at
her now as if its wearer wanted to eat her up. All she needed
to wrap up the fantasy in a big red Christmas bow was a name.

As if reading her mind, he stuck out a broad-backed hand.
"I'm Josh by the way."

Mandy hesitated, and then slipped her hand in his big,
warm one. Glancing down, she considered the many other
"uses" to which the strong, sensitive fingers might be put, and
a jet of warm moisture splashed between her thighs.

Her throat, in contrast, went sawdust dry. Swallowing, she
said, "I'm Amanda…Mandy, actually."

"Mandy, hmm? Pretty lady, pretty name." He glanced down
to their clasped hands, and she realized she'd forgotten to let go.

Palm tingling, she slipped her hand from his. "Sorry."

He stared straight at her, blue eyes blazing. "I'm not."

Suddenly the room was too hot, he was too hot. Too hot to
handle, though images of her doing just that, running her hands
over him from head to foot with some studied stops in between,
sped through her mind like racers on a NASCAR track.

A cough from behind had her glancing over her shoulder.
A Roland Park grand dame stood at her back, silver-blue hair
piled into a bouffant and liver-spotted hand wrapped about an
empty champagne glass.

Geez, lady, ever heard of AA? She turned back to the bartender, Josh, and said, "I guess duty calls."

"I guess so." He rolled his eyes, letting her know he didn't welcome the intrusion any more than she did. "Hey, I've got another hour to go and all the nonalcoholic carbonated beverages you can drink, so don't be a stranger, okay?"

"Okay, I won't."

She stepped aside and half walked, half floated back to the check-in station. Throughout the next hour, beautiful people in beautiful clothes milled about quaffing drinks, noshing on appetizers, and pretending to study the mosaics while not-so-secretly studying each other and yet Mandy's eyes kept coming back to one person. Him. Josh. And the most amazing, unbelievable and altogether wonderful part was that every time she looked over, she caught him looking back. Who would have thought she'd meet her dream man behind a makeshift bar pouring out rotgut chardonnay to blue-haired old ladies?

By 8:05 p.m., most of the crowd had dispersed. Despite the few stragglers, the caterers were breaking down the setups, including the bar. Her spirits, which had been dancing on air, started to plummet. Both the evening's assignment and the fantasy were about to end.

By the time O'Brien returned to sign her out, her feet were planted squarely back on terra firma. Pulling out his fountain pen, he asked, "How'd your night go?"

Ordinarily it would have seemed an innocent enough question, and yet Mandy felt her face heat. Flirting on the job wasn't exactly unethical, but it wasn't the most professional behavior, either. Hoping he hadn't seen her hanging around the bartender, she said, "Fine, thanks. Yours?"

He handed back the signed overtime slip. "It went fine, but I'll be glad to get home to my family. It's hard leaving the wife and kids on a holiday. What about you, Mandy? Got any kids?"

A telltale lump lodging smack dab in the middle of her throat. "No, not yet anyway."

They said their goodbyes and there was nothing left to do

but head for home. Still, Mandy couldn't help sending one last look in the vicinity of the bar. The stock had been packed up onto a cart, and it looked as though Bartender Josh had packed it in as well. He must have slipped out through a rear exit door while she was finishing up with O'Brien. Holding in a sigh, she pulled her cell phone out of her belt clip. It was early yet, and she didn't really feel like going home and being pressed into tree decorating duty. Maybe her friend, Suz, would feel like grabbing a bite to eat.

A tap on her shoulder sent her spinning around, the cell clattering to the floor as she reached a hand toward her gun holster, the palm of her other hand coming smack up against a very broad, very firm chest.

Josh slid his gaze down to her firing hand and then slowly back up. "Easy, you. There's no need to pull a Dirty Harry on me." He bent to retrieve her cell. Straightening, he handed it over. "I just didn't want to give you the chance to sneak out without saying good-night."

Feeling like an idiot, she slipped the phone back into the clip at her waist. "I wasn't sneaking out. I was signing out."

It was the first time she'd been near him without the portable bar as a buffer. Except for the rumpled white tuxedo shirt, he'd changed out of his uniform. If possible, he looked even sexier in softly worn jeans, scuffed boots and a faded black leather jacket than he had in the formal wear dangling from the dry cleaner's hanger in his hand.

When he seemed in no hurry to go, she found herself searching her sex-soaked brain for something smart to say. "You're, uh…done for the night, too, then?" *Brilliant, Delinski, really stellar. You'll make detective yet.*

He nodded, rolling his broad shoulders. "Yeah, thank God." Thinking of how amazing he must look without the shirt and jacket, without clothes at all, made her mouth water in a way usually reserved for chocolate or some decadent dessert.

Lifting long-lashed eyes to hers, he added, "Any chance I could persuade you to grab a drink or a cup of coffee with me?"

Oh my God. Had he just asked her out? For the second time that night, Mandy had to resist the urge to look back over her shoulder. *Okay, a) I have a brain tumor that's causing me to hallucinate, b) I've hit my head and gone into a coma or c) I'm already dead and hanging out in Heaven. Pick any of those three, and as long as I don't have to come to or come back, I don't care.*

"Don't tell me you don't fraternize with civilians?" He raised one sandy-colored eyebrow and regarded her, waiting.

Set at ease by his teasing, she found her voice. "I can't drink in uniform but, uh…coffee sounds good. Only it's Christmas Eve. There won't be much open at this hour."

There it was again, that sexy, half-cocked smile that had her heart doing somersaults—and more southern portions of her anatomy going very warm and very wet.

"In that case, I should probably mention I make great coffee."

Holy Mother Mary, he wasn't just asking her out, he was asking her back to his place! Talk about moving with lightning speed. But as much as she'd been fantasizing lately about sex with a red-hot stranger, thinking and doing were separate activities. Beyond giving up her good-girl self-image, there was the very real, very deep-seated fear that because of her weight he might consider her desperate, an easy mark.

Reining in the heat, she took a step back. "Actually, I know of this great locals' place, The Daily Grind. It may still be open."

If he was disappointed, he hid it behind a smile. "In that case, officer, lead the way."

2

Monday, December 25
1:00 a.m. (Too excited to sleep…)

Number of hunks potentially available for sucking
face with under the mistletoe: one—but then how many
does a girl need? Countdown to New Year's Eve, the
hands-down worst night of the year to be thirty and
single: still exactly one week, but feel particle of
optimism creeping in to disperse black cloud of despair
as consider possibility may not have to ring in the new
year alone after all.

Maybe not alone after all…

MANDY LIKED TO THINK of The Daily Grind as the anti-Starbucks.
A kitschy little locals' enclave in the heart of Fells Point, the city's
historic waterfront district, it catered to lovers of coffee and conversation in an eclectic, low-key setting showcasing local art and
a gumball machine that dispensed chocolate-covered espresso
beans by the handful for twenty-five cents. In the warmer months,
you might just as easily encounter a whacked-out homeless
person occupying one of the restaurant's two café tables and
chatting with imaginary friends as a buttoned-down business
executive carrying on a virtual meeting from his or her cell
phone. But it was Christmas Eve, as well as bitterly cold, and the
outside tables were deserted for good reason.

Off-duty use of the squad car didn't permit taking on un-authorized passengers, so they'd driven separately, Josh following in his beat-up Buick. On the drive over, Mandy had worried they might not have anything in common—other than the sexual chemistry drawing them together like twin magnets—but the opposite proved to be true. Within the first five minutes, they'd discovered shared passions for classic black-and-white films, Art Deco antiques and any dessert with Death by Chocolate in the title. Settled inside with two large café mochas, their second round, set on the table between them, they couldn't seem to *stop* talking.

Mandy took a sip of her drink and set the porcelain cup down on its saucer. "Audrey Hepburn is probably my all-time favorite film actress. Even playing an escort in *Breakfast at Tiffany's* she came off as so elegant and self-possessed—and well, so skinny. I'd kill for a figure like hers." She looked down at her cup. The thought of all the calories in the whipped cream alone had her holding in a sigh even as she dug in her spoon.

Josh shook his head. "She was a great actress, no doubt about it, but too skinny for my taste. When it comes to body types, I'm more of a Marilyn Monroe fan. Did you know she was a size sixteen?"

Mandy looked up from sipping whipped cream from her spoon. "Get out of here, really?"

He nodded. "That was back in the day when women had curves and were proud to show them off." His gaze slid over her, openly appreciative rather than leering, and Mandy felt her heart tip over on its side like an overloaded cart.

Oh my God, is this my dream guy or what! Before she fell any more head over heels, she ventured to ask, "You never did say where in New England you're from—or do I have to guess?"

Again, that hint of hesitation from him that she'd picked up on at the museum. Even in the throes of a full-on hormone blitzkrieg, her police-trained mind kicked in, wondering what he might have to hide.

"Boston," he answered after a longer than usual pause. "I grew up in the 'burbs, though."

Watching his chiseled features for signs of deception, Mandy said, "I went there once on an overnight school field trip. Tenth grade American History with Sister Anne Marie."

His smile dimmed and some of the sparkle seemed to leave his eyes. "It's a great city as long as you don't mind snow. You should go back sometime. If, make that *when* you do, let me know. I make a great tour guide."

She held in a breath. Was he implying they'd be staying in touch, that coffee on Christmas Eve might be a prelude to something more? "Getting time off can be tricky sometimes but sure, that would be great."

Elbows propped on the table's edge, he leaned across, close enough that she could taste the rich chocolate and cream on his breath. "If you don't mind my asking, what made you decide to be a cop?"

Usually she resented the question if only because her male colleagues were seldom asked to explain their career choice. Females in law enforcement weren't the anomaly they once were, but men still represented the vast majority.

But looking into Josh's eyes, she didn't see censorship, only genuine interest, and she found herself reaching beyond her pat fifty-words-or-fewer answer. "Growing up, I was always watching cop shows, anything from reruns of *Dragnet* to *Barney Miller*. After high school, I floated from one dead-end job to another—restaurant manager, retail sales clerk, limo driver. Believe it or not, I even did a stint as a cosmetologist."

"Why wouldn't I believe that? You're beautiful."

Unused to compliments, she wasn't sure what to say, so she only shook her head and pretended interest in the whipped cream melting into her cup. "Five years ago, my cousin, Vince, was killed during a robbery at his convenience store."

A pained look crossed his face. He shook his head. "That's awful. A violent death affects so many people—family, friends, even coworkers. For what it's worth, I'm sorry."

Warmed by his understanding, she said, "Thank you. It was awful for our family but especially for his wife, Theresa. She'd just had a baby and they had two little girls, twins, who barely remember their dad. What made it even worse was they never caught the guy who shot him. I wanted so badly to do something to help. Not Vince—it was too late for him and his family—but the crime situation in the city. Working patrol lets me help people hands-on, work with community leaders to come up with crime prevention programs for at-risk kids, that sort of thing. There are good days and bad, but overall I wouldn't trade the badge for any other job in the world."

He looked at her, gaze thoughtful. "You're fortunate then to have a job you love. Most people I know hate what they do. They're just in it for the money."

She couldn't help chuckling at that. "Well, I can definitely say I'm not in police work for the money. If anything, I'm in it in spite of the pay."

One corner of his mouth lifted in a wry smile. "That good, huh?"

"I'm pulling as many overtime shifts as I can get to save up to buy a house. In the meantime, I'm back living with my folks." What was in her drink, truth serum? As turn-offs went, admitting to living at home about topped the chart. It was just that he was so easy to talk to, she forgot to censor herself.

Instead of making a beeline for the door, he stayed put and asked, "Bad breakup?" He looked sympathetic, even a little sad.

"Yes, but with my so-called financial advisor. An old… friend from the neighborhood was working as a broker at the time. He convinced me to put my savings in the stock market—the month before the last big crash." Thanks to that jerk, Lenny, she'd lost everything—her self-respect along with all the money she'd saved up since her babysitting days.

"That's tough. If you ever consider reinvesting, you might think about diversifying your portfolio to include telecommunication technologies. WiFi networks are literally the wave of the future—the radio wave."

Mandy recalled that several popular downtown coffee spots recently had expanded into Internet cafés, providing customers access to their wireless networks while sipping their lattes and chatting on their cell phones. Until now she hadn't thought much about how the technology worked or that it might constitute big business.

Her ignorance must have shown on her face because he elaborated, "Wireless fidelity devices connect to the Internet at high speeds via radio waves instead of the old, cumbersome fiber optic cabling." He flashed an apologetic smile that set her heart on its side. "Sorry, I'm sort of a geek when it comes to this stuff."

"No, not at all, it's interesting." It *was* interesting though at this point interesting pretty much summed up everything about him. Fact was, he could pull out a newspaper and read her the weather report, and she'd be spellbound. "And thanks for the investment tip, but a money market is probably about as adventurous as I'll ever get again."

But there were areas of her life other than finance where she was prepared to shake off her old conservatism and be adventurous indeed, her sex life for starters. Earlier, he'd slipped off his black leather jacket. Watching the rise and fall of his chest, the broad planes outlined by the fitted shirt, was an amazing, make that an *orgasmic* sight to behold.

Realizing she must be staring like the cliché of the gauche Catholic schoolgirl she'd once been, she grabbed her drink and took a small, scorching sip. "Ouch!" She pulled back, setting her cup down with a clang.

All concern, Josh said, "You didn't burn yourself, did you?"

She could already feel the roof of her mouth peeling but rather than admit it, she shook her head. "I'm okay."

Staring at her mouth, he said, "You have a spot of whipped cream just…there." Reaching across, he gently swiped the pad of his thumb across her bottom lip, slowly tracing the arc. He brought his thumb to his lips and, holding her gaze, licked it very slowly and very thoroughly clean. "Hmm, you taste great."

Oh my God. Talk about blistering! Watching him, Mandy felt the wetness between her thighs heat to molten lava, the twinge of sexual awareness spike to full-throttle ache. There was no more ignoring the obvious—she wanted this man more than she'd ever wanted anyone in her adult life.

A throat being loudly cleared drew their attention across the room to the coffee bar. Standing behind it, the two counter workers regarded them with frowning faces and folded arms. A guilty glance around confirmed the other booths and tables were all empty. They were closing down the place—literally.

Wearing a cop's badge carried certain perks but keeping merchants past closing on the biggest holiday of the year was definitely pushing the envelope. She turned back to Josh. "It is Christmas Eve. I guess we should let these folks go home."

"Before they throw us out, you mean?" Standing up, he reached around to retrieve his jacket, giving her a close-up shot of his denim-clad butt, which definitely qualified as Grade-A American booty. Wow!

Swallowing hard, she pushed back from the table and stood. "Yeah, that."

"In that case, I'll walk you to your car."

Under ordinary circumstances, Mandy might have pointed out that she was, after all, the one packing the pistol. But this was no ordinary night. Having a hot hunk with a heart of gold act as her self-appointed bodyguard was an experience she was determined to savor for however many more minutes it lasted.

They stepped out into icy air and bluster, the exterior shop lights cutting off as soon as their feet struck the sidewalk. Hugging their coats, they crossed Thames Street to where Mandy had parked.

Josh dragged a hand through his hair, pushing it back from where it had blown over his brow. Watching him, Mandy couldn't help wondering how that thick thatch of corn silk might feel against the sensitive skin of her inner thighs as he kissed her intimately. Though the wind chill made the temperature feel subzero, the fantasy fired off a heated throbbing low in her belly.

Cars keys in hand, she searched for something to say that would wrap up the evening beyond goodbye. "I had a really nice time." *Pretty original, Mandy—not!*

Josh smiled. "So did I." A strong wind blew off the water, hitting them full force. He moved closer, shielding her body with his. "The great thing is it doesn't have to end."

She gulped against the dryness in her throat, a striking contrast to the moisture pooling in her panties. "It doesn't?"

"No, it doesn't." He settled a warm hand on her waist. "I live just about five minutes away in Canton."

"That's…convenient." Five minutes away. Even though she had a pretty good idea of where this was leading, she couldn't shake the feeling she was dreaming. Sexy encounters such as this didn't happen to women like her or at least they hadn't in the past. "You're in my precinct, then." Anticipating his kiss, she moistened her lips.

He smiled. "Yet another reason to love living downtown." The smile faded and in the sketchy light, she saw his expression turn serious. "Look, I don't mean to be forward or offend you, it's just that…" He shook his head as if to clear it and admitted, "I'm not ready to say good-night to you, not yet."

"You're not?"

"No." The hand anchored to her hip slid lower, cupping her trouser-clad buttocks. "What about you, Mandy?"

Oh, she was definitely ready all right, but leaving was the very last thing on her mind. Before she could find a graceful way of saying so, she was pulled flush against a hard male chest, with the cold metal of the car at her backside and the sexy lips she'd been salivating over all night zeroing in on hers.

He hesitated, his mouth a bare whisper from hers, his exhaled breath a warm balm to her cold-stiffened face, his solid body her sole source of comfort in an otherwise cold, cruel world. "Mind?"

"Nuh-uh." She shook her head, dimly aware that some instinct had led her to widen her stance so that he stood inside her parted thighs, the heat and pressure of his erection penetrating their layers of clothes. Instead of visions of sugar plums dancing in her head, it was the vision of what she was certain must be a big, hard, beautifully-shaped cock sliding back and forth inside her hungry mouth, teasing the tip of her tongue and back of her throat, probing the slippery wet slit between her thighs.

She caught a glimpse of his answering smile and wondered what sort of wicked thoughts were dirty dancing inside his head. Before she could find the words to ask, he dipped his head and captured her mouth in the sort of soul-searing, silver-screen-era kiss she'd dreamt of since the age of eight but until now had never experienced. For once in her life she didn't think, didn't hesitate, didn't worry, but gave herself up to the moment. She parted her lips and he deepened the kiss, sliding his tongue inside her mouth, touching the tip to hers and then delving deeper. He tasted of rich cocoa and sinfully sweet whipped cream, and she kissed him back with a hunger that surprised even her, devouring the taste and texture of him, savoring with tongue and lips and nipping teeth.

For the span of several heartbeats, the only sounds on the street came from them—the wet tangling of tongues, the hitching of breaths, urgent hands pulling at layered clothing, seeking access to blood-warmed flesh. A moan, Mandy's, broke the semi-silence.

Trailing kisses along the corded sinew at the side of his neck, she whispered, "Tell me this is real, that I'm not dreaming."

"Oh, baby, if you are then I'm dreaming, too, and I definitely don't want to wake up." He slid a broad-palmed hand upward from her waist to brush the tip of her breast.

Oh my God. Arching against him, Mandy wrapped her arms around his neck and held on for dear life as those hands— big, powerful, long-fingered hands that somehow managed the trick of staying warm without gloves—worked their magic on her breasts, knuckles and thumbs teasing her nipples to exquisite awareness, a state that had nothing to do with the cold. Because even though the temperature must be dipping well below twenty, Mandy had never felt so hot, so wet, or so alive in all her years. And if the hard ridge of jeans-clad erection pressing into her was any indication, her "partner in crime" was feeling pretty lively, too.

Wrenching his mouth away, he pulled back to look at her. "Sorry, but I just had to do that." Gaze holding hers, he hesitated. "Actually, I'm not really all that sorry." He took another deep breath and admitted, "Actually, I'm not sorry at all." The sheepish bad-boy look he sent her had her heart skipping beats and the wetness seeping through the crotch of her silk panties.

She ran her tongue over her bottom lip, sensitized from the contrast between cold air and hot kisses, and admitted, "I'm not sorry, either." If she was sorry about anything, it was that they were stopping.

He lifted her chin on the edge of his hand. Thumb stroking the edge, he said, "Then come home with me. Along with making great coffee, I make amazing cinnamon rolls and a pretty decent spinach-and-feta omelet."

Mandy stared up at him, his tousled hair backlit by ambient light, his chiseled features a mask of shadows, and realized she was more tempted to say yes than ever before in her life. She'd never before engaged in casual sex, let alone a one-night stand, but an encounter with a sexy stranger had been figuring into her fantasy life more and more of late. Josh didn't exactly qualify as a stranger, but she'd only known him a couple of hours. Even so, in many ways she felt more connected to him than she did many of the friends she'd grown up with, which was crazy when she considered she didn't even know his last name let alone why he'd decided to up and move from Boston to Baltimore. If she took him up on his invitation, she'd likely find out the answer to that question and so much more—what the hard body wrapped around hers looked like beneath his clothes; how and where he liked to be touched, tasted, sucked; what his favorite positions were and how he moved in bed…slow and steady or fast and hard or some combination of the two.

But tomorrow wasn't just any day. It was Christmas. She tried to imagine waking up in a stranger's bed on Christmas morning and then slinking home in the wee hours before her family stirred, sin oozing from her every pore, and somehow she just couldn't. Yet standing before her was the hands-down best Christmas gift she'd ever gotten even if it—he—didn't come wrapped in a bow.

She stepped back from his embrace, her every corpuscle quivering like the Jell-O cubes she'd starved herself on as a teenager. "I like you, Josh. I like you a lot. I like kissing you and well, I'm pretty sure I'd like doing, um…other things with you, too but…" In the wake of his steady-on gaze, her voice trailed off, small and weak and anything but sophisticated and self-assured.

The corners of his mouth flattened. "But?"

"Well, tomorrow is Christmas and my folks are…well, kind of traditional." Talk about an understatement. She might as well say the Pope was *kind of* Catholic.

He shook his head, his hair mussed from the wind and her fingers. "You're right. I was being selfish. Of course you'd have plans." He looked sad suddenly, and she was reminded that in all likelihood he didn't have anywhere to go.

Like Christmas tree lights, the idea, the solution, came to her in a flash as though someone had flipped on an invisible switch. Maybe she didn't have to choose after all? Maybe she could have her holiday hunk *and* the holiday at the same time.

"Why don't you come over to my folk's? My mom has a big open house for family and friends and neighbors starting around two." Subjecting him to her big, rowdy Polish-American family would be a gamble, but then again he'd as good as said he didn't have anyone to be with or anywhere to go. "No pressure," she added quickly, not wanting to scare him off. "I'll introduce you as a friend I met on the job. I just don't think anyone should be alone on Christmas."

He stroked the side of her face, the tenderness of the gesture as much a turn-on as his passionate kisses. "You're sweet to include me in your plans, and I really appreciate the invitation…"

When he left the sentence unfinished, it was Mandy's turn to interject. "But?"

"The thing is I'm not…I'm not so good at parties."

That took her aback. "But you're a bartender."

He hesitated, and then shrugged. "Mostly I get bookings through an event planning service like the one tonight. I have a regular gig a couple nights a week at a bar in Canton but even then most of the time bar patrons want to tell you all about themselves, not the other way around."

"So you're saying you're shy?" Prone to shyness herself, she couldn't entirely strip the skepticism from her voice.

He must have picked up on it because for the first time since initiating that sexy kiss, he shifted away. "Uh, I guess you could say that. But give me your number, and I'll call you."

I'll call you—otherwise known as Famous Last Words. How many times in her adult life had a guy said "I'll call you," only never to be heard from again? Saying "I'll call you" was a lot like telling a retail clerk you'd "have to think about it" so you could get the hell out of the store before you were cornered into buying the vintage lava lamp or butt ugly couch. Basically, "been there, done that, bought the T-shirt."

To save face, she decided to play along. "Sure, that'd be great." Fingers clumsy from the cold, she took out one of her department issue business cards and handed it to him.

He slipped the card into his back jeans pocket, and for the first time she noticed the pager he wore at his waist. That was an odd accoutrement for a bartender. Before she could ask him about it, he looked back at her, serious expression catching at her heart.

"Hey you, if I say I'm going to call, it means I'm going to call, okay?" He laid a broad palm on either side of her face and gently turned her to look at him. "Look, Mandy, I like you. I like you a lot, and what's more, I'd like to put in the time to get to know you better. Is that so hard to believe?"

It was and yet how she wanted to believe—in him, in herself, and more than anything, in magic moments that led to fairy-tale endings.

As if in answer, a church bell chimed, striking out the hour. Twelve o'clock. No longer Christmas Eve but Christmas Day.

Josh smiled. "Merry Christmas, Mandy."

She smiled back. "Merry Christmas, Josh." And it was a merry Christmas, not to mention the hottest, sexiest holiday she'd ever had.

He leaned in to kiss her again. This time when their mouths met it was definitely good-bye or at least goodnight, a feather-light caress that had her heart melting to the gooey consistency of a chocolate chip cookie still warm from the oven.

Something cold and wet struck her nose. Josh must have felt it too because they stopped kissing at the same time to look up. Above them, fat, feathery snowflakes fell fast and furious. Snow on Christmas Day. If that wasn't a positive sign, what was?

She turned back to Josh. His shoulders wore a sprinkling

of pristine white powder that made her think of the glitter that her mom had once glued to the wings of her angel's costume for the fourth grade Christmas pageant. Back then she'd believed in angels and miracles and the special magic of Christmas snow. Could it be time to believe again?

Speaking her thoughts aloud, she said, "A white Christmas, it doesn't get any better than that."

He shook his head, a smile playing about the corners of his mouth. "Oh, it gets better, Mandy. It gets lots better. I have a hunch this New Year is going to be the start of something wonderful, a fresh start in more ways than one." He kissed the tip of her nose before stepping back. "I'll call you after the holiday. In the meantime, have a good one—and drive safely."

She hesitated, not sure of how much to say, of how much to hope. "Okay, you too," she said and then turned to open the car door.

Hands shoved into his pockets, he waited until she was safely inside the car with the engine started before turning to go, one hand raised in a wave. Watching him fade to black, his tight Bon Jovi butt filling out the seat of those jeans in just the right way, his booted feet leaving impressively large prints in the powdering of snow, she vented a sigh. *It might be a record cold night, but there's no need to switch on the heater, that's for sure.* Backing out of the space, she caught a glimpse of a smile, hers, in the rearview mirror and shook her head. Maybe her luck wasn't changing for the better; maybe it already had.

3

Christmas morning, hurray! Barely closed eyes all night but when did, was to visions of blond-haired, blue-eyed hunk dirty dancing through dreams. Come awake awash in optimism and hormone-induced euphoria. Put energy boost to use in Christmas gift to self: getting rid of puke pink wall color reminiscent of scary high school prom dress and repainting to soothing sage green fit for cool, sophisticated Woman of the World. Afterward, floated downstairs to find mother holed up in kitchen, too busy fretting over preparation of Christmas Open House feast to comment that youngest daughter (me) is still languishing in chaste, childless singledom, frittering away supposed "best years" and dwindling supply of "baby eggs" on cold-blooded pursuit of police career.

But for first time in a long while, maybe forever, feel like the best is yet to come. Embracing power of positive thinking, am keeping cell phone close at hand so as to be ready when, not if but when, He calls.

Please, dear God, let him call. Let him call soon…

WATCHING MANDY DRIVE OFF, Josh could only shake his head at his life's latest ironic turn of events. Just his luck, he finally met his dream woman—Mandy Delinski of the Titian red hair, soulful amber-brown eyes and Rubenesque body-to-die-for—and he couldn't even tell her his real name.

Ever since he'd discovered that his new brother-in-law, Tony, was embezzling money from Thornton Enterprises, his family's Boston-based telecommunications company, his life hadn't been his own. When Grady Stone, the company's chief financial officer, first came to him with his suspicions that Tony was faking project invoices, Josh had brushed it off as the workings of an overly active imagination. Grady might have a great head for crunching numbers, but he read way too much true crime crap for Josh to accept such a wild accusation on faith alone. True, he'd never been all that crazy about Tony, but he was still Martie's husband. He wasn't ready to hang the guy out to dry purely because their personalities had clashed on occasion.

Still, Grady was the CFO. Josh had agreed to check out a few things behind the scenes, namely the accounts on which Tony served as project manager. Once he started digging, it wasn't long before he hit pay dirt—literally. No run-of-the-mill embezzler, Tony was a high-level Mafia plant. He'd used his marriage to a Thornton as his entrée into the firm and had been feathering his nest—his crime family's nest—by selling WiFi networks to corporate clients at triple the cost, and then funneling the illegal profits back to the mob. The depth of the deception still blew Josh away. Not sure where to turn, he'd contacted the FBI's Boston field office. The feds had lost no time in faking Josh's death, assigning him a new identity as Josh Thorner, and relocating him to Baltimore. Three days later, Grady had turned up as a floater on the Charles River.

As far as the public was concerned, Joshua Sedgewick Thornton the Third had drowned in a tragic sailing accident that summer. At first Josh had objected to the ruse until his FBI contact, Special Agent Walker had pointed out that playing dead was his best guarantee of staying alive.

Looking back over the past six months, he admitted that in all likelihood Walker had been right. And though Baltimore wouldn't have been his top pick for a relocation locale, once you went underground, geography pretty much lost its meaning.

As for bartending, he'd been skeptical at first of the Bureau's choice of temporary occupation, but the service industry had proved to be the perfect cover. Bar patrons might share every detail of their lives, no matter how embarrassing or minute, but they rarely thought to ask questions about yours. Beyond that, he couldn't help appreciating the honest, hands-on nature of the work. In a bar, a satisfied customer was just that—no if, ands or buts. If someone didn't like the product, they told you so to your face, and you had the chance to make things right then and there—no corporate backstabbing or political infighting to navigate. At the end of the day, or rather, night, you left work behind and went home with a head uncluttered by spreadsheets or quarterly productivity reports. If it weren't for the estrangement from his family and friends, and the guilt he felt about letting them believe he was dead, he would be savoring his sabbatical from the dog-eat-dog world of corporate America.

Other than his FBI contacts, the only person who knew he was alive was his former fiancée, Tiffany, and given the unsavory circumstances surrounding the disclosure, his secret should certainly be safe with her. On his way to rendezvous with the two agents assigned to protect him, he hadn't been able to resist stopping off at the Beacon Hill town house they shared to let her know he was okay. He'd entered through a rear door, the sounds of a woman's whimpering drifting down the back stairs. Thinking she must have heard the bogus bad news already, he took the stairs two at a time and rushed into the bedroom—and found her sprawled atop the sheets, the curly brown head of the lawn care kid wedged between her splayed thighs.

Sickened, he'd backed out of the room before the kid had

registered his presence. An hour later, he was hunkered down in the back seat of a car with two FBI agents driving south toward Maryland. Even after six months, the gut-dropping feeling of walking into that room never entirely left him, replaying in his head like a bad TV rerun and putting him squarely off women—until tonight.

Mandy Delinski was someone very special. He'd felt that from the moment he'd locked eyes with her across the crowded museum event, and their coffee date had only enhanced the attraction. Gorgeous, curvy ladies with passions for old movies, Art Deco and Death by Chocolate ice cream didn't just walk into a guy's life every day of the week. Beyond her obvious physical attributes and their shared interests, there was something about her that tugged at him, a crazy dead-on chemistry he'd never felt before in his thirty-two years of planetary living. Her full figure molded to his body like a custom-made glove and man-oh-man, could the woman kiss. He knew he must be wearing the lion's share of the fiery red lipstick that had accentuated her luscious mouth and rather than rush to wipe it off, he couldn't stop grinning—or fantasizing about where those red-hot kisses could lead, namely to a thorough, head-to-toe exploration of every amazing inch of her.

So far the only thing about her he wasn't head-over-heels crazy about was her job. With her cop's training, she'd been all too quick to pick up on the mismatch between his supposed shyness and his bartending occupation. When, not if, he saw her again, he'd have to be more careful, at least until he testified. The trial was scheduled for January second and afterward he would have his life back. It was too soon to know how a certain lovely lady cop from Baltimore might fit into his future, but he didn't intend to let her slip away without first exploring the possibilities.

Coming up on his car, a beat-up Buick he'd named Betsy because it was the automotive equivalent of a swayback mule, a vehicle so antiquated even the lowliest carjacker could be counted on to pass it by, he slipped the key into the door lock. Typically it took at least three failed tries before the engine would start, and with the extreme cold temperature, it would more likely take four. Yanking open the rusted door, he admitted that what he'd done tonight went against the three cardinal rules Walker and his colleague, McKinney, spoke of as The Holy Trinity of witness protection. "Don't give out personal information, no matter how innocuous, to anyone you meet—and that includes admitting you're a federally protected witness. Don't make contact with family or friends or coworkers back home under any circumstances—and that includes your mother calling for you on her deathbed or your childhood dog getting run over by a truck. And above all, don't get personally involved."

He'd settled onto the cracked leather seat and reached up to adjust the rearview mirror to check out his lipstick status when he felt something cold and hard jam into the back of his head.

"Well, well, Thornton, what's a nice Boston Brahmin like you doing in a crap blue-collar town like this?"

The gravelly voice coming from his back seat sent Josh's heart dropping to Betsy's rusted floorboards. He looked into the rearview mirror and glimpsed a man's partial profile, the skin pitted with acne scars. The slicked-back dark hair, deep-set eyes, and craggy features, including an obviously broken nose, fit the Hollywood stereotype of a Mafia hit man.

Futile as it was, he found himself saying, "Whoever you are, you've got the wrong guy."

A belly laugh erupted from the vicinity of the back seat. "Oh, I don't think so. Your hair may be longer and you're definitely dressing down these days, but it's you, no doubt about it. Joshua Thornton the Third."

Oh shit, oh shit, oh shit...

"What do you want with me?"

His life, of course, but the longer Josh kept him talking, the longer he had to go on breathing. And life, every freezing, fearful second of it, had never felt more precious. Ordinarily he might have held on to the hope that someone, anyone, might happen by. But it was after midnight on Christmas and the normally bustling downtown bar district was deserted. Unlike George Bailey in his favorite Christmas movie, *It's a Wonderful Life,* there would be no guardian angel sent down to save Josh in the nick of time. This was real life, not reel life.

And the reality was he was about to die.

The hit man leaned in, the warmth of his exhaled breath striking the back of Josh's neck, an eerie contrast to the icy pistol butt prodding his skull. "Put the key in the ignition and drive."

"Why should I? Either way, I'm a dead man."

"True, but if I do you here, I'll have to pay a call on your cop girlfriend afterward. By the way, nice lipstick, Romeo." A beefy hand adorned with several chunky gold rings reached around, slapping his cheek.

Face stinging, Josh froze. He was going to die, that was a given, but how could he take Mandy down with him? He'd made choices along the way, including ignoring Walker's third rule and asking her out, but she was an innocent bystander. Now that he'd gotten her caught up in the web of his fucked up life, he owed it to her to try and save her.

The thug knocked the pistol into his head again, hard enough this time that he forced back a groan. "Clock's ticking. It's your call, rich kid. What's it going to be?"

Beneath his leather jacket, Josh felt the sweat running down his ribs. Without answering, he stuck the key in the ignition and turned it clockwise.

Just his luck, old Betsy fired to life on the very first try.

THE ANNUAL DELINSKI Christmas Day open house was a twenty year and counting tradition looked forward to year-round by the hundred or so persons counted as guests. The doorbell had started ringing promptly at two o'clock, and by two-thirty the narrow row house was all but splitting at the seams with family members and friends and neighbors, many of whom showed up with covered dishes of their own. Mandy's mother pulled out all the stops, serving up turkey with all the trimmings as well as signature Polish dishes like kielbasa and dumpling soup and stuffed cabbage with mushroom sauce. There was enough food to feed the proverbial army and yet every year Mandy's mother fretted they might run short.

For one of the few times in her life, Mandy was too excited to eat.

Stationed near the door in case the bell rang again, she felt someone watching her. Afraid it might be her old boyfriend, Lenny, she quickly looked up, relieved to see not Lenny but her mother marching across the packed living room toward her.

Materializing at her side, she gestured to the untouched food languishing on the paper plate in Mandy's hand, a frown lining her high forehead. "You've been carrying that plate around for the past hour like it was luggage. You on one of your crazy diets again or what?"

"Nah, Ma. I'm just not hungry."

"Not hungry!" In the Delinski household, lack of appetite counted as an eighth Deadly Sin. One of the hazards of being born into a family for which eating was the antidote to every ill was that nearly all Mandy's relatives were stout as barrels. "But it's Christmas. After morning mass, what is there to do but eat?"

Mandy could think of a few other things to do, several of them fairly aerobic and all involving getting a certain blue-eyed, blond-haired hunk naked and horizontal. Feeling her face heat, she ducked her head and forked up a bite of stuffed cabbage.

Predictably, her mother relaxed. "That's better. I'll thank you to remember you're an attractive Polish girl with a beautiful full figure and you ought to be proud. Not everybody likes skinny-skinny, you know. Lenny, for one, appreciates a girl with a healthy appetite." She nodded toward the far side of the living room to where Lenny Borkowski hunched over his plate, shoveling food into his mouth.

Skinny as the proverbial rail, Lenny could never seem to get enough to eat—especially if the meal was free. If he was the type of man her full figure attracted, Mandy had better start on a juice fast straightaway.

Catching her eye, he smiled over at her, food rimming his front teeth and red sauce dribbling his chin. Disgusted that she'd been desperate enough to date him even after the investment fiasco, Mandy sent him a halfhearted nod and turned back to her mother. "That's because he eats like a pig and looks like Ichabod Crane."

One eye monitoring the food table, no doubt to determine if replenishments were required, her mother asked, "Who?"

"You know, Ma, the skinny schoolmaster who got his head lopped off by the Headless Horseman."

Her mother drew back, expression horrified. "Really, Amanda, I'll thank you to remember it's Christmas. Can't you keep from bringing your violent work home with you one day out of the year?"

Mandy started to explain that Ichabod Crane was a fictional character from Washington Irving's Halloween classic, *The Legend of Sleepy Hollow,* but then thought better of it. Why waste her breath? Besides, it was the wrong holiday.

Apparently the food supplies were holding steady because her mother turned back to her. Casting a significant glance across the room, she leaned closer and confided, "Lenny wants to get back with you. He told your brother Jimmy so just before you came downstairs. And I hear his business has picked up. Rumor has it he's doing very well for himself now."

Mandy set down her plastic fork on the plate's edge, well and truly finished with her food. Lenny was from the neighborhood, which meant he was Catholic and Polish. They'd both been raised in traditional blue-collar families but beyond being still single and thirty, they had absolutely nothing in common.

Holding firm, she said, "Great, then he can pay me back the money of mine he lost. And frankly I don't care if he's suddenly Donald Trump, because I have absolutely no interest in getting back together with him, not now and not ever."

Not only was Lenny physically unappealing with no apparent head for finance, but worst of all, he was a deadbeat. The last time they'd gone out, he'd made a big deal of impressing her parents by taking her to dinner at Tio Peppe, one of the city's priciest restaurants. He'd ordered the most expensive items on the menu, including a bottle of Dom Perignon, and ended the night with one of the restaurant's signature flaming desserts. But when the bill arrived, he announced he'd forgotten his wallet. Fortunately she'd had her credit card with her, not that he'd ever paid her back for even his share of the meal. That little encounter had set her dream of home ownership back by several hundred dollars.

Her mother's gaze lifted to the velvet painting of the Virgin and Child hanging over the living room couch. "You got somebody better on the string, then?"

Here we go—again. Mandy paused. Part of her wanted to shout out that *yes, yes* she did if only to get her mother off her back, but superstition held her back. Ridiculous as it was, she didn't want to risk jinxing her chances of Josh calling her by mentioning him too soon to her well-meaning but nosy family. Besides, the first questions they'd ask were what he did for a living and who his parents were. If she had to admit he was a bartender and that she didn't even know his last name, all hell would break loose. And by keeping mum, if he didn't call, at least she'd be spared rehashing the episode around the dinner table for the next ten years.

Arms folded across her full bosom, her mother demanded, "Well, do you or don't you? Which is it?"

Mandy's pager went off, saving her from answering. Seeing her mother's scowl return, she shrugged and said, "It's the job, Ma." Actually, she hoped it was Josh. Her pager number was part of her contact information on the card she'd given him.

Please, let it be him, let it be him, let it be…

Heart racing, she handed her mother the sagging paper ware. "Gotta go."

Before her mother could answer her back, she turned and cut through the living room packed with siblings, aunts and uncles, cousins including Mikey, the family's official black sheep, nieces and nephews, and assorted neighbors and friends to the stairway.

Upstairs, she headed for her bedroom—and sweet privacy. Pulling the door closed against the clamor, she felt calm washing over her. It could be years yet before she was able to afford a house of her own, but in the meantime she'd turned her bedroom into a haven, a space she felt good about coming home to at night. She'd spent the past weeks stripping away most of the girlish vestiges of her teen years, including changing the wall color from the Pepto-Bismol pink she'd picked out as a thirteen-year-old to a soft sage green. She'd put on the final coat of paint this morning, her Christmas present to herself.

Hands shaking, she sat on the edge of her bed and pushed the pager's call-back number. Her heart plummeted when she saw it was the switchboard number for the precinct, not a personal call. No Josh calling to wish her Merry Christmas or to set up another date or even just to say "Hi, I'm thinking about you."

Swallowing her disappointment, she picked up her cell and called back. "Delinski here. You paged me?"

The shift commander on the other end of the line didn't bother with "Merry Christmas" or other festive preamble. "You're needed down at the morgue, pronto. Homicide. It's a federal case, so get a move on, okay?"

A federal case! Could this be her long-awaited "red ball," the high-profile, career breakout case she'd been hoping for? Balancing the cell in the curve of her shoulder, she was already reaching for the locked drawer that held her badge and gun. "Don't worry, Sarge. I'm as good as there."

4

Christmas night, almost midnight

Consoling gal pal, Suz just left with bottle of Chianti and box of Kleenex, both empty. To say bubble of happiness has burst is like calling atomic bomb dropped on Hiroshima "a little hand grenade." On leaving Medical Examiner's Office earlier, briefly considered heading to Penn Station and tossing self on train tracks à la Anna Karenina, but discarded as messy and melodramatic, plus would involve traumatizing civilians, so made SOS phone call to Suz instead.

Not really sure what to do with self at this point but one thing's for certain: no longer in position of having to wait and wonder whether or not he'll call. No call's coming now. Not now, not ever...

THE MEDICAL EXAMINER'S OFFICE, known among cops as the ME's Chop Shop, was located on Penn Street near the train station in heart of the downtown. Mandy arrived to find two federal agents waiting in the reception area. Dressed in nondescript dark suits, pressed white shirts, and red-and-navy striped ties, they might have passed for twins except for the obvious difference in their ages.

Pulling the outside door closed behind her, she said, "I'm

Officer Delinski. I'm sorry to have kept you waiting. I just got the call to come down twenty minutes ago."

The agent with the salt-and-pepper hair reached out to shake her hand. "I'm Special Agent Walker." He inclined his head to the younger man flanking his side. "And this is my colleague, Special Agent McKinney."

With his cropped hair and flawlessly symmetrical features, McKinney reminded Mandy of the Ken doll she'd got for Christmas one year as a kid—plastically perfect to the point of blandness. "I'm afraid you've left your family on Christmas for no reason, officer. In fact, I'm going to have to ask you to leave."

Leave, my ass. Digging in her heels, Mandy braced herself for a battle. Unfortunately turf wars were part and parcel of the landscape of modern day law enforcement. Rather than combining their resources and skills to bring closure to a case, more often than not federal and local authorities spent a ridiculous amount of time, energy and even taxpayers' money butting heads over jurisdiction. It was too bad, really. The FBI might have the fancy crime lab and National Crime Information Center database for tracking fugitives, but no one had a better handle on the terrain of the city, including its criminal culture, than the street cops and detectives who knew just about every drug dealer, thief and snitch by face and name.

Pulling back her shoulders, Mandy looked the fed straight in the eye. "With all due respect, the murder occurred in the southeast precinct of Baltimore City. By definition, the BCPD's already involved."

"You misunderstand me. If Baltimore City Police wants to ride our coattails on this one, it's fine by me. It's not your precinct's involvement we object to but yours."

"I'm sorry, but I don't follow you."

"This is a federal case, Officer Delinski, and your card on the victim's body makes you part of the investigation. I don't know whose call it was to send you down here, but your presence could compromise the evidence."

A sinking feeling hit her squarely in the stomach, making her glad she'd eaten lightly. "Hold up, *my* card turned up on the vic?"

Both feds nodded. Mouth pulled into a grim line, McKinney advanced on her, and she had to resist the instinct to back up. "Yes, *officer,* but surely that's no surprise to you. You must have given it to him."

His accusatory tone had her mentally reviewing her work activities over the previous week. She'd given out her contact information to any number of individuals, including a pimp claiming to have inside information on a drug deal about to go down. It certainly wasn't unheard of for an informant to turn up dead, but she didn't see why the feds would involve themselves in a local homicide case.

Walker laid a hand on the young hotshot's shoulder. "Let her stay. As long as she's not left alone with any evidence, there shouldn't be a problem. Besides, we need her to go on record as identifying the body."

The body. No matter how many years Mandy logged in on the force, that phrase would never lose its ominous sound.

The attendant on duty, a gaunt young man with dark-circled eyes and a head of curly black hair, stepped inside. Hands stuffed into the pockets of his stained lab coat, he said, "Dr. Matthews, the M.E. on duty, is waiting for you in the crypt. I'll show you to the elevator."

They filed out into the hallway, a stark affair of linoleum floors and gray-white walls, to the bank of elevators. The attendant punched the down arrow button, and the metal doors opened at once. The three of them stepped on, the federal agents holding back for Mandy to enter first. Gaze fixed on the light bar registering the descending floors as they dropped downward, Mandy considered that so far no one had mentioned the victim's name, only his gender. Not knowing who he was—or rather, had been—only that he was someone with whom she'd interacted recently was a lot more anxiety-provoking than dealing with the bad news upfront.

Stepping out into the basement hallway awash in bluish neon, she felt as if she were in Batman's fictional Gotham City rather than Baltimore City. *Quiet as a tomb,* she almost blurted out to break the tension, but glancing between the agents' stern, square-jawed profiles, she decided neither was likely to appreciate the stab at humor.

A short, balding man dressed in a white lab coat and green surgical scrubs met them at the door. "I'm Dr. Matthews. You're here for the Thorner case?"

Walker answered, "Yes, Doctor, that's correct. Only the last name is Thornton."

Dr. Matthews hesitated, and then nodded. "Very well, then. If you'll follow me…"

They stepped inside the crypt—the climate-controlled chamber where bodies awaiting autopsy or identification were stored until claimed by relatives or otherwise disposed of. Mandy had pulled morgue duty a few times before, but if she lived to be a hundred, she'd never forget the signature smell. The close air was rank with formaldehyde, Lysol and alcohol, the windowless room flanked on three of its four sides by floor-to-ceiling metal drawers that held the remains of those who had experienced their last earthly Christmas.

The M.E. snapped on a pair of latex gloves and reached for the handle on one of the midlevel drawers. The slab slid out almost soundlessly, the victim's body enclosed in a plastic body bag. He unzipped the bag, and Mandy braced herself. Whomever that drawer contained would be someone she knew, someone with whom she'd shared anywhere from a passing word to a relationship of days, months, or even years. Even with five years as a beat cop under her belt, she'd never gotten used to this part of the job, not entirely, and a part of her hoped she never

did. No matter how many corpses she came across—and she'd
seen her share—she couldn't look down on a victim's bloodless face and unblinking gaze without wondering about favorite
colors and favorite foods, secrets fears and passions, victories
celebrated and losses mourned—all the trappings of a life, a
human life, cut short by senseless violence.

Moment of truth time, Delinski. No guts, no glory.

Mandy dropped her gaze—and froze.

Oh, God, no. Please…no.

The face was waxen, the chiseled features frozen stiff rather
than mobile and yet there was no mistaking the dead man's
identity. He was Josh, *her* Josh, or at least she might have had
the chance to make him hers if he'd lived. Josh of the laughing
blue eyes, sexy smile and strong, knowing hands. When she'd
stepped out of his arms last night to go home, she'd never
guessed their next date would be at the morgue.

"Officer Delinski, do you know this man?" McKinney, impatience sharpening his voice, hovered over her.

The plummeting sensation in her stomach reminded her of
riding the Twilight Zone Tower of Terror attraction at Disney's
MGM Studios theme park as a kid—a drop of thirteen gut-
wrenching stories experienced again and again. Fighting the
urge to be sick over the tops of her polished shoes, Mandy
considered the question. Had she known Josh? In one sense,
she hadn't known him at all, not even his last name let alone
why he'd left his home in Boston. In another sense, though,
she'd known him well indeed—his favorite ice cream flavor,
his favorite movies, how he liked to be kissed, held, touched.

"Officer Delinski, please answer the question. Do you or
do you not recognize this man?" McKinney again, louder this
time, as though she were deaf instead of stunned to speech-
lessness from looking on at a lost life—a life that had touched
hers intensely albeit briefly.

Slowly, like a coma victim coming into consciousness, she

nodded. "He introduced himself as Josh. I never knew his last name. We met last night at an event at the Baltimore Museum of Art. I was working an overtime security detail, and he was tending bar."

"I see." McKinney's gaze honed in on her, and Mandy felt a blush creeping up her throat.

A horde of heated memories rushed her, an oddity in this cold, cold place—the melting stares coming across the atrium from a pair of blue bedroom eyes; the way he'd swiped away the whipped cream smudge below her mouth and pronounced her, not it, to be delicious; that ready hard cock rubbing against her, driving her crazy, until she hadn't known what she wanted to do more, spread her legs and take him inside her in a single, satisfying thrust or open her mouth and spend the time to taste and suck and savor.

She heard the M.E.'s voice as if it came from the opposite end of a tunnel. "Cause of death was a gunshot wound to the back of the head, a classic execution-style hit." He slid an arm beneath the victim's head, Josh's head, turning the body onto its side to reveal the wound. "We dug out a .22-caliber slug from the left occipital lobe. The bullet transected the bone and lodged in the soft tissue, so there was no exit wound. The mechanism of death was massive traumatic hemorrhage of the brain."

Forcing the cop part of her brain to kick in, Mandy focused on the facts of the case. A .22-caliber pistol was frequently the firearm of choice among mob enforcers for practical reason. Because of its small size, the bullet lacked the velocity to penetrate the skull a second time; instead ricocheting around inside and bringing about massive brain hemorrhage and death. With a clean, close shot, victim fatality was virtually guaranteed.

Sounding like a museum docent reciting the details of a particular piece, the M.E. continued, "Note the ragged, star-shaped wound. That tells us that the weapon was fired at close range, likely with the barrel pressed directly against the skin. The gases shoot under the skin, expand, and the explosion of expanding gas causes the tissue to split."

Walker spoke up, "We'll need to rule out suicide. If there's a murder trial, the defense may try to con the jury into thinking Thornton could have just as easily shot himself as been murdered. Any chance the physical evidence could be construed as indicative of a self-inflicted wound?"

Reclaiming his arm, the M.E. shook his balding head. "Suicide shots are almost always to the temple, through the mouth or into the front of the chest. In this case, the angle of the bullet, the degree of gunpowder tattooing on the skin around the wound, the absence of any trace residue on the victim's hands, and the fact that no weapon was found at the scene all rule out suicide. No, gentlemen…pardon me, I meant to say *lady* and gentlemen—" He cast an apologetic look at Mandy before continuing, "Joshua Thornton was murdered. I'd stake my professional reputation on it."

For the first time since she'd met him, Mandy saw McKinney break into a semi-smile. "Good to know, Doc, because you may have to do just that. When we collar the bastard who carried out the hit, I'll be calling on you to testify as an expert witness—unless he flips, of course, in which case we'll offer to cut a deal in exchange for the name of his boss. The trigger man is just a hired gun, after all."

Swallowing against the sourness coating her throat, Mandy interrupted to ask, "So that means he didn't suffer, right?"

"Excuse me?"

"Josh…I mean the vic, he didn't feel any pain, did he?"

The three men turned to look at her as though she were newly landed from Mars. Beyond providing physical clues to closing the case, the victim's suffering was considered inconsequential at this point. It didn't matter to the white-lab-coated medical examiner or the two dark-suited FBI agents whether

Josh had died instantly or languished for hours, but it mattered to Mandy. It mattered enormously.

"There were no other marks found on the body to indicate torture or even a struggle. In all likelihood, death would have been instantaneous."

Mandy let out the breath she'd been unconsciously holding back. As far as homicide went, a clean shot was a relatively humane death. It wasn't much in the way of comfort, but it was all she had to hold on to.

Expression grim, McKinney shook his head. "When he didn't check in this morning, I paged him, but he didn't respond. I knew then they must have gotten to him. It's a damn shame, too. He was almost to home base. The case was scheduled to come to trial the day after New Year's Day. If only he could have held out just a little longer."

Josh's words came back to her. *"I have a hunch this New Year's is going to be the start of something wonderful, a fresh start in more ways than one."*

Agent Walker added, "If my twenty-five years with the Bureau have taught me anything, it's that the last week is critical. When we lose them, typically the hit goes down within the last seven days. We tell them to lay low and for a while they do, but then they're almost to the finish line, and something or someone comes along and they get careless or antsy or just plain bored and they slip up."

Something or *someone* comes along. Mandy clamped her mouth closed against the bile burning up the back of her throat. *One more week, Josh. You probably would have made it, too, if I hadn't come along and screwed everything up for you.* If only she'd turned down that offer of coffee. If only she hadn't kept him hanging around on the deserted street waiting for her to start her car. If only she hadn't been such a prude and had gone back with him to his apartment. *If, if, if…*

"Wait a minute, are you saying Josh, I mean Mr. Thornton,

was a federally protected witness? But why would the mob take a contract out on a bartender?"

"Joshua Thornton is, or rather was, no bartender. That was just his relocation cover. He was heir to Thornton Enterprises, one of this country's largest telecommunications firms."

Josh's words, which she hadn't thought much about at the time, came back to her as vividly as if he were standing beside her, whispering clues in her ear. *If you ever consider reinvesting, you might think about diversifying your portfolio to include telecommunication technologies. WiFi networks are literally the wave of the future….*

"Telecommunications? So they would sell stuff like WiFi networks?"

The agents nodded. Walker explained, "Life was smooth sailing for Mr. Thornton here until he stumbled across evidence that his new brother-in-law was cooking the books. It turns out the brother-in-law was a Mafia plant. Marrying the sister was just a means to infiltrate the firm. He'd been selling the company's WiFi network products to corporate consumers at triple the cost, and then funneling the illegal profits back to La Costa Nostra as well as using the firm as a vehicle for laundering mob money from other…*ventures.*"

Mandy wouldn't have thought of high-speed Internet access as a commodity organized crime would set out to steal—or kill for—but when she imagined the millions of dollars that must be involved, it made a crazy sort of sense.

Pulling her scattered thoughts back to the present, she asked, "If you had evidence of the embezzlement, why didn't you pull him then?"

"Because there still wasn't enough hard evidence to link the brother-in-law back to the Mafia, in this case, the Romero family. They've been running their operation from Boston's North End since the fifties and aside from a few petty drug busts, no prosecutor has ever been able to make a conviction stick. Thornton agreed to stay on and work for us undercover, even wear a wire, until we had enough evidence for a search warrant. When his coworker turned up as a floater in the Charles River, we knew we had to get him the hell out of Boston to some place big enough that he could get lost but close enough so we could get him back to testify without any major hassles. Baltimore seemed to fill the bill on both counts, or so we thought."

Poor Josh, no wonder he'd worn that hunted look when she'd asked even the most basic questions about his background. At the time she'd wondered if there might be something shady in his past he was trying to hide. The truth was, he'd been a hero.

Voice quivering, she asked, "Where…where did the hit go down?"

Dr. Matthews answered, "A homeless man came across the body behind a Dumpster inside the Recreation Pier Building in Fells Point and used a pay phone to call 911. We found his car parked a block off Thames. Given the splatter on the side of the Dumpster, it's safe to say the hit went down there."

Recreation Pier was in the seventeen hundred block of Thames Street, the same block as The Daily Grind. Poor Josh, he apparently hadn't lived to see much of Christmas Day.

McKinney spoke up. "Do we have an estimated time of death?"

Midnight! Mandy's mind screamed. *Just after midnight.*

The M.E. rocked back on his heels, expression thoughtful. "That's difficult to pin down. Postmortem changes are strongly affected by environmental factors. With the extreme cold last night, and the snowfall, decomposition would be notably slowed."

McKinney knocked together the heels of his polished wing tips. "Listen, Doc, we don't need a forensics lesson, just give us a time frame for the murder, and we'll take it from there."

Frowning, the M.E. said, "My best estimate is that Joshua Thornton has been dead between twelve and eighteen hours."

Agent Walker glanced down at his Timex. "It's almost six o'clock now. That would put the hit on Thornton at sometime between…midnight and one o'clock this morning?"

Matthews nodded. "Correct."

Mandy's heart leaped into her throat. Even though she'd surmised as much, the M.E.'s confirmation that Josh had died within minutes to an hour of her turning down his invitation for red-hot sex and cinnamon rolls hit her like a sucker punch.

"We know Thornton showed up for work at the museum at 4:30 p.m. and clocked out just after 8:00 p.m., but we can't account for the time between eight and midnight. Maybe he grabbed a bite to eat somewhere?"

Matthews answered, "His stomach contents yielded the remains of coffee and liquid chocolate, probably cocoa. I'm having one of my CSIs pull a data run on all coffee spots within a ten-mile radius of the museum that stayed open after 8:00 p.m. on Christmas Eve."

Heart drumming, Mandy spoke up, "That won't be necessary."

McKinney stared at her, his thin ribbon of upper lip curling with what could only be contempt. "Do you mean to say you don't think reconstructing Thornton's last few hours alive are germane to the case? Really, officer, for all we know, that cup of cocoa could be the key piece of evidence that leads us to the killer."

Feeling as though she were standing within the chamber of a beating heart, Mandy shook her head. "No, that's not what I'm saying." She divided her gaze between the three men staring her down and admitted, "From the time he left the museum at around eight o'clock until midnight, Josh Thornton was with me."

SEATED ON THE STAINED SOFA in the M.E.' s private office, Mandy reached for the paper cup of water Special Agent Walker held out. "Thank you."

She'd barely gotten the first sip down when McKinney jumped on her. "Just what the hell were you doing hooking up with a federally protected witness, *my* witness, while you were on duty?"

Great going, Delinski. So much for making detective— ever. "I wasn't on duty. I was signed out for the night. If you don't believe me, then check my overtime slip."

"We will, make no mistake, but for now go on. Where did you go after leaving the museum?"

"The Daily Grind on Thames Street—that's on the Fells Point waterfront in the same block as the Recreation Pier. Right across the street, in fact," she added, reminded they might not know the city well or even at all. "We drove in separate cars. Department policy prohibits our taking on any unauthorized passengers in the squad car without written permission."

"And then?" McKinney pulled a pen and notepad out of his inside coat pocket and started scribbling notes.

"We ordered, got a table, and sat talking."

The pen stilled. McKinney looked up. "Are you telling me you spent nearly four hours talking…over coffee?"

"Mochas, actually, but yes, that's correct. It turned out we have—had—a lot in common."

"Okay, so after this four-hour chatfest, what happened?"

"He walked me to my car, and I left to drive home." No point in going into the details of that steamy good-night kiss or to how close she'd come to letting good-night turn into good morning.

Screw the promotion. I'll be lucky to keep my current job.

Tone gentle, Special Agent Walker intervened. "We'll have to include this in our report to police Internal Affairs."

McKinney piped up, "Damn straight we will."

Shooting a glare in the younger agent's direction, Walker

added, "Is there anything you'd like to add, Officer Delinski? Anything at all?"

Ah, so they were playing her or at least trying to. Good cop, bad cop, Mandy knew the shtick. "Nothing I can think of at this time." Out of the corner of her eye, she saw the two agents exchanging glances. "I assume I'm free to go?"

Tucking his notes inside his coat pocket, McKinney answered with a grudging nod. "Just don't plan on taking any extended vacations or sudden trips out of town."

She set her water down on the coffee table and got up on shaky knees. "Relax, gentlemen, I'm no flight risk. These days I can barely afford dinner and a movie."

And given the way things were turning out, it would be a while—a long while—before she went out on any more "coffee dates," either.

5

New Year's Eve, oh joy! Number of hunky potential boyfriends lost to violent homicide over the past week: one. Calories consumed: don't know but as am swearing off men for remainder of life, who cares. Glasses of champagne downed to dull grief at grizzly death of sex god and potential soul mate: lost count after first bottle.

MANDY FILED HER REPORT with the department and then went about the rest of the week in a sort of functional daze. Until she could sort things out, including her feelings, keeping herself busy—and numb—seemed like the best solution. For the most part it worked. Well, sort of. In a feeble attempt to feel better, she reminded herself she hadn't really known Josh, not really. Beyond a shared a love for old movies, Art Deco antiques and anything chocolate, he'd been a stranger to her. Until the episode at the M.E.'s, she hadn't even known his real name, let alone who and what he was. Sure, they'd only spent a handful of hours together, a blink of time, and yet there'd been this crazy chemistry, a connection—invisible, indefinable, and yet real nonetheless.

Taking a step back to assess the situation objectively, she could see that things never would have worked out between them. Cinderella fantasies aside, in the real world New

England blue-bloods didn't find their girlfriends from among blue-collar immigrants one generation removed. In all likelihood, he'd found himself alone on Christmas Eve and had been making time with her for lack of something better to do. All he'd wanted with her was a fling or less than that, a one-night stand. Whatever fleeting attraction he'd felt had been brought on by the holiday blues or, given his situation, just plain loneliness. If he'd lived, he would have joined the mounting list of men in her life who said they would call and then didn't. The let-down would have been enormous but even getting used for sex and then dumped would have been preferable to the shock of finding your fantasy man stretched out on a morgue slab on Christmas night. She thought about the speed with which he'd asked her back to his apartment, how close she'd come to accepting, and couldn't help wishing she'd gone with him—and not just to save him, either. She couldn't forget the way he'd smiled at her, not just with his mouth but with his eyes, too; the sensual magic of his kisses; the easy way she'd fit in his arms as though she was meant, just *meant* to be there. No matter what she'd found out, she had to believe that part had been real at least. She just had to.

And now it was five o'clock on New Year's Eve, and she was curled up on the plaid living room couch—encased in its clear vinyl cover—a bowl of microwave popcorn in her lap and jumbo bag of Reese's Pieces on the coffee table in front of her. She leaned over to reach for the TV remote when the doorbell rang.

It was Suzie Plotnik, her best friend since they'd met as fifth-graders at St. Agnes School. Standing in the doorway, she gave Mandy the once-over, taking in the baggy sweatshirt and mismatched drawstring sweatpants, and shook her short cap of razor-cut blond hair. "I can see I got here just in time."

Without waiting for an invitation, she stepped past Mandy and strolled into the living room, casually elegant in a cream-colored angora turtleneck sweater and slim-fitting jeans.

Feeling like a blob—a blob with unwashed hair and no makeup—Mandy followed her over to the couch.

Plopping down on the cushion, she held out the popcorn bowl in offering. "Since you're here, dig in."

Kicking off her suede slip-ons, Suz shook her head. "No thanks." She'd lost a boatload of weight on Jenny Craig the year before, and Mandy hadn't seen her swallow much more than air since.

Shrugging, Mandy dug in a hand. "So are you checking up on me or what?"

"Actually, I came to invite you to the New Year's Eve party I just decided this morning to have. I figured since I didn't get invited to any cool, hip party, I'd throw one myself. Since it's a last minute thing, I'm following the K.I.S.S. rule and keeping it simple—munchies and a couple of party platters from Giant Food, wine and beer, and of course, champagne. And the really great part is I'm just a few blocks away, so you won't have to worry about driving. You can spend the night if you want or walk home afterward, your call."

Licking butter from her thumb, Mandy shrugged. "It sounds great, really, but I'm not really in much of a party mood."

Suz sent her a sympathetic look. "The dead hunk still got you down, huh?"

In the course of their twenty years as best friends, she and Suz had shared not only clothes and music CDs but also hopes, secrets and dreams. After Mandy had gotten home from the M.E.'s office on Christmas night, Suz had been the only person she'd even considered calling.

Voice hitching, she'd said, "I met this really great guy on Christmas Eve, at least he seemed really great and really into me, *me,* if you can believe that. Only guess what, I just ran into him again and the only thing he was wearing other than his birthday suit was a toe tag."

Even on the brink of tears, she'd deliberately held back any mention of Josh being a federal witness. There were some things, classified case information especially, that a cop couldn't share, not even with her best girlfriend.

A true blue buddy, all Suz had said was, "Hold tight, girlfriend, I'm on my way." She'd shown up on the Delinskis' doorstep fifteen minutes later with a bottle of Chianti and a jumbo box of Kleenex, neither of which had gone to waste.

With Suz's clear green eyes looking straight through her, Mandy knew denial was pointless no matter how pathetic her situation might seem. "I know it sounds crazy, but I really thought I'd finally found him. You know, *the* guy, Mr. Right. We only spent a couple of hours together, but we had this chemistry thing going and well, as nuts as it sounds that a guy like that would be into me, he really seemed like he was."

Crossing her long legs beneath her campfire style, Suz shook her head. "It doesn't sound crazy and stop putting yourself down. You know what you felt. Just because he's, uh…passed on, doesn't make what you experienced any less real."

"I don't know, Suz. It was Christmas, after all, and he was…new in town. Maybe he just couldn't face the holiday alone. Maybe he just wanted another warm body to cling to. Make that a *big,* warm body to cling to." She tried for a laugh but it fell flat. Like leftover New Year's Eve champagne, there was no sparkle, no fizz.

Looking exasperated, Suz dragged a hand of hot pink nails through her hair. "Look, Mandy, you're a great woman at any weight. You're pretty, and funny, and smart—don't roll your eyes at me like that, yes, you are. Some guy's gonna come along and sweep you off your feet when you least expect it, you wait and see."

A lump of sadness moved into her throat, and Mandy set the popcorn aside. "But I thought this was him, you know, The One."

Suz reached across for Mandy's hand. Giving it a squeeze, she said, "I know you did, sweetie, but there are other great guys out there just waiting to meet someone like you." Letting go, she sat back and added, "But one thing's for sure, you're not going to meet anyone holed up here watching *Dick Clark's New Year's Rocking Eve*. Besides, I've invited actual living, breathing men tonight including some real hotties."

Suz was back to doing a sales job on the party. Holding in a sigh, Mandy reached for the candy. "It sounds great, really, but I still think I'll pass."

Snatching the bag away, Suz said, "Come on, Mandy, it'll be fun. It'll do you good to get out. All your sitting here gorging on chocolate will accomplish is wrecking your skin and blowing your diet."

"I'm not on a diet and even if I were, I don't have anything to wear—anything that fits, that is—unless you count my current ensemble." She pulled on the elastic waistband of her sweatpants and let go, snapping it back. Was it her imagination or did the fit feel tighter than it had that morning?

Looking like the cat eyeing the dish of cream only in Suz's case, that would be the fat-free soy milk, Suz smiled. "Remember that black velvet cocktail dress of mine you always said made me look twenty pounds thinner and volumes hotter?"

"Uh, huh." Mandy made a swipe for the candy bag, but Suz shoved it behind her back. "The one you're too skinny to fit in now. Yeah, I remember."

"Well, consider it yours. I have it out in my car hanging in the plastic dry cleaning bag. I'll go out and get it, and you can try it on." When Mandy stayed put, Suz tugged at her arm. "Come on, Mands, if you stay home you'll just get even more depressed, eat every Reese's Piece in that bag, and then start on the can of fudge frosting hidden in the back of the fridge."

Damn, but Suz was the one who should be trying for detective. "How'd you know about the frosting?"

Grinning, Suz shrugged. "I'm your best friend, remember? I know you always hit the frosting when you're really down."

Mandy shook her head. "It doesn't matter because from this moment on, I am permanently swearing off men. Consider it my New Year's resolution."

Suz untucked her legs and popped up. "I don't believe in New Year's resolutions, I believe in goals. Come on, let's go check out that dress."

FOUR HOURS LATER, Mandy was pulling off her snow boots and slipping on her high-heeled sling-backs on the stoop of Suz's East Baltimore row house. The shoes were a painful proposition, but they went perfectly with her borrowed Little Black Dress. The slinky black fabric fell well above the knee, much shorter than she'd ever worn before, but she had to admit if only to herself the dress did look pretty good on her. She'd even gone to the trouble to do her makeup and use heated rollers on her hair, which fell past her shoulders in loose, finger-combed waves. Entering, she caught Suz's eye from the opposite side of the room, and her friend's face lit up like a Christmas tree.

Dressed in a glittery gold stretch top and slinky Chinese silk cocktail pants, Suz pushed a path toward her and greeted her with a hug. Drawing back, she said, "You look hot, girlfriend. Make that smokin'." She touched an index finger to Mandy's shoulder and made a sizzling sound.

"Okay, okay, I get the point. Thanks. You look pretty amazing yourself." Self-conscious, Mandy darted a look around to the twenty- and thirtysomethings congregating in the living room and camped out around the dining room food table before slipping off her three-quarter length belted black wool dress coat, a loan from her sister, Sharon.

Without the outerwear, she felt if not exactly naked, certainly closer to that state than she usually came, in public anyway. The dress's low neckline left little to the imagination, especially with the lacy black push-up bra underneath. She couldn't help wishing Josh had gotten to see her like this, looking her best—okay hot—rather than in her sexless police uniform, not that he'd seemed to mind.

Suz took her coat and hung it inside the jammed closet. Turning back, she said, "Beer and wine are in the kitchen along with someone I want you to meet."

Another fix-up, oh shit. Some detective she'd turn out to be, she hadn't even seen that one coming.

Mandy shook her head so hard she nearly knocked off one of her mother's vintage faux pearl-and-diamond clip-ons. Reaching up to secure the earring, she said, "I told you, I'm swearing off men."

"Not in that dress you're not." Grinning, Suz hooked her arm through Mandy's and started towing them toward the back of the house.

Mandy tried digging her heels, her *high* heels, into the beige wall-to-wall, but it was no use. Her friend was on a mission. They came up on the kitchen alcove, and Suz dropped her voice and said, "See the Italian hunk standing by the beer cooler talking to my brother Joey?"

Mandy followed the less than subtle head jerk to the beefy bodybuilder sipping from a bottle of Miller and talking to Suz's younger brother. "Italian *hulk*, you must mean."

Standing at medium height, the man had the tree-trunk neck and wide-legged stance of someone who pumped iron in a serious way. She doubted there was an ounce of fat on him, and yet he looked as though he might split the seams of his black T-shirt and trousers at any minute. At one time, she might have found all that bulky muscle a turn-on, but now she couldn't help thinking how much sexier Josh's taller, leaner body had been.

Leaning in, Suz whispered, "His name's Danny Romero, and he owns a gym downtown."

"A gym, huh?" One look at her and he'd probably tell Suz to lock up the party food. "That's nice."

Suz scowled. "Nice! Show a little more enthusiasm, can't we? He's gorgeous, owns his own business and, Mandy, he's single—never married, in fact."

"I guess that makes him almost a relationship virgin, huh?"

Rather than answer, Suz shoved her through the kitchen door and into the hulk's granite chest. "Danny, this is my best friend in the world, Mandy Delinski. Mandy, this is Danny Romero, a buddy of Joey's."

Before anyone had the chance to say another word, Suz grabbed her baby brother by the arm and all but dragged him out of the kitchen.

Stranded, Mandy stepped back from the hard slab of chest and looked up. "Hi."

"How you doin'?" His gaze slipped to her breasts, recently flattened against him, and stayed there. "So you're Suz's friend, the woman cop?"

The woman cop. Nice. Teeth gritted, Mandy answered, "Yeah, at least until those sex change hormones kick in."

He hesitated and then threw back his head and chuckled, a loud braying that made her want to cover her ears even as she thought how much nicer Josh's laughter had sounded. "You're funny. I like that."

So glad I have your approval. "Thanks. If this *woman* cop thing doesn't work out, I figure I can always fall back on stand-up comedy."

He grinned, revealing what had to be professionally whitened teeth. "Want a drink?"

What the hell, it was a New Year's Eve party. If she was going to be trapped here until midnight, she might as well partake and, at any rate, she was walking home. Perusing the bank of open wine bottles set out on the kitchen table, she said, "Sure. I'll have a—"

She stopped when he reached down into the cooler, pulled out a Miller Lite, and popped the cap without asking her preference. Murmuring a thank-you, she accepted the beer, thinking how politely Josh had treated her on their short but sweet date, opening doors, carrying her coffee to their table along with his, standing around in the cold to make sure she got her car started.

As the night wore on, the comparisons continued. Whereas Josh had wanted to know about her, it was obvious Danny was more interested in having an audience, a *captive* audience of one, hear all about him. Knocking back the beers he kept handing her, Mandy listened in silence as he went on about his problems keeping a decent aerobics instructor on staff— they were all "bimbos," according to him—his plans for expanding the facility to include a juice bar and separate rooms for spinning and yoga classes, his personal diet and weight training program because hey, you don't get to look like this without workin' at it. When the latter segued into a bragging fest on how many pounds he could bench press, Mandy decided she'd heard more than enough.

Alcohol buzzing through her bloodstream, she set down her empty beer bottle—was it her third or fourth—and said, "You know, it's a little warm in here." *Must be from all the hot air.* "I'm going to step outside for a moment."

"Get some fresh air, that's a great idea. I'll keep you company seeing as how I'm, uh…hot, too." His leer and the fact that his eyes were still pinned to her breasts left no doubt as to what kind of company he was offering.

Conceited asshole, he was so stuck on himself he probably thought she was hinting she wanted to make out with him. *I may be a fat woman but as far as making out with you goes, fat chance, buddy.*

"Thanks but I'm kind of a solo breather. My…er, yoga instructor likes me to keep it that way."

His smile dropped to the ground like one of his precious

barbells. For one of the few times that night, he actually looked her in the eye. "But it'll be midnight in five minutes. You can't tell me you want to ring in the New Year all by your lonesome. Might be unlucky or…something." He reached for her, but she took a quick step back.

"I'll take my chances." She snatched her evening purse off the Corian counter and made a beeline for the doorway.

Out in the living room, guests wearing paper party hats and pre-testing noisemakers and confetti congregated around the big screen TV, tuned in to the countdown for the ball to drop in New York's Times Square. She made her way over to Suz, who was circulating with a bottle of champagne.

She looked up from the plastic glassware she was filling and grinned. "Is that Danny something else or what?"

Mandy nodded. "He's, uh…definitely something all right."

Suz must have caught the sarcasm in her voice because her smile fell. "You two hit it off, right? You must have because you've been standing in that same spot for hours."

"Only because it took me that long to get a word in, and once I did I decided to make it goodbye." Mandy dragged a hand through her hair, too frustrated to care about messing up the curls. "It's a great party, really it is, but I'm just not in a party mood. I shouldn't have come. Look, I'll call you tomorrow, okay?" She turned to go.

Suz trailed her to the front door. "But Mandy, you can't go now."

Fed up with being told what she could or couldn't do, Mandy swung around. Flinging her arms out at her sides, she said, "I know, I know, it's almost midnight, and who wants to ring in the New Year alone, right? Well, you know who? Me. I do. Call me Garbo, but the truth is I want to be alone." Taking the silver screen diva's famous quote as her exit line, she turned her back on Suz and the roomful of suddenly silent guests and yanked open the front door.

She stepped out onto the marble steps, her breath forming whitish clouds in the frigid air. Rubbing her bare arms, she asked herself what the hell was the matter with her. Had she suddenly become the biggest bitch on the planet or had the events of the past week taken a heavier toll on her than she'd cared to admit? Either way, there was no excusing her rudeness, especially when Suz had been trying to help. As soon as she pulled herself together, she'd go back inside and apologize, grab her coat and head for home. Hell, while she was on a roll, she might as well track down Danny, Mr. Wonderful, and apologize to him, too, before her buzz wore off.

Overblown ego aside, Danny was what most women from her neighborhood would consider a catch—good-looking, single and a successful business owner. He'd even seemed sort of interested in her, her breasts at least. The bigger problem wasn't him, she admitted, but her. Even if he'd been the greatest conversationalist on the planet, she still wouldn't have been able to look at him without mentally morphing his dark eyes into blue ones, his black hair into sandy blond, and his stocky build into a leaner, taller frame. Because no matter how great Danny or any other man might be, he would never be Josh. No one would. There was only one Josh Thornton and the damned shame was that by now he was planted six feet underground somewhere in Boston.

A splash struck her cheek. She looked up, expecting to see rain or snow, but the sky was clear and after a few seconds she realized what she'd felt wasn't precipitation but her own tear. Wiping it away, she noted the absence of the moon in the canvas of black sky. Recalling the lunar notation on her wall calendar, she knew it was a new moon, that time of the month when it cycled through all the other signs of the zodiac to align with the sun. The start of the next lunar phase, it was supposed to be the optimal time for pursuing fresh starts and seeking future possibilities.

In the past, she'd written off astrology as New-Age woo-woo, but standing on Suz's stoop, she desperately needed to believe in something—in the possibility of happy endings and magic and make-believe; in the power of wishing. Only what she wished for wasn't to move forward with her future but instead to retrace her steps and go back—back in time. Back one week to that magical, fateful Christmas Eve, only this time when Josh asked her to come home with him, she'd answer yes, yes, *yes!* Hindsight being twenty-twenty, she'd do everything possible and then some to make sure he stayed safe and alive for that Boston trial even if that meant locking him in a room and herself right along with him—especially if it meant that.

"Ten, nine, eight, seven…" From inside the house, collective voices chanted out the countdown to a new year.

She squeezed her eyes tightly closed. "Please, God, and Mother Mary, too, if any of you are up there listening, this wish is for Josh, and for me, too, I guess."

"Six, five, four…"

"If there's anything you can do to intervene, anything at all, please make him not be dead."

"Three, two, one—Happy New Year!"

Mandy opened her eyes, an explosion of noisemakers and joyous shouts sounding off at her back. Holding her breath, she looked down at the watch on her right wrist. It was indeed midnight. The date on her digital watch had flipped forward to January 1, 2007. Forward, not backward. Had she really expected it to say 2006?

Those beers must have hit me a lot harder than I thought.

Not only was she on a crying jag, but she apparently was delusional, too. She'd actually had herself believing she could turn back time just by wishing, or actually, praying. *Man, I had better get home and fast.* She dug a Kleenex out of her purse and dabbed it beneath her eyes. Dropping the balled-up tissue inside, she snapped the bag closed and chanced one last look up at the sky.

"Happy New Year, Josh, wherever you are."

She turned to go back inside and say her other goodbyes.

6

Monday, January 1, New Year's Day, or December 24 (Christmas Eve round two)—take your pick.

Cases of drinker's remorse: one but worst since morning after high school prom when woke up in lawn chaise at public pool wrapped around gross Lenny Borkowski and missing panties. (Okay, on second thought, maybe not as bad as that). Likelihood of carting around brain tumor size of Harborplace or being knocked out cold in coma like friggin' Connecticut Yankee in King Arthur's Court: very likely but with hot fantasy to liven up vegetative state, decide consciousness definitely overrated.

Number of hunky potential boyfriends raised Lazarus-like from the dead: one but hallelujah and praise be!

"'I CAN'T GET NO SATISFACTION. No satisfaction…no, no, noooo…'"

Mandy awoke to the Rolling Stones' "Satisfaction" blaring out of her radio alarm clock. *I can't get no satisfaction, how fitting.* With eyes squeezed shut, she unfurled from the fetal position she'd curled into and reached out to shut the music off. Ah, so this was a hangover. It had been so long, senior year in high school, that she'd almost forgotten what the experience felt like. She'd certainly earned it, following up on the beers she'd downed with several plastic glasses of champagne Suz kept refilling and not leaving to stumble home until sometime around 2:00 a.m. *Ringing in the New Year with a ringing head—great going, Mandy.*

Since she'd already faced the music, so to speak, she might as well get up and face what would likely prove to be a pretty scary reflection in the bathroom mirror. She cracked open an eye—and felt her cotton candy-colored bedroom spinning like a carousel.

Oh, shit. She closed her eyes and held still, waiting for the sickening dizziness to wind down. Wait a minute, pink? Whatever happened to the sage green she'd painted just before Christmas? She'd heard of cases where alcohol poisoning had brought on blindness but color blindness?

I must be hallucinating, or still dreaming. She opened her eyes again. Nope, still pink.

Could someone have crept in after she slept—make that passed out—and repainted as some sort of joke? But no, there wasn't a trace of odor. Just to be sure, she rolled out of bed and stumbled across the room to touch the wall. The old paint was dry as bone—and still pink. How could that be? She glanced over to the corner where the can of paint and new brushes she'd bought sat. One hand to the wall for balance, she squatted down to examine them. The seal on the paint canister was unbroken and the brushes not just clean but untouched. And yet she'd gotten up early on Christmas Day and put on the final coat. What the hell was going on?

The alarm went off again, this time a contemporary tune by the group, Third Eye Blind. She must have hit the snooze button rather than off. One hand pressed to her pounding temple, she staggered over to the night table when the alarm's electric date display caught her eye. The digital numbers read 12/24/06—only it was January 1, 2007. Piece of shit alarm must be broken, had to be. She'd pick up a new one on her way home from work that night.

Work. Oh shit, she was on duty today. Fighting nausea, she grabbed her robe and hurried down the hallway to the bathroom, stripped off her sweats, and stumbled into the shower. Forty-five minutes, two Advil and a large Starbucks coffee to-go later, she was driving down Eastern Avenue to the tune of "Jingle Bells," the roaring in her head muted to a manageable mewling.

Christmas carols on January first. Some people just didn't know when to put the season to bed. The music ended and the DJ broke to a commercial. "Attention, holiday shoppers, Smith and Company is keeping its stores open until midnight tonight. Yes, that's right, midnight. Take advantage of this last chance to get those low, low, *low* sale prices before the holiday, and come on down to…"

Holiday shoppers? Mandy slammed on her brakes, narrowly avoiding running the red light, coffee sloshing onto the floor mat.

Okay, visual hallucinations are bad enough but auditory… that definitely signals trouble.

Shaken, she pulled into the precinct, parked and entered the building with five minutes to spare before roll call. Ordinarily working the holiday would have sucked, but given the weirdness she was experiencing, she was glad to have a routine to fall into.

Betty, the widowed receptionist with the dyed black beehive and penciled-on brows, smiled at her as she walked through the door. "Good morning, Mandy. Would you like a cookie? I took them out of the oven right before I came in to work."

Glancing down at the foil-covered plate on the desk, Mandy knew that a cookie was likely the last thing she needed. On the other hand, she had skipped dinner last night—unless Reese's Pieces had been added to the Department of Agriculture's food pyramid. Besides, Betty lived to bake.

"Sure, I'd love one."

Beaming, Betty whisked off the foil wrap. Mandy reached

down to make her selection and then froze. From red-nosed reindeer to red-capped Santa Clauses to button-eyed snowmen, the cookies were all formed in festive holiday shapes, *Christmas* holiday shapes. Had poor Betty gone off her rocker or what?

Hand hovering, Mandy looked up at Betty, searching that sweet smile for signs of early onset dementia or at least extreme stress. "You mean you reheated these, right?"

Betty's smile folded into a frown. "Do you think I would serve stale cookies to my friends and coworkers? What kind of a person do you think I am?"

"Betty, I didn't mean—"

"If you don't believe me, then try one. Go ahead."

Mandy picked up a snowman and bit off the head. Chewing, she had to admit there was no doubt about it. The cookie was warm and gooey and well, oven fresh.

Tapping a red acrylic nail on the faux wood desktop, Betty demanded, "Well?"

Feeling as if the cookie was sticking in her throat, Mandy swallowed. "It's delicious, Betty, but then I always say you could enter your sugar cookies in any cooking contest and come home with the blue ribbon."

Betty nodded, her smile returning. "Roll call's next door in five minutes. You want one for the road?"

"Thanks, but no. I'm trying to slim down—New Year's resolution and all that."

Betty pushed the plate toward her again. "Oh, go ahead, hon. You might as well live it up for the next week. There'll be plenty of time to diet after the holidays."

After the holidays, there it was again. *Oh my God, what's happening to me?* Had that Danny guy slipped something into her beer last night when she wasn't looking?

The squad room was filling up with suits when Mandy entered. Boblitz took the roll and then handed out the day's assignments—all identical to the ones she'd received on

Christmas Eve the week before, right down to checking in with the mother of an armed robbery suspect who'd gone missing along with the cash.

The day progressed, the coincidences piling on until she could no longer ignore them or deny the apparent truth. As impossible, okay, crazy, as it sounded, she'd lived this day before. She felt like an actor in a TV drama, knowing the script by heart because she and the other players had blocked out the scenes. Only this was no walk-through. She was living it all firsthand—again.

The finale came at the end of the day. As if responding to a stage manager's cue, Sergeant Boblitz belted out, "Yo, Delinski, not so fast."

Oh God, oh God, oh God. Either I've lost my mind, completely flipped out, or it must really be true, it must really be happening. She'd gone back in time but only a week. It was Christmas Eve, *the* Christmas Eve Joshua Thornton had asked her out for coffee, kissed her and then turned up dead on Christmas Day.

Heart pounding, Mandy turned slowly around.

"Somethin's come up, special detail at the BMA. I need you there pronto. There was a bomb threat earlier this week, totally bogus but the museum director, who is stuck way up the mayor's ass, is pissing in his pants to make sure nothing goes wrong tonight."

Reciting from memory, she said, "But it's…Christmas Eve. What, uh…could be going on tonight?"

He shrugged. "I dunno, one of those artsy fartsy shindigs, and seeing as the museum is one of the city's leading cultural attractions, et cetera, et cetera, the department has a vested interest in making sure tonight goes off without a hitch—make that a *boom*. Seeing as you're so gung-ho on making detective, I know you won't want to pass up this opportunity to distinguish yourself."

"Okay, I'll do it."

Mandy raced out of the squad house, jumped into her squad car, and drove to the museum as fast as she dared.

JOSH CAST AN APOLOGETIC LOOK to the elderly couple who'd strolled up to the bar, expecting their champagne glasses to be refilled. "I'm pretty sure we're out, but if you'll give me a minute, I'll check again."

He ducked behind the portable bar and flipped open the cooler concealed by the bar's covering of white skirting. Fingers raking the ice, he asked himself what kind of bush league event ran out of champagne in the first hour. Back in Boston a champagne drought at an arts function would have been the catalyst for a mass guest exodus if not an outright revolt. Then again, Boston had been the stage for one hell of a tea party whereas Baltimore was tamer ground. Still, to borrow a line from Agatha Christie's Miss Marple, how could you celebrate a champagne occasion without…well, the champagne?

He was just about to give up when his frozen hand came upon the object of his search—a magnum bottle of high-end champagne the caterer had reserved for VIP guests. Well, anybody who'd stuck it out this long for charity rated as a VIP in his book. Bottle in hand, he stood up. "Here you go, sir, ma'am. Merry Christmas and enjoy."

He splashed bubbly into their glasses, earning the woman's smile and a generous five-dollar tip from her husband. Once five dollars would have seemed a pittance, but the days when he'd pulled down a six-figure salary were fading to a distant memory. It was all relative, he supposed.

Why was it standing in the same spot for hours on end left him feeling more tired than when he'd crossed the finish line of the Boston Marathon? At least working the bar of the crowded Canton pub, his regular gig, kept his hands and mind engaged, but these formal functions were deadly whether you were a guest or the hired help. Time always felt like it was standing still. He looked across the atrium courtyard in search of a wall clock—and found himself staring into a pair of thickly lashed chocolate-brown eyes. The eyes stared back at him from the oval-shaped face of a drop-dead gorgeous redhead with a porcelain perfect complexion and a mouth fashioned for sin. Tall and curvy, she somehow managed to look both sexy and feminine in the buttoned up uniform of a Baltimore City street cop, no small feat. His gaze returned to her mouth, full lips painted a deep, rich red reminiscent of a silver-screen-era starlet, and suddenly images of all the things they might do together to smudge that perfectly applied cosmetic ricocheted through his mind. As if on cue, he felt himself growing heavy and hard.

Easy, Josh. Down, boy, down.

Granted it had been a while, okay, a very long while, since he'd gotten down and dirty—or even down—with a woman, but the depth of his reaction took him by surprise nonetheless. Grateful for the ledge of bar that came above his waist, he willed his breathing to relax, his heartbeats to slow, and his hard-on to soften. He was a Thornton, after all. Thornton men prided themselves on their business acumen, their principles and, above all, their self-control.

But he was also an O'Malley on his mother's side, and those passionate and unruly Irish genes would not be denied either, not entirely. And so in a very un-Thorntonlike gesture, he filled an empty champagne flute, raised the glass in a toast, and meeting the police woman's wide-eyed gaze, mouthed the words "Merry Christmas."

She hesitated and then smiled back, a dazzling smile that showed off straight white teeth and matching dimples flanking either side of her slightly cleft chin. Holding her gaze, he silently willed her to cross the room toward him.

"Tanqueray and tonic."

He broke eye contact to regard the sixtysomething woman

standing before him, a diamond choker clasped about her bony throat and a sense of entitlement oozing from her every patrician pore.

Covering his annoyance at the intrusion, he said, "My apologies, ma'am, but the only gin we're serving tonight is Beefeater."

"Beefeater!" From her shocked tone and indignant expression, one would have thought he'd just suggested savagery on par with draining the life's blood from infants or drowning puppies in the city's Inner Harbor. "And well you should apologize. Do you have any idea what a sponsor-level membership runs these days?"

Squelching the impulse to ask who might give a damn, he pasted on a stiff smile and reminded himself that he'd dealt with his fair share of difficult clients in the telecommunications industry. These days the consequences of an unhappy customer were pretty insignificant stacked up against multi-million dollar accounts at stake—or his very life.

"Would you still like that gin and tonic—with Beefeater— or would you prefer another beverage?"

She hesitated, nostrils flaring. "I'll have a white wine."

"Chardonnay, coming right up."

He grabbed one of the newly opened bottles of Kendall-Jackson and filled a wine glass to the rim if only to delay her coming back. Looking up to hand her the drink, he froze. All too often dreams died on the vine, but once in a great while wishes still came true.

Standing directly behind that tower of stiffly sprayed gray hair was the redheaded cop. If possible, she was even prettier up close than she'd appeared from across the proverbial crowded room.

Taking a sip of her wine, the older woman wrinkled her nose. She reached a liver-spotted hand into her beaded evening bag, plunked a quarter into his tip jar, and moved on.

Glad to see her go, Josh suddenly found himself face-to-face with the object of his lust—a doe-eyed, full-figured redhead conjured straight out of his most X-rated dreams. "Can I get you something to drink…*officer?*" He was pretty sure he knew what her answer would be, but he couldn't resist flirting, or at least he didn't want to. There was something about her, a rare innocence that made for an intriguing combination with all those sexy curves.

She shook her head and blushed as though he'd suggested stripping her naked and having her on top of the bar—a lovely fantasy and like most fantasies, highly impractical—but, oh, so fun to think about. "Can't…I'm on duty."

Not yet willing to let her go, he pressed, "Coke, then?"

He had the eerie déjà vu feeling of having asked her that question before, which was crazy since they were meeting for the first time. Shrugging off the been there, done that sensation as an occupational hazard of bartending, he waited for her answer.

Again, that shake of her head, those big brown eyes riveted on his face as though she couldn't quite believe he was real. "N-no thanks, I'm good. You're not…you're not from around here."

That remark was the equivalent of plunging the semi-erection he'd got going straight into the drink cooler of ice. "What makes you say that?"

She shrugged, which did amazing things to the beautifully shaped breasts molded to her high-buttoned uniform top. "Your accent, it sounds kind of New England."

Josh relaxed fractionally. It was an innocuous observation for anyone to make, cop or civilian. He must be even more on edge than he'd thought. Paranoia was a fairly normal symptom of cumulative stress, in his case the stress of spending six consecutive months in hiding. And now of course it was Christmas, the absolute worst time of year to be alone, separated from family and friends and…home. Thank God the ordeal was coming to an end in just a little over a week. The trial date was set for January second. The night before, the feds would fly him up to Boston, he'd give his testimony the next morning, and then he'd be home free.

Free. Keeping that beautiful thought foremost in his mind, he found his smile—and his flirt. "Oh, it's *my* accent, is it?"

All that smiling must have been contagious because she smiled back, revealing a dimple on either side of her sexy, upturned mouth. "If you're saying I have a *Bawlmer* accent, then I'm guilty as charged. I can't help it. I grew up in the city."

He shook his head. The last thing he'd meant to do was offend her or seem to put her down. "I like your accent. It's distinctive…like you."

"Thanks, *hon*," she said with a wink.

He'd been in Baltimore long enough to recognize those truncated vowels, especially the infamous Baltimore *O*. Charmed by her ability to poke fun at herself, he tossed back his head and let loose with a belly laugh that would have done Old St. Nick proud.

Recovering, he held out his hand. "My name's Josh."

She hesitated, and then slipped her much smaller hand inside his. "I'm Amanda…Mandy, actually." She gave his fingers a slight squeeze, and suddenly he found himself bombarded with images of all the other places he'd like to let that soft palm and pretty pink-nailed fingers travel.

"Mandy, hmm?" he repeated even as his semi rocketed to full-out hard-on. "Pretty lady, pretty name." He glanced down at their joined hands. One of them, maybe both, had forgotten to let go.

A throat clearing saved him from behaving like a complete idiot. Dropping her hand, he looked beyond her and saw that the blue-haired lady with the scary hair had returned. She held up her empty wineglass as if to say, "Fill her up."

"I guess duty calls," the cop, Mandy, said, brown eyes sparkling.

"Yeah, I guess so." He made a show of rolling his eyes, letting her know he didn't welcome the intrusion anymore than she did. "Hey, I've got another hour to go and all the nonalcoholic carbonated beverages you can drink, so don't be a stranger, okay?" He winked.

Josh spent the rest of the evening pouring chardonnay, champagne and the occasional mixed drink to a steady stream of thirsty patrons. Throughout, he kept one eye on the wall clock and one eye on the pretty lady cop, Mandy, stationed at the door. Mandy. Ever since she'd introduced herself, the Barry Manilow song of the same name had been playing nonstop in his head, only now it struck him as kind of nice rather than goofy.

When eight o'clock rolled around, he made double time in closing down the bar, packing up the stock and storing the used glassware in the plastic crates. He ducked into the men's room and changed out of his uniform into jeans and his leather jacket. Stepping out, his uniform on a hanger, he spotted Mandy standing at the security check-in area. He came up behind her and touched her lightly on the shoulder.

She whirled, the cell phone he hadn't seen dropping from her hand to hit the floor as that same hand went to the holster at her hip.

Man, he thought he was tightly strung these days. Taking a step back, he held his arms out from his sides in mock surrender. "Hey, easy you. There's no need to pull a Dirty Harry on me. I just wanted to say good-night before you snuck out." He dove for the cell and handed it to her.

She took it and slipped it into the clip at her waist. "I'm not sneaking out, I'm just signing out." She hesitated. "You're, uh...done for the night, too, then?"

He rolled his shoulders, thinking how good those small, capable hands of hers might feel on his back, and said, "Yeah, thank God." He paused, reaching for his nerve. "Any chance

I could persuade you into grabbing a drink or a cup of coffee with me…or don't you fraternize with civilians?"

Actually given his situation, he was the one who shouldn't be fraternizing. On the other hand, if the mob boys hadn't found him yet, chances were they wouldn't. In another week, he'd go back to Boston, testify at his mobster brother-in-law's trial, and be home free. Almost to the finish line, he felt like celebrating—only not alone. Besides, it was Christmas Eve.

Flushing, she shook her head, and he felt his heart drop along with his hopes for the evening. "I can't drink in uniform, but uh…coffee sounds good. Only it's Christmas Eve. There won't be much open at this hour."

God, she was pretty. She smelled good, too, some light floral fragrance underlying a spicier scent that had his head spinning—and his mouth opening to blurt out, "In that case, I should probably mention I make great coffee."

Jesus, had he really just asked a complete stranger to go home with him? What the hell had gotten into him? He liked women, okay he liked them a lot, and though he'd logged in his share of sexual exploration, he'd never been a one-night stand kind of guy. Getting to know a woman first wasn't only the health-conscious thing to do, but it also built the anticipation to make the inevitable conclusion all the more satisfying.

But there was something about this night and this woman that was different from any other encounter, borderline magical. He wasn't acting like himself, not at all, and as much as he wanted to blame it on Christmas and being lonely, he knew that wasn't the explanation, not really. Truth was he'd never been this red-hot, this on fire for a woman, and he was badly in danger of losing his head.

If he'd shocked her, she hid it well. She took a small step back but didn't bolt. "Actually, I know of this great locals' place, The Daily Grind. It may still be open."

Amazed she wasn't turning him down flat after the way

he'd behaved—make that, *misbehaved*—he hid his relief behind a smile. "In that case, officer, lead the way."

SITTING IN THE DAILY GRIND across from Josh, Mandy felt as though she'd rewound a rented movie and was watching it again from the start only instead of looking on, she was living or rather *reliving* it. Knowing in advance how the evening would play out should have dampened her excitement, but instead it only heightened her anticipation. It was like stepping back into a lovely dream, a magical memory you got to live again only in the moment.

Looking across the table into Josh's warm-eyed gaze, she couldn't shake the feeling she must be hallucinating or, barring that, still asleep in her bed at home in the throes of a crazy, hung-over dream. The last time she'd seen him, he'd been a stiff on a morgue slab, as bloodless and inanimate as a figure in a wax museum.

Unfortunately time, even time in reverse, wasn't prone to standing still. If anything, it seemed to sprout wings and fly by. Josh had been killed shortly after midnight. Glancing down at her wristwatch, she saw it was eleven forty-five. Shit.

"I can't help noticing you keep looking at your watch. Am I keeping you from something?"

No, but I am trying to keep you alive. Panic hit her, and she shook her head. If he left the coffee shop without her, he was as good as dead—again. "No, not at all, it's just a habit I've gotten into, a cop thing, I guess." She lifted her porcelain cup and chugged the contents like a frat boy chugging beer.

"Ouch." She slammed the cup down, mouth on fire. Damn, but if she hadn't burned herself—again.

He reached across to wipe whipped cream from her chin, his moist mouth parted in a sexy, half-cocked smile, and there was no denying that he was very real and, for the moment, very much alive. Although it went against all logic, she could no longer ignore or pretend that what was happening to her, to him, to *them,* was anything less than one hundred percent real. By whatever power, she'd been granted her New Year's wish, thrust into the role of guardian angel with the mission of saving Joshua Thornton's life.

Watching her set the empty mug down, he asked, "Would you like another?"

She shook her head. "No thanks. I'm good. Any more caffeine and sugar, and I'll be bouncing off the artwork." The truth was she was all but jumping out of her skin, but the two large mochas weren't to blame. "It is Christmas Eve. I guess we should let these folks go home." She nodded toward the counter where the two employees regarded them with familiar, fuming looks.

"Before they throw us out, you mean?" He got up and turned to grab his jacket off the chair back.

There it was again, an up close view of that incredibly tight ass. Mandy licked her lips, feeling as if the thermostat had just knocked up several notches. Sure, she was on a mission, a life-saving mission, but the fact was she was hot for him, hotter than she'd been the week before even because now she'd had a week of regret to live down.

Remember, he has a life and, for all you know, a serious girlfriend back in Boston. Do not, under any circumstances, lose your head—or your heart. Even so, she couldn't help thinking what a gentleman he was, how eager to please. She'd bet anything he was like that in bed, too. If she had anything to say about it, she'd be finding that out very soon.

And there they were again, standing out on the darkened street alongside her parked squad car, the coffee shop fading to black behind them like the backdrop in a movie set. Only this was no movie, but rather reality on instant replay.

But altering the night's outcome, and saving Josh, called

for her to take a decidedly more proactive approach than she had before. Wrapping her arms about his neck, she crushed her mouth against his, letting loose all the passion, all the *hunger,* she normally kept locked inside.

Coming up for air, she stared into his startled eyes and blurted out, "Take me home with you—now!"

7

December 25, Christmas Take Two

Like Dr. Alexander Fleming discovering penicillin or astronaut Neil Armstrong stepping out of the spacecraft for that first moonwalk, feel as if am standing on brink of "brave, new world"—new to me, at least. In past, sex has been like dining at an all-you-can-eat buffet where the dishes are all overcooked or soggy in the middle—you never leave hungry but never exactly satisfied, either. Based on the kiss alone, can tell sex with hot hunk, with Josh, will be amazing experience akin to progressive chef's dinner at fine French restaurant—a slow awakening of the palate through carefully prepared courses culminating in a sinfully rich, totally decadent flambé.

For first time in life, am in no rush to get to "dessert."

JOSH LIVED just off Boston Street in a studio apartment occupying the upper floor of an old Formstone row house. The peeling wall paint and dated avocado-green kitchen appliances were offset by interior features such as crown molding and real hardwood floors. Below them was a bar, a real locals' hangout, where he told her he filled in a couple nights a week.

Locking the dead bolt behind them, he turned around to Mandy and said, "It can get pretty loud on weekends when they have bands in, but usually they shut down around the same time I get off, so it's not a problem."

"I thought you said you were shy in crowds." She searched his face for the telltale signs of deceit.

Sure enough, they were there in full measure. Gaze darting away, he hesitated before answering, "That's the great thing about working the club scene. It's too noisy to do much talking." He took a step toward her. "Speaking of which, you're doing a lot of talking tonight."

Heart pounding with anticipation, she said, "I guess you could say it's an occupational hazard."

"Yeah?" He reached for her, his big, warm hands enclosing her waist, gently pulling her to him. "I can think of a lot better uses for that amazing mouth of yours."

Startled, she said, "You really think my mouth is amazing?"

"Uh, huh." He slid his hands to her shoulders, slipping her coat downward and off. "Perfectly shaped and very, very kissable, it goes with the amazing rest of you." As if to demonstrate his point, he angled his face to hers, drew her bottom lip between his teeth, and gently sucked.

All in the line of duty. Flexing her shoulders, she let the coat fall to the floor.

Glancing downward, he asked, "Do you want me to hang that up?"

Lost in sensation, she shook her head. "Nuh-uh."

Against her mouth, she felt his lips curve into a smile. "Good because I don't want to stop kissing you or touching you for even a minute."

His hands went to the necktie at her throat, tugging loose the knot, slipping the fabric free and then off. Behind them was his bed, a metal four-poster that had seen better days. Along with the tie, the spindled headboard set a host of provocative images firing off inside her brain, including her bound to the bedpost and straining to meet him as he moved back and forth inside her.

"Your hair, I want to see it down." He paused, a hand at the braided bun secured at her nape. "Mind?"

"Nuh-uh."

He gently pulled out the pins, sending them pinging to the floor.

"Better," he said, sinking strong fingers into her braided hair, freeing the waves to pool around her shoulders. He turned his attention to the buttons fronting her shirt. One by one, he undid them, laying her bare. Snagging her gaze, he said, "You're stunning."

Blushing, she looked down to where her shirt gapped open, revealing the lacy Victoria's Secret peach-colored bra—sexy lingerie, her secret indulgence. Generous breasts were the upside of being full-figured—okay, overweight. If her luck held, he would switch off the ceiling light before he went any farther—and discovered that big boobs came with a matching set of hips.

When he made no move toward the wall switch, she said, "Turn the light off, okay?"

His gaze zeroed in on hers, and he shook his head. "Not a chance. I intend to see, kiss and lick every glorious inch of you between now and morning." He ran the knuckles of his hand over the tip of her bra-clad breast, bringing the nipple to life and raising the throbbing between her thighs to an exquisite ache.

She felt a blush burning its way from her cheeks all the way to her scalp line. "It's already morning, Christmas morning, in fact."

He smiled, crinkle lines appearing about the corners of his bedroom blue eyes. "In that case, I'd better get busy unwrapping my present." He dipped his head to kiss her throat and, at the same time, reached behind to unhook her bra.

Her breasts swung free. Josh's long, sensitive fingers slipped beneath the lacy straps, carrying them down her shoulders to her elbows and then finally off. "So soft, so beautiful," he whispered, his breath hot against her neck, his hands warm and strong and gentle, almost reverent, as he filled his palms with her. He bent his head to her breast, circling her areola with the point of his tongue, sipping at the nipple, and then drawing it between his lips with a gentle tug that sent her world reeling.

Oh-my-God. Tipping back her head, Mandy told herself she could consider herself off-duty for the present at least. For the time being, Josh was safe. After the holiday, she would get to work rooting out the Mafia hit man before he could make his move (again). In the interim, there was nothing more she could do beyond keeping the quarry, Josh, out of harm's way, which meant within her sight and occupied at all times. Never before in her life had duty and pleasure been so closely aligned.

"Is that a pistol in your pocket, officer, or are you just happy to see me?"

She followed his downward gaze to her gun belt and blushed. For the first time in five years on the job, she'd forgotten she was wearing her weapon. It was the one article of her attire she would definitely need to remove herself.

"I could ask the same of you." She touched the pager at his waist, fingers skimming the leather belt to which it was clipped.

Gaze on her stroking hand, his smile dimmed. "Yeah, well, catering is an almost 24/7 business these days. I never know when I'm going to get a call to show up for a job. I'm so used to being on call sometimes I forget I'm even wearing a pager." He lifted her hand from his belt and pressed a warm, sexy kiss into her palm.

Mandy shivered, the hot tingle in her palm mirrored in the moist heat mounting between her legs. Though she had a pretty good idea why he wore a pager, rather than spoil the moment, she said, "Well, I am definitely off-duty for the night, and I'm taking mine off." Backing out of his embrace, she sidestepped the bed and went over to the scarred oak dresser.

She unbuckled the holster and secured the safety on the pistol before putting it and her pager and cell inside a drawer.

She caught her reflection in the cracked wall mirror above the dresser and stopped. With her long hair streaming over creamy bare shoulders and full breasts, the woman staring back at her was scarcely recognizable as herself. Bold, pagan and sexually free, she resembled the red-haired, full-figured goddess in Boticelli's "Birth of Venus." Mandy had first seen the famous painting as a slide in Sister Judith Marie's eleventh-grade Art History class. The very nude Venus had set off a chorus of snickers and nervous giggles amongst the students, her included, but poised on the brink of new discoveries and new beginnings, she was able to appreciate the work's innate sensuality as well as her own.

Emboldened, she turned away from the mirror and walked back over to Josh. He'd shed his leather jacket, but considering she was topless, he still wore far too many clothes for comfort, hers at least.

When he started for her pants zipper, this time she pushed his eager hands away. "My turn, I want to see you, too."

He obeyed, holding his arms out at his sides, and suddenly her bondage fantasy expanded to encompass him lying on his back beneath her, wrists lashed to the bed's metal posts as she straddled him, driving him deeply inside her and lapping at the sweat running down his straining neck and sides.

Fingers clumsy with impatience, she started on his shirt buttons, following the downward trail of gradually exposed flesh with kisses, the crisp golden hairs teasing her lips and tongue.

"You're the one who's so beautiful." Pushing the shirt down over his broad shoulders and powerful arms, she stood back to admire him.

Indeed, it wasn't often that reality exceeded fantasy but this was definitely one of those rare times. She'd known from the firm feel of him through his clothing that he would be well-muscled yet lean, but he was even more beautiful than she'd imagined, with broad shoulders, sculpted pectorals and a perfect six-pack abdomen. She found the disc of one flat, brownish nipple with her mouth and circled it with her tongue. Looking up, she saw his eyes darken, and then his lids flutter closed. Taking that as a sign she was pleasing him, she drew him into more fully her mouth, laving the tight nub with her lips and tongue, sucking gently then gradually increasing the pressure until he groaned, eyes flying open and chest heaving.

He sank hard fingers into her hair, pulling her closer. "Oh baby, do you know what you're doing to me?"

If what she was doing felt anywhere near as amazing as the attention he'd given her own breasts, she had a pretty good idea. Changing tacks, she laved warm, wet kisses along the line of V-shaped breast bone and then downward, following the path of dark-gold hair leading like a very adult Yellow Brick Road from the center of his taut midriff to the waistband of his jeans and beyond.

She settled her hand over the hard bulge at his crotch and gave it a gentle squeeze. Feeling deliciously wicked and wholly alive, she lifted her gaze to his and asked, "What about you? Is this a pistol in your pocket or are you happy to see me?"

In answer, he covered her hand with his and pushed hard against her palm. "I'd say I'm definitely happy to see you. Feel how hard I am for you, how much I want you?"

The way he kept saying "you, you, you" had her almost believing he wasn't just horny in general, but hot for her in particular. Even if that wasn't strictly the case, it made for a pretty steamy fantasy.

And that's what this was, a fantasy. She was actually living the previous week, so in a way none of this was really happening. The sense of suspended reality brought with it enormous freedom—the freedom to say and do and feel things that until now she'd only said and done and felt in her fantasies.

"Yes, you certainly do feel hard, only..." She let the sentence trail off unfinished, a deliberate sensual tease.

"Only?"

A frown marred his high forehead and he looked desperate, a bit wild-eyed even, like a little kid afraid his candy might be snatched away—only there wasn't anything "little" about him. Judging from the bulge crowning his jeans, he was well-endowed, possibly enormous. At one time, that might have caused her some concern. In this case, she was so wet, so utterly drenched, that she was confident that no matter his size, he'd slide right inside her.

"Only I don't just want to feel you. I want to see you. And smell you. And taste you." Massaging him through his jeans, she almost purred the words. "Hmm, I especially want to taste you. I'll bet you taste incredible." To emphasize the point, she ran her tongue along the curve of her bottom lip, watching his pupils pop, darkening the irises of his blue eyes to black.

Gaze riveted on her mouth, he reached for her. "Oh, baby, where have you been all my life?"

Though it wasn't really a question, Mandy paused to consider it. Where *had* she been? Camping out in her childhood bedroom rather than risk striking out on her own again. Hiding her hopes and dreams and yes, desires behind the extra flesh she'd accumulated since high school, using her weight as an excuse to watch life from the sidelines instead of crossing the line and really living it.

Kissing, they backed across the room until her backside bumped up against the low lying bed. Sitting on its edge, she reached for his jeans zipper and very slowly, very deliberately, slid it down.

Josh sucked in his breath. "When I asked you out, I figured I'd be the one doing the seducing."

She anchored her hands to his narrow hips, pulling him closer. "Hmm, do you mind?"

"Mind?" Letting out a laugh that was part groan, he shook his head. "Not at all, seduce away."

He wasn't wearing underwear and when she opened the fly of his jeans, his erection poured out into her hands. He was large as she'd suspected, but what she hadn't counted on was how beautiful he would be. Perfectly shaped and fragrant with musk, he literally made her mouth water. She wrapped the fingers of her right hand around him, moving slowly up and down, learning the feel of him, experimenting with what pleased him.

He pushed against her palm, rock hard and ready for her. That something so silken to the touch could also be so hard was a wondrous thing to behold and hold. Only Mandy wanted to do a good deal more than just look at and hold him. She wanted to take him inside her, all the way inside, starting with her mouth.

"I'm dying to lick you and suck you and make love to you with my mouth. Pretend you're inside me. Inside my…" She hesitated, vestiges of her outward good girl warring with the sex goddess within, the one who'd waited thirty years to break through that prison wall. "Pretend you're inside my pussy, Josh." There, the p-word, for the first time ever she'd said it out loud. Another milestone made.

Angling her face to his groin, she guided him into her mouth, savoring him inch by precious inch. At the same time, she slid her free hand beneath to cup the firm fruit of his testicles, giving them each a gentle squeeze.

Licking her lips, she looked up into his feverish gaze. "Hmm, you do taste amazing."

Muscular chest rising and falling, he shook his head. "It's you I can't wait to taste."

He tried to tip her back on the bed, but she backed away from his reach. Still wearing the bottom half of her clothing, she felt sexy, femininely powerful. Taking off her trousers to reveal her rounded belly and full thighs and, worst of all, her big butt would burst the bubble of fantasy and quite possibly Josh's libido, too. She wasn't yet ready to come down to earth and be that vulnerable, not just yet anyway.

"You're going to have to wait for a little while at least. I'm just getting started, and I have a feeling I'm going to take a very long time."

She flicked the pad of her thumb over the moist slit crowning his cock, drawing his shudder. Biting his bottom lip, he ground out, "I'm not sure I can last all that long, not with you doing…that and…well, that."

"Oh well, what's life if not a challenge, hmm?"

Head at the crescent of his thighs, she slowly sucked him inside her mouth. "Hmm, so good," she murmured, drawing him deeper inside, the tip of his member tickling the back of her throat.

Josh snagged a hand through her loosened hair and surged into her mouth. "Oh Mandy, you're making me crazy."

Drawing away, she looked up into his taut-featured face, feeling more powerful and sexy than she'd ever felt before. "Good, because I want to make you crazy. I want to make you come."

He reached down and wrapped a staying hand around her wrist. "Later. For now, it's your turn. Tell me what you want, Mandy. Better yet, show me."

Startled, she stared up. Josh on the cusp of his climax, his eyes and chiseled features stark with desire, his powerful chest damp and glowing, had to be one of the most beautiful sights she'd ever seen. "Show you?"

He nodded, a slow, sensual smile spreading over his face. "I want you to show me what feels good to you, exactly how and where you want to be touched, tasted."

More comfortable in the role of giver than receiver, she'd been bold up until now. But the prospective of shedding her remaining clothing and inhibitions, of opening herself to him completely, drew a host of mixed emotions—excitement and foreboding, eagerness and fear.

What if I'm not pretty enough, not slim enough, not...good enough? Feeling hesitant, she suddenly couldn't bring herself to look up into his eyes. "What if...I'm not sure?"

He reached down and cupped her cheek. "I'm not buying that for a minute. I think you know exactly what you want from me. And I'll give it to you, Mandy, I'll give you whatever you want for however long you want it, only first you have to say the words."

Mandy took a deep breath. Feeling as though she were in a roller-coaster car poised atop the precipice, she hesitated and then lay down on her back. Slowly, very slowly, she lifted her hips off the bed and slid her trousers and lacy panties down and then off.

Tossing them aside, she said, "I want you, Josh. I want you to touch me and taste me like...like this." Her voice trailed off, leaving the sentence unfinished, the good girl stifling the erotic words her inner bad girl wanted to scream to the rooftop.

Slowly, very slowly, she slid her hand from her breast to her belly, stopping just above the triangle of curls crowning her thighs.

He nodded his encouragement. "You're doing fine, sweetheart. Go for it."

Josh's smile was all the prompting she needed. Opening her legs wider, she slid her hand between her thighs and found herself with her fingers. He'd been right when he said she knew exactly what she wanted. She'd touched herself enough times that her dampened finger went straight to the spot.

The nub of her clit was firm beneath her fingertip and achingly sensitive. She slid another finger inside herself and brought it out, using her essence to moisten herself. Squeezing her eyes closed, she moved her finger back and forth, up and down, and then circled.

"Mandy, open your eyes and look at me." The mattress

dipped as Josh joined her. She felt his breath strike the side of her neck, smelled the musky tang of his sweat-scented skin.

The tingle was fast building to a full-blown ache. She moved her hand faster now, a steady rhythmic pressure.

Almost there, almost, but not quite...

"Look at me, baby. I want to see your eyes when you come."

This time, she did as he asked and opened her eyes. She looked up and saw him leaning over her, a hand braced on either side of her head. Their gazes locked and the warmth of his eyes, the obvious pleasure he was taking in watching her, sent her careening toward the pinnacle and beyond, her world exploding in a starburst of pulsing, radiant heat. She squeezed her eyes closed again if only because the sight of him above her was too blindingly beautiful to bear.

When she opened her eyes again, she saw that he'd shed the rest of his clothing. Gloriously naked, he reached across to the night table, yanked open a drawer, and took out a foil-wrapped condom.

Mandy's orgasm was ebbing from full-throttle combustion to the batting of butterfly wings, but the sight of him rolling the latex over his erection had her forgetting to breathe.

She pushed up on her elbows. "Hurry, Josh, hurry. I want you."

Even in the midst of her passion, she took note of the slight trembling of his hands, and her heart warmed at the sight. Surely a player, someone for whom sex was just a game, wouldn't have shaking hands, would he? Before she could answer that question, she was sprawled on her back, Josh's body covering hers, his cock—so beautiful, so hard, and so sublimely ready—sliding inside her, filling her as, until now, she'd only fantasized about being filled.

He stopped, holding himself utterly, tantalizingly still. Palms anchored to either side of her head, he speared her with his gaze. "You want me to what?"

She lifted her hips in a silent appeal, hoping it would be

enough, but he still refused to budge. Perspiration filming the backs of her knees, she ground out, "You know what I want."

He didn't deny it. "Say it, Mandy. I need to hear you say the words as much as you need to say them."

"Please." On the brink of a second climax, she held back, desire warring with what she'd always thought of as basic decency.

Tipping the scales was the amazing sensation of Josh still inside her. Looking up into his stark gaze, demanding yet tender, she knew that this once in her duty-driven life, desire would win out. And suddenly, she no longer cared. If anything, she was glad.

"Please what?" He stared down at her, waiting.

"Okay, you win. Please, fuck me, Josh. Please…fuck me *now!*"

He pulled out and then thrust into her again, burying himself in one sweet, sure stroke that had her gasping for air, experiencing for the first time the ecstasy of complete, tran-scendent connection. Sliding an arm beneath the small of her back, he raised her higher still, the tilt of her pelvis and his buffering arm absorbing the shock of his thrusts as he drove deeper still, again and again.

"Come for me, Mandy. Step off the edge of that cliff and come. I'll be on the other side to catch you, I promise."

"You promise?" The question emerged as a moan.

Chest rising and falling, he managed a jerky nod. "Go ahead and try me." He reached down between them and found the bud of her clitoris with his thumb, circling it once, twice…

"Oh, God. Oh, Josh…" Mandy dropped back against the lumpy mattress and came and came and came.

8

Living breathing sex gods nailed: one. Orgasms reached: multiple (okay 3.5, but even sex goddesses-in-training must sleep sometime). Calories consumed: negative. Who needs chocolate when can feast on ambrosia of sex god fallen-to-earth? Times mother has looked up at velvet painting of Virgin Mary and Baby Jesus and asked when will settle down and have babies like a good Catholic girl: don't know because didn't make it home last night.

MANDY CAME awake to a moist mouth nibbling her neck and a full-on erection pressing against her backside. Against her ear, a man's low, morning voice rumbled, "Merry Christmas, sleepyhead."

Cracking open an eye, she found herself looking across to a sea-foam green wall, the paint peeling off in patches like week-old sun-blistered skin. *Where the hell am I?*

As if in answer, a sinewy arm wrapped about her waist, drawing her up against a rock-hard cock. Damn. Opening both eyes, she looked down to one very large, very masculine hand fanned across her left breast. The second identical hand rested on her waist just atop her pubis, tapered fingers pointed decidedly downward. Beyond the hands, her only covering was the rumpled white sheet riding her waist.

Oh-my-God. She felt a jet of warmth splash between her

thighs and a flush that was part embarrassment and part turn-on spread over her body like a Southern California brush fire.

Before things burned out of control, she rolled over onto her back. "Merry Christmas right back at you."

"I hated to wake you, but it is Christmas. What would you like for breakfast before you head out?"

Before you head out. Judging from the words alone, it sounded as though he couldn't wait to boot her out the door, and yet his rueful smile and the boner pressing against the outside of her thigh gave her the confidence to say, "You. I want you for breakfast." Turning to face him, she reached beneath the covers and found him with her hand. The little telltale bead of moisture on the head of his cock confirmed he was more than ready for her.

"Hmm, definitely you for breakfast." She gave him a playful squeeze, her thumb slipping in his slickness.

"As much as I would love to spend Christmas Day in bed with you, I don't want to make you late for your plans." He reached down and gently disengaged her hand. Carrying her hand up to his mouth, he kissed the palm before giving it back. "So what's to going to be—French toast or omelets or cinnamon rolls or all of the above?"

She tucked the sheet around her, her post-coital glow doing a rapid fade-out. It wasn't like hit men took holidays. If she left Josh alone, chances were she would have just delayed his death by a matter of a few hours—a few, red-hot sexy hours, to be sure but hours all the same. Blowing a second chance to save a man's life balanced against her embarrassment over exposing a blue-blooded guy like him to her very blue-collar family made the choice an easy one.

"None of the above. Listen, my folks have a big open house every year for family and friends and neighbors starting around two o'clock. No pressure, I'll introduce you as a friend I met on the job."

His gaze shifted away. Using a strand of her hair to tease her nipple, he said, "I don't know, Mandy, I'm not so good in big groups."

It was hard to concentrate with him playing with her breast, but she reminded herself that a life was at stake, Josh's life, and keeping him alive required all her due diligence and then some.

"Right, you're shy. Well, no worries. My parents' place is on the small side—okay, tiny—and they invite a hundred or so people every year. I guarantee it'll be as packed as any bar and even noisier. No one will be able to hear themselves speak let alone you."

The hand toying with her breast slid down her stomach and lower, settling between her legs. "It sounds like a family affair. I don't want to intrude."

He cupped her pubis, gently squeezing, and Mandy bit back a moan. "You're...you're, uh, coming, and this time I'm not taking no for an answer."

He stopped to stare, face an open question. "What do you mean, *this time?* You just invited me."

"It was just a figure of speech. A colloquialism, I guess you could say. What I meant to say is you're coming home with me, no ifs, ands or buts."

"In that case, the least I can do is make you breakfast." He sat up, the sheet sliding to his narrow waist, and Mandy admitted that killer or not, there was no way she was letting him out of that bed, not yet anyway.

She pushed up on one elbow and wrapped an arm about him, pulling him back down. "My mom makes tons of food, literally. If we have breakfast, we'll spoil our appetites. The one requirement of any Delinski family function is that every guest eats her..." She slid her palm down over his washboard stomach, impossibly sculpted and firm and flat, and admitted she knew exactly what she wanted for breakfast, not to mention lunch and dinner, too. "Make that, *his* share."

Grinning, he turned over and eased her back down on the pillow. "In that case, what do you say to a noncaloric breakfast?" Showering kisses on her throat, collarbone, breasts and stomach, he moved down the length of her. He looked up at her from the tent of her raised legs and smacked his lips. "Suddenly I'm starving. Mind?" Without waiting for her answer, he dipped his head and kissed the inside of first one thigh and then the other.

Mind? She sucked in her breath. The only mind she could think of was the one between her ears, and she was on the fast track to losing it. The softness of his lips provided an exquisite contrast to the sandpaper roughness of his beard stubble, landing the warm, fluttery feeling in her belly even lower.

"Are you kidding? This has got to be the all-time best Christmas ever. Better even than the year my parents splurged and got me the Barbie town house."

Mouth curving into that sexy, lopsided grin she was coming to like entirely too much, he slid a long finger inside her. "Better than the Barbie town house, huh? That's one hell of a compliment."

Biting her bottom lip to keep from moaning, she shook her head. "I'll have you know it came with an elevator and the full complement of amenities."

Even with a mob killer on their trail, she felt happier than she could ever remember feeling, not to mention turned on as hell. Gorgeous, sexy, kindhearted and fun to be with, Josh was her fantasy lover come to life—and she meant to keep him alive no matter what she had to do.

"Amenities, huh? That's some pretty stiff competition." Finger still inside her, he found her with his mouth, settling the tip of his tongue over the spot where she'd pleasured herself the night before, circling and sucking until what little sanity she'd managed to hold on to threatened to break away. "My God, you taste amazing. I could have you for breakfast every day of the year."

Every day of the year. She sank hard fingers into his hair and lifted her hips, her world for now reduced to the rhythmic pull of his warm, wet mouth, the back-and-forth movement of his stroking finger, and the possibility of promises yet to be realized.

He paused to look up at her, gold-tipped lashes brushing the high bones of his cheeks. With his blond hair wildly rumpled and golden beard, he was the embodiment of every sexy fantasy lover she'd ever dreamed up only a hundred times better because he was real. "What time did you say your folks' open house started?"

Mandy scoured her sex-soaked brain for the answer, time having lost any immediate meaning. "Around...around two, I think. Why?"

He glanced down to his wrist watch, an expensive Rolex a Baltimore bartender could never afford, and his smile broadened. "It's only ten-thirty. We have hours yet."

Perspiration filming the backs of her knees, Mandy lifted her hips, wanting more, wanting all of him. "Whatever will we do with all that time?"

She caught the flash of his grin just before he lowered himself between her legs once more. "I know a broken-down bed in a cheap rental probably seems like a poor substitute for a swank town house like Barbie got. Just remember, Ken may have deeper pockets, but at least I'm anatomically correct."

SEVERAL HOURS LATER, Mandy found herself admiring the way Josh navigated her parents' packed living room. Whether it was talking sports with her brothers, listening to her Aunt Clarice complain about her bunions, or helping himself to the buffet-style food, he gave the impression of being right at home. Despite his assertions of shyness, he was more than able to hold his own in a roomful of strangers. Indeed, she imagined he could accommodate to just about any environment, even one as nuts as this.

By the time four o'clock rolled around, he'd talked to every member of her immediate family and most of her neighbors, let himself be dragged down into the basement by her older sister, Sharon, to assemble her son's Spider-Man Electronic Pinball Machine, and gone back for seconds on dessert, earning her mother's approving smile. But when Mandy caught herself fantasizing about them having a future of holidays together, Christmas jingle bells turned into an internal warning siren. *Reality check time, Delinski. Boston Brahmins don't pick their girlfriends from among blue-collar Polish families.* Hadn't she already made peace with that cold, hard fact? He was good at slumming was all, one of those rare people who could not only make the best of any and every situation, but rise to the occasion and shine.

Still, it was Christmas, a time for celebrating miracles and wishes come-true, a time for believing. When he'd gotten down on the carpet on all fours for Theresa's five-year-old, Lizzie, to climb up onto his shoulders, sending the child and her twin siblings into spasms of delight, Mandy's heart had squeezed in on itself like a fist. A piggyback ride, what better Christmas gift to give a trio of fatherless children than that? He even liked little kids, how much more wonderful could a guy get? Actually, he seemed to genuinely like everybody and everything. So far, he hadn't shown signs of minding nosy questions (her mother's), thunder thighs (hers), or noise and chaos (the Delinski clan and guests in general). And to top it off, the cherry on the hot fudge sundae, he was absolutely amazing in bed. If only he really was a bartender, or some other working class occupation, he really would have been perfect to a T.

"Want a bite?" Startled from her thoughts, Mandy looked up to find her father sidling up to her side, a slab of chocolate cake resting on the plastic plate he held out. Aside from accumulating some extra pounds and gray hairs, he looked much as she remembered him growing up—a big, raw-boned man with a penchant for sideburns, button-down cardigans, and clip-on bow ties.

She shook. "No thanks, I'm good."

He lifted an eyebrow. "You sure? It's chocolate cassata from Vaccaro's."

Devil's food cake layered with chocolate cannoli cream and garnished with chocolate drops around the outside, the Italian confection defined sinfully delicious. Mandy remembered it all too well if only because she still wore last year's serving on her thighs. "Yeah, I'm sure, but thanks anyway."

"Hot in here, huh?" He pulled on the knot of his Christmas tie, a gift from her mother. Like her sweater, the annual Christmas tie was a tradition to be suffered through with a smile but never questioned. This year's selection featured polar bears wearing Santa caps. "What's your best guess on the temperature in the living room, huh? Seventy? Seventy-five?"

Uh-oh, small talk. In the Delinski household, chitchat was a red flag that a major interrogation was about to go down. Eager to escape before it could, she said, "I honestly don't know, Pop, but I'll go downstairs and bring up the floor fan."

She took a step toward the basement door, but he caught at her sleeve. "No, your mother will just complain she's cold. I've been married to that woman for thirty-five years, and you know, I've never seen her break a sweat."

Stopped in her tracks, she turned back around. "I guess I take after you, then?"

"Guess so." He scooped up a forkful of cake and popped it into his mouth. Chewing, he said, "That young man of yours, Josh, he has a funny accent but otherwise he seems like an okay guy. Where'd you say he's from?"

Oh shit, here it comes—the Spanish Inquisition sans *the rack and thumb screws.* "Boston."

"Boston, huh? Your aunt Cessie went there once. Snows a lot, she said."

Mandy hid a smile. Her parents' idea of travel was limited to an annual summer vacation to the beach in Ocean City, Maryland. Outside of that, they rarely ventured beyond Baltimore. "Only in the winter, Pop."

He shrugged. "How'd you two meet, by the way?"

"On the job."

"So he's a cop, too?"

Feeling all of twelve, she looked down to the toes of her shoes. "Not exactly."

Talk about being caught between a rock and a hard place. On one hand, if she said Josh was a bartender, her father would dismiss him on the spot as a player and a deadbeat who couldn't hold down a "real" job. On the other hand, if he knew they had a high-powered telecommunications executive in their midst, he'd be running out the door to find a priest to marry them— so long as she left out the part about Josh being on the run from the mob. Not that it mattered because no way would she dream of blowing Josh's cover by telling her pop the truth, a truth she wasn't even supposed to know. Besides, it wasn't like Josh was going to be sticking around long enough for her to worry about how he was going to fit into her family. If all went according to plan—meaning she managed to keep him alive to testify— he'd be back to his old life in Boston by January second.

Her father's frown deepened. He forked up more cake. "Not exactly? Just what is *not exactly* supposed to mean?"

Hoping the best defense was indeed a good offense, she countered with, "Why are you giving me the third degree? He's just some guy I met who's new in town and didn't have anywhere to go for Christmas. I thought I'd bring him home for a little hospitality, a little Christmas cheer is all. That's what open houses are for, right?"

"Hospitality. Is that what they're calling it these days?"

Feeling like she had a scarlet *A* glowing on her breast, she backed up a step. "Pop!"

He let out a huff. "If he's just some guy, then tell me why you're looking at him like that?"

Okay, back to feeling twelve years old, not a great feeling, but it beats feeling like Hester Prynne. "Like what?"

"Like you're about to melt into a puddle of wax on the floor any minute, that's how."

"I told you, Pop, I'm hot is all." She made a show of pulling at the neck of her sweater.

"Hot, huh. Hot to trot, don't you mean? Speaking of which, you should know I covered for you with your mother."

Shit, she really was busted. "Covered for what?"

"You know very well for what." He shook his head. Leaning in, he whispered, "When you didn't come downstairs for breakfast, I told her you were sleeping late. She was so busy in the kitchen, she never saw you waltz in."

"I didn't waltz, I tiptoed…but only because I didn't want to wake anybody."

"At noon on Christmas? What are we, vampires? Come on, Amanda, you may be thirty years old and a police officer, but I'm still your father. You can't pull the wool over my eyes, so don't even try. You like this guy, you like him a lot. What I want to know is what are his intentions?"

His intentions. Suddenly she felt as though she'd traveled back in time not one week but a good fifty years. She fitted a hand over her forehead which had begun to throb. "It's too early to say, okay. Right now, I'm just taking it slow and seeing what happens."

"You call spending the night with a stranger taking it slow?"

She felt herself flushing with guilt and something more. She'd never before had a one-night stand, let alone propositioned a man to get into his bed. There was no way she could explain to her pop, to anyone for that matter, that she'd gone home with Josh to save his life. Well, okay, maybe that wasn't the only reason, but certainly saving him had been the catalyst.

The hot sex they'd shared had surpassed her wildest, craziest fantasies, but it was the tenderness afterward, the way he'd held her close and let her lay her head on his shoulder that had her thinking last night must have meant something special to him, too. Maybe she was just kidding herself but even though he was tall and built and good-looking—okay, hot—he didn't strike her as a "player," someone who went after sex for the thrill of the conquest or well, for the hell of it.

It was obvious that further denial was pointless, a waste of energy, and so she tried tossing off the subject with a shrug. "It's a brave new world, Pop, and I'm not a kid anymore. What do you want me to say?"

His expression softened. "You're a grown woman, Amanda, I know this. Sometimes it may seem we forget that because you're the baby of the family. Sometimes maybe we do, but it's only because we love you and want what's best for you."

This was the very last conversation she wanted or needed to be having right now. "I know, Pop, I know. I just need some space, a little room to breathe, okay?"

"All I'm saying is this, don't sell yourself short. You're a beautiful young woman with a good brain and a big heart, and I'm not just saying so because you're my daughter." Eyes holding hers, he tapped his fork on the hunk of half-eaten cake. "Don't settle for crumbs when you deserve the whole cake, okay?"

It was just like her family to set her up for the kill and then go all mushy on her at the last minute. She nodded, embarrassed at how choked up she was becoming. "Okay, Pop, got it."

"Good, that's my girl." Flashing a watery smile, he chucked her under the chin. The habit had used to annoy her, but in the last few years she'd come to find it endearing, comforting even. Dropping his hand to his side, he started to step away, and then stopped. "By the way, this cake, it's the only store-bought pastry your mother will let me bring into the house, but then Vaccaro's has been in business since 1956 when I was still a kid with a paper route. It's solid, dependable." He gestured to his plate. "Trust the word of someone who's lived a lot longer than thirty years, Amanda. A marriage partner is like a bakery—choose wisely and you'll be surprised at how what looks like a plain chocolate cake on the outside can turn out to be filled with rich, wonderful surprises."

9

Times mother looked up at velvet painting of Virgin Mary and Baby Jesus and asked when would settle down and have babies like a good Catholic girl: don't know as have been avoiding maternal evil eye, along with diet-busting Italian chocolate cassata cake, all afternoon. Number of battery-operated electronic gifts received as "Christmas cheer": exactly one, which really, *really* could have used as, um..."stocking stuffer" last year, but may no longer need. (Mental note: donate either to women's prison or convent as need level likely to be about same.)

Number of hunky potential boyfriends available for sucking face with under the mistletoe: one, but then how many does a girl need?

FROM THE FAR SIDE OF THE ROOM, Josh saw Mandy and her father in the midst of what looked to be a serious heart-to-heart. Mr. Delinski stepped away and Josh caught Mandy's eye and winked. She smiled back though he thought she looked a little sad or at least wistful, emotions that seemed out of step with the boisterous celebration.

The Delinski Christmas Day Open House turned out to be every bit as loud and chaotic as she'd warned, not that he minded. Classic Christmas carols blared from the old turntable hi-fi, mingling with the sounds of children playing, the chug-

ging of the miniature train doing loop-de-loops about the wide
Christmas tree in the corner, and the clamoring of neighbor
women jockeying for counter space and microwave moments
in the tiny kitchen. By comparison, his family and friends
back home seemed colorless, almost monochromatic, stereo-
typical New England stuffed shirts.

He'd been on edge when they'd first arrived, not from
culture shock but from anticipating what questions might be
asked of him and how he would respond. For once, his anxiety
proved to be unfounded. His hosts and fellow guests were in-
fallibly warm and welcoming, more focused on having a good
time than on grilling anyone, including him. When someone
did ask a question of him, it was invariably, "How do you
know *our* Mandy?" As the afternoon wore on, it was obvious
there was more than one would-be matchmaker in the room,
and that "our Mandy" was very dear to family, friends and
neighbors alike, not that he was surprised. True, he'd known
her fewer than twenty-four hours, but in that time he'd found
her to be warmhearted and generous, caring and giving, both
in and out of bed.

As for the in bed part, once she'd gotten over her initial
shyness, the sex had been phenomenal, the best of his life.
Moving in perfect sync, they'd made love for hours. Given
how out of shape he was in the bedroom department—the
condoms in his apartment were left over from the summer
before in Boston—he'd bet money he'd wake up tomorrow
with a stiff back and hips, a small price to pay for that level
of pleasure. Given the intensity with which they'd gone at it
that morning, he suspected Mandy would be feeling sore in
certain places as well, not that he expected her to say so. She
still hadn't lost all her reserve, especially when it came to
asking for what she wanted in bed, but she was uncannily good
at anticipating his desires—and then fulfilling them beyond
his wildest fantasies. What inhibitions she still held on to all

seemed to be focused on her body image, specifically her weight. That was a damned shame, he thought, and something of a mystery because she looked beautiful to him—okay, hot—a full-figured version of a Victoria's Secret angel. Even dressed casually in a Christmas sweater, jeans and boots, she managed to shine.

Truth be told, he didn't much care for the sweater, a gift from her mother. The snowman motif and baggy construction hid the shape of her beautiful breasts, but he loved that she wore it with a smile, obviously to make her mom happy. Christmas gift or not, Tiffany would have tossed the hideous sweater aside without a thought for anyone's feelings beyond her own. The boot-cut jeans on the other hand were awesome, or more to the point they looked awesome on Mandy. Her softly flaring hips and perfectly shaped ass filled out the denim to perfection. Of course he preferred her wearing nothing at all—nothing beyond his bedsheets, that is—but then again this was Christmas and definitely a family affair, so he'd have to keep his lust in check…until later, at least.

A tall man with slicked-back honey-colored hair, a gold-capped front tooth and cotton undershirt visible beneath his satiny striped dress shirt strolled up. Sausage roll in hand, he gave Josh the once-over and asked, "So how do you know our Mandy?"

Our Mandy. There it was again. Before Josh could answer, the subject of everyone's adoration materialized at his side. "We're just friends, Mikey, so ease up, okay?"

Munching on the appetizer, Mikey shrugged. "Geez, can't a guy ask a simple question about his favorite cousin without getting his head bitten off?" He punctuated the question by tearing off another bite of the roll.

"Sorry, Mikey. Merry Christmas and lay off, how's that?" Before he could answer, she took Josh's hand and steered them through the room of wall-to-wall people toward the kitchen.

On the way, he asked, "Just how many siblings and cousins do you have?"

"I'm the youngest of five. As for cousins, well, to be honest, I've lost count."

"Wow." He shook his head. "When you said you came from a big family, you weren't exaggerating."

A cloud crossed her face. "You can't say I didn't warn you."

He reached out and lightly squeezed her shoulder. "Hey, I didn't mean it like that. I like your family and your friends." With the exception of the creep, Lenny, who kept staring at her breasts and swiping sweat from his upper lip, that was true enough. "They're great, really warm. My family is much more...reserved. That's not always a good thing." He dropped his hand to his side as it occurred to him that touching her so publicly might not jive with her "just friends" story. It was just that touching her came so naturally to him that he did it without conscious thought, sort of like breathing.

"Sometimes I wish my family wasn't quite so in my face, but most of the time they're pretty okay. The bottom line is there's not a person here who wouldn't rush out to help me at 3:00 a.m. if I was in trouble."

"Well, that's a lot. That's just about everything."

Family and friends and that special someone with whom to share it all, the good, the bad, and all the moments in between. At one time, he'd thought that special someone was Tiffany but looking back, he could see he'd deluded himself from the start. Oh, she'd looked the part of a Thornton bride with her pedigreed ancestry, spa-sculpted body, and couture clothes. And she could be very charming when it suited her, which was usually when she wanted something. If he could have overlooked the absence of a soul, she would have made the perfect wife, the perfect *Thornton* wife, he supposed. But spending the night with Mandy had opened not only his eyes but his heart, as well. Now that he'd experienced what it was to be with someone truly generous—generous with her heart and body and feelings—there was no question of going back. Not back to Tiffany, certainly, nor to any Tiffany-like clone, either. He wanted more from a woman, a wife, than a social-ite to host his dinner parties, bear his babies and pretend interest in his lame golf stories in front of guests. He wanted someone warmhearted and kind, passionate and real. He wanted someone like Mandy. But there was only one Mandy, and he'd started out their relationship based on a lie.

From the far side of the house, a bell sounded. They looked across the room to where Mandy's sister, Sharon, squatted beneath the Christmas tree, rifling through the pile of gifts beneath. She gave the hand bell another ring and called out, "Listen up, people, it's time for the Secret Santa gift swap. Get your butts in here."

Josh turned to Mandy. "I feel badly. I didn't bring a gift to exchange."

She shrugged, looking anything but concerned. "Don't worry about it. It's Secret Santas, not really a gift swap. In a family as large as ours, buying a present for everyone just isn't affordable, so instead all the adults exchange names on Thanksgiving and buy one gift—except for the kids, that is. They still rake it in. There's no way I'm going to miss out on buying Barbie paraphernalia."

He shook his head. "Like the Barbie town house, you mean?"

She waved a hand. "Oh, the Barbie townhouse is old news. Now there's the Barbie Totally Real House complete with a working doorbell, spinning washer and dryer, and, believe it or not, shower and flush toilet. Compared to it, the town house was a rent-controlled hovel. Right now I get my fix by buying for my nieces and cousins."

"I take it you want kids, then?"

Mandy hesitated. Until now, she'd been enjoying the light flirtatiousness of their conversation, but the seriousness of the question set her on her guard. Having kids was a hot button topic if only because for her that meant marriage first, which of course meant finding the right man. Mr. Right, in so many ways she was looking at him now, and yet she couldn't see any way a future together could be possible. Forget possible, she didn't even know if a future with her or anyone, was even on his radar screen. Given the pressure he must be under just to stay alive, she doubted it.

Choosing her words with care, she hid her feelings behind a shrug. "Someday, if things work out, sure, I'd like to have a family. What about you?"

It was his turn to shrug. "I always assumed I'd marry and have kids eventually. I'm not so sure now. A lot of things are pretty...up in the air for me right now."

He'd only confirmed what she'd known in her heart and yet the admission made her feel sad suddenly, a little empty inside, and more than a little lonely.

From across the room, her sister, Sharon rang the hand bell she was using to keep order and called out Mandy's name. Glad for the opportunity to exit before their conversation became any more personal, she turned back to Josh and said, "Duty calls. I'll be right back."

She marched across the room to where Sharon stood holding out an exquisitely wrapped gold foil box. "Merry Christmas, Mands, and for God's sake don't open this here or Mom and Pop will have coronaries."

Taking the gift, Mandy gave it a shake. "That good, huh?"

Leaning in, Sharon whispered, "Actually, it's something for your goody drawer, if you know what I mean."

"I don't have a goody drawer."

Sharon grinned. "You do now, although by the looks of the hunk over there in the corner, maybe you don't need this after all."

"He's just a friend."

Sharon rolled her eyes. "Uh-huh, sure he is. And this is just a body massager."

Taking the package, Mandy shook her head. Her big sister might look like a conservative, middle-aged mom, but inside her plump, Laura Ashley jumper-clad body beat the heart of a porn star. "Thanks, I guess."

Sharon caught at her arm. "He likes kids, I know that much. You should have seen him with Jimmy assembling that pinball machine."

A lump in her throat, Mandy tucked the package under her arm. Amidst group shouts of "Open it, open it, let's see what you got" she shook her head. "Like I said, he's just a friend."

Josh was standing in the same spot where'd she'd left him, a funny look on his face. Glancing at the package under her arm, he asked. "Aren't you going to open it?"

Face heating, she shook her head. "I have a pretty good idea what it is. I'll wait and open it in private."

"In private, huh? Now you've really piqued my curiosity." His slow smile brought back memories of their sexy night together, and she felt her blush spreading along with the heat pressing between her thighs.

Setting the package aside, she said, "Let's just say my older sister has a perverse sense of humor."

Expression turning serious, he said, "I wish I had a gift for you."

How could she tell him that he'd given her so much already, great sex, to be sure, but so much more than that— tenderness and passion and the precious reassurance that she was sensual and sexy and maybe, just maybe, loveable, too. No matter if she lived to be one hundred, their beautiful night together would live on in her dreams, and her heart, for the rest of her life.

"I'm thirty years old, Josh. At this point, the things I want from life don't come out of a box, no matter how pretty the wrapping."

He searched her face with his eyes. "What is it you want, Mandy?"

You, I want you. "I want experiences, I want to feel things and know things and share things. I want time, Josh, time with you." Before she lost her nerve, she hurried ahead. "I have some vacation left over, not much, just about a week's worth, but if I don't use it before the first of the year, I can't carry it over. It'll be lost." Actually her plan had been to cash it in, but money, even money saved toward the worthy goal of home ownership, seemed so very trivial compared to a life at stake. "If I take this week off from work, this time between Christmas and New Year's, would you spend it with me? No strings, no promises. I know…that is, I'm guessing Baltimore is just a pit stop for you, that you'll be going back home to Boston…eventually." When he didn't deny it, only watched her in silence with solemn eyes, she felt a stab in the vicinity of her heart. Determined to ignore it and make the most of what time they did have, she said, "My New Year's resolution for 2007 is to start living in the moment, to start living, period. What I'm asking you for is a week's worth of moments. What do you say, Josh, do I get my Christmas wish? Will you stay with me until the New Year?"

Expression unreadable, he said, "Before I answer that, have you noticed where we're standing?"

She'd just poured out her heart to him knowing he could as easily say "no" and walk out of her life—and straight to his death—as he could say "yes" and stay. What she hadn't prepared herself for was ambiguity. Flustered, she shook her head.

"For a cop, you're not all that observant of your surroundings." He reached above them and tapped the ribbon-tied greenery and waxy white berries hanging over the archway. "What is this, do you think?"

"Mistletoe."

His mouth curved into a smile mirrored in the warmth of

his eyes. "That's right, mistletoe, and you know what that means. Merry Christmas, Mandy." Without so much as a glance around to see who might be watching, he leaned in and kissed her.

10

December 26, "The Day After" (Christmas)—again!

Number of hunky potential boyfriends brought back from the dead: still one and seems to be very definitely alive. Calories consumed: negative but food no longer important as am now living on sex and air. Descent from Size 16 to Size 6 is surely matter of mere days. Time remaining to track down Mafia hit man bad-ass before he can strike again, killing boyfriend and successful new diet plan with single (.22 caliber) shot: one week exactly. Oh, shit! Had better get off fat ass, make that "lush" ass, and get back to business...

WALKING DOWNTOWN the day after Christmas, Mandy reminded herself that though she'd succeeded in altering the course of events so far, this was no time to rest on her laurels— or her ass. Until Josh showed up in Boston and testified at the trial, he was a marked man. Whoever had accepted the contract to take him out was still in town, still watching, and still waiting for an opportunity to strike. The situation called for 24/7 vigilance, and the only way she knew to accomplish that was to move in with him.

First thing that morning, she'd called in and explained to her supervisor that a family emergency had come up and she would be using her week of vacation time after all. Boblitz wasn't happy about the last-minute notice, but then what else was new? The time was hers to take and fortunately the squad's docket was running light.

As for her parents, they were predictably horrified when she returned from Josh's that morning to pack a bag and explain they shouldn't look to see her again until after the New Year. Going off with a man she barely knew…what had come over her? She was making a terrible mistake, a whopper, her mother tearfully told her. Rather than argue, Mandy reminded them she was a grown woman, not their little girl. She had thirty years of mistakes under her belt, such as getting hooked up with a creep like Lenny and entrusting him with her finances, but so far she'd managed to survive. At this point, her making another slipup was akin to an Aussie tossing another shrimp on the barbie—what was one more?

The only other person with whom she'd had to square her plans was Josh. Sex was a great way to keep him under watch, but short of handcuffing him to the bed, a tantalizing prospect even if he wasn't in danger, she couldn't expect to keep him indoors indefinitely. That was too bad because the apartment was the hands-down safest place for him. The FBI had selected the location in Canton specifically. For all she knew, the bar below was a federal front operation. Regardless, in her police academy days she'd read enough briefs on how federal cases were conducted to surmise that the two special agents she'd met at the morgue would be stationed close by, watching the comings and goings like a pair of hawks. Even with great sex and great gab in between, she couldn't expect to keep Josh indoors indefinitely. Eventually he would want to go out and when he did, he would be a walking target.

The only real way to head off the hit was to take a proactive approach and turn the hunter into the hunted, to smoke the hit man out of his hiding hole before he could make his next move. And so while Josh was back at the apartment re-

pairing a leaking kitchen faucet—a task he'd apologetically
told her would take several hours—she seized the opportunity
to pay a call on her cousin, Mikey. If anyone had his ear to the
ground and his finger to the pulse of the seedy underbelly of
Charm City, it was her ex-con cousin.

Mikey worked as a bouncer and fill-in bartender at Club
Strip-Tease, one of the more popular spots on The Block, Baltimore's red-light district. The two-block stretch of East Baltimore Street was home to sundry strip reviews, porn and sex
toy shops, and miscellaneous adult entertainment venues from
the landmark Gayety Theater to Larry Flynt's new Hustler
Club. Advancing down the street past neon-lit clubs and glass
storefronts of mannequins modeling the latest in S&M wear,
an occasional catcall came her way but otherwise the street
stragglers left her alone. It was just after twelve noon, early
for sin, and most of the Block's merchants and clients were
still resting up for another big night.

She opened the smeared glass door to Club Strip-Tease, the
stink of stale cigarettes hitting her in the face as soon as she
stepped inside. Taking in the empty stage with its metal poles
and the floor of tables with the chairs still up, she made her
way over to the bar, the heels of her boots catching on the
sticky floor.

Standing behind the bar restocking the shelves, Mikey greeted
her with his gold-toothed grin. "Hey, Mands, what's up?"

The black sheep of the Delinski clan, Mikey had a rap sheet
as long as Mandy's arm, but it was all petty stuff—stealing
office computer equipment after hours, forging driver's
licenses and fake IDs for college kids, stripping stolen cars for
parts. As far as she knew, he'd never physically harmed anyone,
man or beast. During his last stint at Lorton, he'd become
active in the inmate program to feed and care for the feral cats
living on the prison grounds. Since his release, he'd been the
main caretaker for a colony that resided behind the club's trash

Dumpster. Just about every time she saw him, he tried to give her a kitten. Criminal record aside, he was a real pussycat.

She shrugged. "Oh, you know, this and that. Mostly working, picking up as much overtime as I can to get the bucks together for a down payment on a house."

Looking sympathetic, he nodded. "Yeah, me too. There's this culinary school in Philly I've got my eye on. It's a six-month program, and tuition ain't cheap."

Ever since she'd known him, he'd loved to cook. She'd never say so in front of her mother, but the mushroom sauce he made to go with his cabbage rolls beat hers hands-down. Still, as much as she wanted him to succeed, there was a time when she would have questioned his ability to fit in with the canapé crowd. With his craggy face, gold-capped front teeth, and streetwise swagger, he looked more like a mobster from *The Sopranos* than he did Emeril. But making an extraordinary wish and having it granted, experiencing the man of your dreams come back to life before your very eyes changed a lot. It changed everything. Living the miracle firsthand, only now did she see how cynical she'd become over the past five years as a beat cop. At some point, she'd stopped dreaming, stopped hoping altogether. Until Josh had come into her life, she'd given up on second chances, miracles, and yes, herself.

If culinary school was Mikey's dream, his ticket to a new life, then she was all for it. "Just keep yourself clean and you'll get there. You're doing good, Mikey. We're all really proud of you."

"Thanks, Mands. That means a lot to me, especially coming from you." He hesitated, staring her up and down. "You lose weight or something?"

Taking a seat on one of the vinyl cushioned stools, she shook her head. "I wish."

"Well, you look… I dunno, different, like you got this glow about you or somethin'."

"Thanks."

She felt the heat of what surely must be a Day-Glo blush spreading over her face. Any glow she had was the direct result of one and one thing only—spending time with Josh. After leaving her parents' house on Christmas night, they'd gone back to his apartment and made love for hours. At this rate, they'd run through the gamut of possible sexual positions before the week was out, not that she was complaining. Whether he took her hard and fast up against the wall or slow and gentle in his lap on the side of the bed, he was completely committed to ensuring her pleasure. Knowing he would never hurt her, or pressure her into doing something she wasn't comfortable with, allowed her to let go as she'd never done or thought to do before. And of course it didn't hurt that she was so crazy about him she wanted to lick him from head to toe like an ice-cream cone, and then devour him in one sitting like a coveted chocolate dessert.

"Get you somethin' to drink?"

The question brought her out of her lusty daydream and back to the practical present. Reminded this wasn't a social call, she shook her head. "No thanks. I'm good." She looked around the empty bar. Other than the skinny Asian kid mopping the floor, she and Mikey appeared to be alone. Still, you couldn't be too careful. Even though she was in civilian clothes, jeans and a black turtleneck sweater, sitting at a bar *sans* drink might raise suspicion. "On second thought, give me a Diet Coke?"

"You got it." He filled a glass with ice and soda and slid it across the bar to her.

Eyeing the smudged drink ware, she tore the paper off a plastic drink straw and used it to take a sip. She set the glass aside and admitted, "I need a favor."

He paused in wiping a glass with a dish towel to look across the bar at her. "Listen up, 'cause I'm only going to say this once. You stood up and spoke for me at my probation hearing. I know you took heat for that at work, but you did it anyways, and I don't forget that. I owe you big time. Whatever you need, you got it."

"Thanks, Mikey." Sipping her soda, she ventured another glance about before turning back. "You notice anything weird going down over the past week?"

He rolled his eyes. "It's The Block, Mandy. When isn't something weird going down?"

He had a point there. "What I mean is have you noticed anyone hanging out not part of your regular clientele, anyone who might look or seem like they're from out of town, like I don't know…Boston?"

"Boston, huh? You got somebody specific in mind?"

"Maybe, maybe not. It's too soon to say. I got a lead on a mob hit that's supposed to go down before January second, and I need to check it out. Just remember, any New England accents walk in, you page me, okay?"

"Okay, you got it."

She slipped off the seat and stood. "Thanks for the soda. You take care now, keep focused on school." She turned to go.

"I will. Hey, Mandy?"

She turned back around. "Yeah."

"Tell your mom I appreciate her having me over to the open house the other day. Her dumplings were delish."

MANDY RETURNED to find Josh's apartment empty. Oh, shit. She raced down the set of back stairs to the bar, but he wasn't there either. Anxiety fisting her gut, she tried calling him on his cell. When she only got his voice mail, panic flared into full-blown alarm.

She was pacing his apartment, trying to figure out what her next step should be, when she heard the key turning in the lock. She swung around just as the door opened and Josh stepped inside, a sheepish grin and a hot pink shopping bag dangling from one hand.

Relieved beyond words, she rushed across the room and threw herself into his arms.

"Whoa, that's some greeting. I guess I don't have to ask whether or not you missed me." His broad smile told her that her missing him pleased him indeed.

Pulling back to look up at him, she got a whiff of some spicy scent overlaying his own. Needing to focus on something, anything, beyond her recent fear, she said, "You smell good, different though."

He raised an arm and sniffed the inside of his wrist. Making a face, he said, "Some rep for Ralph Lauren shot me with a cologne sample when I was passing through the menswear section."

"The menswear section...as in a department store?" A host of grim possibilities hit her like a fist in the gut. She threw her arms around his waist and pulled him closer if only to make sure he was still real, still alive.

He nodded, blue eyes twinkling like those of a sexy St. Nick. "I snuck out to Towson Town Center and did some shopping while you were gone."

Holding him tight, she said, "Why didn't you call me on my cell? We could have gone together."

He disengaged from her arms and stepped back, looking at her strangely as though she'd suddenly morphed into Glenn Close in *Fatal Attraction* or at least the most insecure, possessive woman on the planet. "It was no big deal. I figured you had an errand to run and I'd only be gone for an hour or so."

It was a big deal, an enormous deal actually. He could have been shot and killed though she could hardly say so.

Making an effort to tamp down her panic, she raked an ice-cold hand through her hair and asked, "Hit any good sales?"

"I wasn't exactly looking for bargains. I was looking for a Christmas gift—for you." He pulled an exquisitely wrapped box from the shopping bag and handed it to her. "Merry Christmas, one day late. It's not exactly La Perla, but I hope you'll like it."

Resolved to be more vigilant in the future or at least more creative—maybe she'd be breaking in that new pair of department issue handcuffs sooner rather than later—she said, "You didn't have to buy me anything."

He shrugged. "I know I didn't have to, I wanted to. Go ahead and open it."

She carried her present over to the bed and sat to open it. Now that any immediate danger was past, she felt her adrenaline knock down from dizzying rush to slow percolate. The paper was so pretty that rather than tear it she untaped one side and slid the box out. The pink Victoria's Secret box was a familiar sight though until now the only gifts from that store had come courtesy of her.

Anticipation building, she lifted off the lid. Nestled within the perfumed pink tissue paper was a small folded square of black lace. Lifting it out, she saw it was a one-piece teddy scarcely bigger than the disposable diaper her sister, Sharon, strapped on her newborn. She'd never had a man buy lingerie for her before, or shop for her at all, for that matter, and the thoughtfulness of the gesture touched her. She only wished she had a better body to show it off.

Emotions mixed, she looked over to Josh. "It's so beautiful and, um…so tiny."

Grinning, he reached over and slid a hand inside the fabric. "It stretches, see."

"I, uh, see that, only by the time it expands to fit me, it may be more like dental floss than lingerie."

He drew his hand away. "You don't like it. That's okay. I had the salesclerk include the gift slip. You can take it back and exchange it for something you really want."

"No, it's not that. This is beautiful, perfect really. The only problem is…I'm not."

"Mandy—"

She cut him off with a wave of her hand. "Let's face it, Josh,

I'm way too heavy, okay fat, to wear something like this. I mean, I wouldn't want you going blind or anything." When he didn't so much as crack a smile, she added, "That was a joke, by the way."

"Well, it wasn't funny. You're not fat, you're full-figured. Lush—and very, *very* sexy."

This was the very last conversation she wanted to be having with him and now was the very worst time to be having it. She still wasn't fully recovered from the shock of him slipping out on her. "Whatever euphemisms you come up with, I know what I am and what I look like."

Gaze serious, he shook his head. "I don't think you do. At least try it on."

"Now?"

He shrugged. "No better time than the present."

Holding it up again, she was sure that, stretchy fabric or not, he'd underestimated her size. She'd bet her badge his previous girlfriends were all gym rats with model-thin figures.

"Okay, you win. I'll try it on. But remember, don't say I didn't warn you." She got up and carried the lingerie to the bathroom.

He followed her with his eyes. "Hurry back."

Inside, she pulled the door closed and faced herself in the mirror, pulling her sweater over her head and slipping out of her jeans and underwear. Staring at her naked self in the full-length mirror backing the door, she tried to see what Josh supposedly saw. The top half of her wasn't so bad, she had to admit. Her arms weren't skinny by any means but they were toned from all the push-ups she did and her breasts were, well, pretty nice, she had to admit. Her stomach might not be exactly flat, but she had a waist and it cinched more or less where a woman's waist was supposed to. But when her eyes dropped lower to take in the rest of her, all bets were off. She turned sideways to study her profile in the mirror, a depressing sight. Her butt was huge, her thighs way too wide, her ankles definitely erring on the thick side. And God, could she ever use a tan.

From the other room, Josh called out, "Hey, how's it going in there? You didn't climb out the window or anything did you?"

"Actually, I did. I'm halfway down the block by now. This is a recording."

"Hurry up, funny lady. I can't wait to see you."

Oh you can wait, believe me, you can wait. One hand balanced on the edge of the sink, she held out the teddy and stepped into it. Shimmying, she tugged it upward over her hips, steeled for the humiliating sound of tearing fabric.

Only amazingly, it didn't tear, but stretched just like stretch fabric was supposed to do. Encouraged, she pulled it the rest of the way up, slipped the spaghetti straps over her shoulders, and turned back to the mirror.

Oh my God. Until now she wouldn't have thought it possible to feel more naked wearing something than well, nothing at all. The lingerie's plunging V-neckline shot downward to just above her navel, covering little more than her nipples and the sides of her breasts. The sheer lacy fabric left absolutely nothing to the imagination. Her pink areolas shone through as did the triangle of reddish brown hair between her thighs. And then there was the snap crotch that barely covered anything at all. Thong-style, it fitted snugly between her buttocks, a single scrap of lace.

"Hey, you, at this rate, it'll be next Christmas before you come out. Don't make me come in there and get you." It was Josh again, tone tinged with impatience, leaving no doubt he'd make good on his threat if she didn't show herself soon.

Finding her brush, she used it to make a quick pass through her hair. Giving her head a final toss, she called out, "Close your eyes because ready or not, here I come."

Moment of truth time. Bracing herself with a deep breath, she opened the bathroom door and stepped out.

11

Calories consumed: status still negative but light-headedness attributable not to lack of food but to multi-orgasmic rocketing straight to moon. (Think "Ground control to Major Tom...") "Sustenance" has taken on new, powerful, non-food related meaning. Descent from upstanding enforcer of law and potential wife and mother to carnally-crazed sex-aholic: total or, mission accomplished. Weight: haven't been near scale in days, so can't say, but availability of stretchy microfiber wear may make dieting occupation of past.

JOSH WAS WAITING FOR HER in the bed, propped up against the banked pillows and obviously naked beneath the sheet. He caught sight of her framed in the open doorway, and his jaw dropped. "You're stunning."

Reaching for her courage, Mandy crossed the room toward him, the floorboards chilly beneath her bare feet, the thong abrading the sensitive skin of her labia, a subtle, sensual surprise.

Coming up on the bed, she said, "You were supposed to keep your eyes closed until I said you could open them."

He ran his gaze over her from head to toe and swallowed hard. "Sorry, but I've never been much of a rule follower." He pushed the covers away and got up to meet her, gloriously naked and more than ready to fulfill all her fantasies. "And I'm glad, because I wouldn't want to miss out on so much as a minute of looking at you. You look…wow!"

"Really? You're not just being nice?"

He shook his head. "No, I'm not being nice, I'm being honest. I don't say things I don't mean. You should know that about me."

True, she didn't look like the models in the Victoria's Secret catalog ads but then what living, breathing woman did? For the first time she considered that maybe a digitally enhanced model wasn't the only benchmark for feminine beauty. Shedding some pounds was still a goal for her, but in the meantime maybe she didn't look half bad the way she was.

He reached for her, gently tugging her down on the bed beside him. She came down on her knees, the thong doing a quick slide back and forth. "It is a little tight."

"Really? I think it fits just fine. Perfect, actually."

"The thong part is, uh…a little snug. When I walk, it moves up and down."

"Does that feel good?"

What she felt was wickedly sensual, delightfully naughty. Going with it, she held his gaze and nodded. "It feels very good, as a matter of fact. And the crotch snaps."

He ran his hand down her belly to her mons. Cupping her, he gave a light squeeze. "I can see that. I'll bet it unsnaps, too. Shall we give it a try?" Before she could answer, he had the flap open and a finger slipping inside her. "God, you're drenched."

Holding his stare, she said, "I know, and it's all because of you. You make me wet, you make me crazy." Still kneeling, she spread her legs wider.

"You like it when I fuck you with my finger, don't you, sweetheart?"

"Yes, oh, yes." She braced a hand on either of his shoulders and bucked against him.

"Good, I'm glad because I like it, too." He sank a second finger inside to join the first and moved them scissor-fashion.

Mandy let out a moan and grabbed for his hand, willing him to deepen the penetration, increase the pressure. This wasn't sensual playacting calculated to turn him on, this was for real. "Oh, Josh, that feels good, so good. Please don't stop."

"Not a chance." Still working his fingers, he bent his head to her breasts and sipped at her nipple through the lacy fabric. Drawing back, he looked up at her and asked, "You never did open that gift from your sister, did you?"

"Uh…no."

He flicked his thumb over her clitoris, and Mandy felt a tremor of pleasure pulse through her. "What would you say to our opening it together?"

"Now?"

He nodded. "Yes, unless you want to save it for your… private time."

With sex like this, who needed private time? "No, I don't think so. I'd rather share it with you."

"In that case, where is it?"

"Over there." She gestured to the dresser.

"I'll go get it." He took his hand away and Mandy felt its absence like the loss of a newly returned long lost friend.

"Seeing how you're on to my bathroom window escape plan, I guess I'm stuck here." *Stuck on you,* she almost added, but stopped herself in time. No sense in spoiling one of the sexiest moments of her life by putting out sappy sentiment that wouldn't be returned.

"Good, because I'd hate to have to tie you down to the bed. On second thought, I'd love to tie you down only for fun, not necessity. For now, don't you go anywhere, okay?" He kissed her, soft and slow and thoroughly, and then got up.

"Okay."

Pulling herself up on her elbows, she followed him with her

eyes across the room, admiring the backside view of him, all broad shoulders, narrow hips and tight ass. A spasm of desire struck between her legs, followed by a splash of warm wetness. Squeezing her thighs tightly together, she sucked in her breath and dropped back down on the bed. She'd never thought it would be possible to orgasm from just looking at someone, but Josh was so beautiful, so altogether perfect, that for the first time she considered that visual stimulation alone might be enough to push her over the edge.

He crossed back to the bed. Holding out the box, he gave it a light shake. "What do you think it is?"

"I have a pretty good idea it's not a body massager."

He handed it to her. "Here, open it."

This time she tore open the wrapping without a thought for the pretty paper. The contents were no great surprise and yet holding out a sex toy and tube of Joy Jelly in the bright light of day in front of a lover had embarrassment burning her cheeks.

He took the lubricant from her and tossed it on the nightstand. "I don't think we'll be needing this, do you?"

She shook her head. "Definitely not." She'd never felt so hot, so wet, or so sexy in all her life and though the dildo was a diverting novelty, the catalyst was Josh watching her, touching her, mentally stripping the teddy off her with his eyes as, she was sure, his hands would shortly follow.

He flicked the switch on the toy. A soft hum permeated the room, and he came down beside her on the bed.

"Open your legs for me, sweetheart, as wide as you can." He slid a hand beneath each of her knees.

She obeyed, opening wide and bending her knees. Without looking down, she knew exactly what he was seeing—her wet, swollen inner lips and pulsing pink clit fully exposed and begging for his attention.

He slid the hand resting on her waist upwards over her

belly to rest on her breast. Rolling the nipple between his thumb and forefinger, he said, "I want you to tell me everything you're feeling, thinking, wanting. Everything, Mandy, I want to know it all."

With his other hand, he stroked her with the vibrating toy, moving it slowly over the top of her pubis, the sensitized flesh of her inner thigh, the juncture where her thigh and pelvis met—everywhere but where she craved contact the most, a deliberate sensual tease. "I want to know where you want it, how you want it."

Licking dry lips, she pushed upward, craving the toy but craving Josh even more. "You know where."

Mouth teasing the outer shell of her ear, he said, "I do but I want you to tell me, to say the words."

Grabbing for his hand, she lifted herself, willing him to do her silent bidding, frustrated when he refused to budge. Perspiration filmed the backs of her knees, she ground out, "My clit, I want it there."

"Right there, like this?" She heard the smile in his voice as he positioned the vibrator.

"Y-yes...oh, yes." Her body was humming with satisfaction in sync with the toy, the friction carrying her natural libido upwards to a quick, sharp spiral.

"More?"

Eyes squeezed shut, she nodded, a silent yes.

He slid the vibrator lower to the slippery wet slit between her swollen lips. "You're so small and tight. The other night, I was amazed at how I slid right in you."

With the vibrator humming inside her, she shifted her hips, absorbing the thrill of invasion. Eyes still closed, she pretended it was Josh inside her instead of the toy. "It's because you make me so wet."

Indeed, it wasn't the toy making her wet and so wild but knowing Josh's was the hand wielding it. Looking down at his big hand between her legs, she envisioned his cock inside her instead, and a wave of pleasure washed over her, so intense it caused her to curl her toes.

"I like getting you wet. In fact, I can't wait to have a taste. Mind?" Before she could answer, he'd clicked the vibrator off and replaced it with his searching fingers. Dipping one thick digit inside her, he pulled it back out and slid it between his lips. "Hmm," he said, "you taste amazing, but I need more." He slid down and found her with his mouth, tongue lapping at her clit.

The orgasm hit her fast and hard, spasms of pleasure so intense her entire body trembled with the force of it, the contractions deep and powerfully satisfying, gradually fading to a lingering golden glow, the perfect release.

When she opened her eyes and looked back, Josh was on his knees rolling on a condom. "Are you ready for more?"

Even though she'd just come, she didn't hesitate. "I'm ready for more of you."

He nodded, eyes stark with urgent need, powerful chest rising and falling with each rapid-fire breath. "Good, because I can't wait any longer. I have to have you...*now.*"

Unless he was the greatest actor on the planet, he really was turned on by her. Sliding her gaze down the length of him, she saw he was big and hard, potent and powerful. For the present at least, all that loosely harnessed maleness was for her and her alone.

Feeling the full force of her feminine power for perhaps the first time in her life, she reached for him, her fingers trailing the length of his sheathed penis. "I don't want you to wait."

"Then get on your hands and knees for me."

For the first time since coming out in the skimpy lingerie, she hesitated. "But my butt is huge."

"Your butt, your *ass,* is beautiful, and I want to see it up close. In fact, I want it right in my face when I fuck you."

Oh my God. Heart pounding with anticipation, she turned over and knelt, bracing her weight on her hands. She was still wet from coming and his first thrust brought him fully, deeply inside her.

Drawing back, he asked, "Does this feel good? Not too much?"

She reached upward and grabbed the metal bedposts with both hands. Holding on tight, she glanced back at him over her shoulder. All that masculine beauty and strength was hers for the taking, and suddenly it didn't matter if her butt was too big or her thighs too full because in this moment, this perfect moment, she felt beautiful and free, sexy and powerful.

"Not too much. In fact, I want more. I want all of you. Go ahead, Josh, I can take it. Fuck me. Fuck me hard."

Josh's breath was a hot breeze on her neck, his dirty talking a sexy whisper into the shell of her ear. Hands anchored to her hips, he started out slow and steady, increasing the pace and pressure. They moved together in perfect rhythm, perfect unison. He seemed to have a sixth sense about what she wanted, what she needed him to do, to say. All the while he moved inside her, he told her how beautiful she was, how amazing she smelled and tasted, how good she felt around him. And just when she thought she'd reached the pinnacle, that nothing and no one could possibly make her feel this good, let alone even better again, he reached a hand down between them and stroked her clitoris with his thumb.

Mandy's world shattered, spun apart, and then slowly came together again. Opening her eyes, she realized he was still behind her, still inside her, her inner flesh fluttering around his still hard penis. Wanting to please him, to milk his essence, to feel him come inside her, she deliberately contracted her inner muscles, squeezing him as tightly as she could, an invisible embrace.

"Oh God, Mandy."

Josh pulled out and drove into her once more. He came hard

and fast, a hoarse shout announcing his release. Body shuddering, he collapsed against her. With her head tucked beneath his chin and his hands cradling a breast in either palm, they settled into, if not exactly a "long winter's nap," a very sound, very satisfying sleep.

ACROSS THE STREET, the Men in Black hunkered down in the upper storey of a brick row house in a room furnished only with two beat-up Salvation Army straight-back chairs and the state-of-the-art in audio surveillance equipment. Turning to his partner, Special Agent Walker pulled the microphone from his ear. "Looks like all's quiet on the Western front."

McKinney blew out a breath. "Meaning they must be sleeping. Jesus, it's about time. What…what, uh, do you figure he was doing to her in there?" He reached for his foam cup of tepid black coffee, wishing it were ice water instead.

Guarding a federally protected witness was serious business but at times like this it was hard to keep a straight face—or a limp love muscle. If things in Thornton's apartment got any steamier, McKinney was sure his glasses would fog over.

Turning down the audio, Walker nodded. Fatigue had caused him to drop his normal poker face, and he found himself fighting a smile. "I don't know, but whatever it is, she obviously liked it—a lot."

They'd had the apartment bugged before they'd moved Thornton in gratis a local cleaning service that was really a FBI front. Wiretapping a witness's lodging wasn't exactly textbook procedure, but in a high-profile case such as this one it paid to cover all your bases. If the mob got to him in the apartment, they'd have the murder as a digital recording. That was something at least.

The play-by-play sex talk was a new wrinkle entirely. Until just before the holiday, the most risqué sounds to come out of that apartment were Thornton's letting loose with a swear word when a pot boiled over or he stubbed his toe. But ever since a certain red-haired lady cop stepped into the picture on Christmas Eve, the content rating on the daily digital recordings had spiked from PG-13 to full-out X.

McKinney rubbed a fist at tired eyes. "Looks like Rule Number Three must have slipped his mind, huh?"

Walker nodded. "Don't get personally involved. Personal involvements put you off your guard and sooner or later, you slip up. Judging from the sounds coming out of that mike, this particular *involvement* could end up in getting Mr. Thornton killed."

WALKER AND MCKINNEY WEREN'T the only ones to remark on Josh and Mandy's unfolding relationship. In a smoky bar around the corner, two men on the opposite side of the law sat across from each other at a round bar table sipping frosted mugs of Harp and watching the Baltimore Ravens face off against the New England Patriots.

"Fuck, no way was that a fumble." Bull-necked and broad-shouldered, the man in the dark suit shifted his attention from the plasma TV screen to his companion. "The broad who's been hanging out with Thornton, what's her name again?" His voice carried the accent of Boston's North End.

The second man, a local, answered, "Mandy Delinski. She's a Bawlmer City cop." Casually dressed in jeans and a navy cable-knit sweater that hung on his thin frame, he reached for his beer.

One deep-set eye wandering back to the wall-mounted TV, the suit said, "Is that so? I ain't seen many cops that look like her. What a knockout."

Tone sulky, his table mate said, "She's okay if you like that type. You're planning on taking her out too, right?"

The heavy-set man known as Tommy the Terminator answered with an expansive shrug that caused the buttons fronting his double-breasted jacket to pull but only slightly.

Finding suits that fit had used to be a major problem. Fortunately one of the mob-owned businesses back in Boston was a tailoring shop that specialized in custom-made clothing for "big and tall" men.

"Not necessarily," he said, taking a swig of his beer. "It could go either way depending on the circumstances. My contract terms are to liquidate Thornton on or before the first of January. I get paid by the contract, not the head." He paused, squinted gaze narrowing. "Why, you got some beef with her?" He set the mug down and looked his companion dead in the eye, waiting.

His table mate hesitated. He had a beef with Mandy Delinski, a big one, but it wouldn't do to give that away, not just yet. Swallowing hard, he chose his words with care. "Lady cops, the whole situation just pisses me off. Women ought to know their place—on their backs or on their knees if you know what I mean." He chuckled, stopping when the hit man didn't join in.

Index finger pointed out like a pistol, Tommy leaned across the table, prompting the thinner man to arch back in his chair. "That better be all because this is a business arrangement, strictly business and nothing personal. Got it?"

The thin man felt sweat breaking out beneath his L.L. Bean pullover, but knowing that someone with "Terminator" attached to his name must be trained to smell fear, he reached for his cool. "Yeah, sure, man. No problem, I got it."

Tommy settled back in his seat and reached for the bowl of salted peanuts. "You better get it, asshole, 'cause if I end up having to off the broad, too, I figure I might as well go three for three."

12

Calories consumed: steamed mussels clearly whole-some, guilt-free food fit for Trappist Monks if not for pound of butter consumed in double order of garlic butter-and-caper dipping sauce soaked up with second loaf of bread. On other hand, as nearly turned out to be last day on God's Green Earth, might as well let the good times roll. Times mother looked up at velvet painting of Virgin Mary and Baby Jesus and asked when would settle down and have babies like a good Catholic girl: by now likely have been disowned as Mary Magdalene fallen woman, so probably moot point.

THE NEXT MORNING, Josh woke to find himself lying spoon-style beside Mandy. Brushing her silky hair to the side, he leaned over and pressed a kiss to the smooth skin at the juncture of her throat and shoulder. "By the way, in case you have any doubts, last night counts as the most amazing sex of my life."

She rolled on her side to face him, fitting into the curve of his shoulder like a custom-made glove. Tracing his jaw with gentle fingers, she admitted, "Mine, too, though in my case that might be a case of damning with faint praise."

There she was putting herself down again and at the same time painting him as some kind of player. He lifted his head from the pillow to look down at her. "I haven't been with all that many women, you know."

"Come on, with your looks and position, you must have to fight them off."

"My position?" He hesitated, heart diving directly into his stomach. Had he blown his cover already and without even knowing he'd slipped up?

"I just meant that being a bartender you must come into contact with a lot of women."

Picking up on the insecurity in her voice, he settled back onto the pillow, pulling her against his chest. "That doesn't mean I sleep with them all, and I wasn't always a bartender. It's sort of an interim career for me." She opened her mouth as if to say something, but closed it without a word. Before she could ask any more questions to do with his supposed occupation, he changed the subject. "It's supposed to be a beautiful day for December, sunny and a lot warmer than it's been. What do you say to us going out later?"

She snapped up her head, nearly clipping him on the chin. "You want to leave the apartment?"

He'd thought she'd be pleased, instead she sounded anything but. Hoping she hadn't taken his suggestion to mean he didn't like being in bed with her, he moved into damage control mode. "I want us to do something together, a real date. We could walk around the Inner Harbor, catch the Christmas decorations while they're still up, and then take the water taxi over to Fells Point. I still haven't tried Bertha's famous mussels."

She slid a hand beneath the covers and wrapped her hand around his cock which went from semi to full hard-on at her touch. "Are you sure you won't want to just stay in? We could order in Chinese or pizza, and I could try out your muscle—again."

She was so incredibly sexy and warm and generous, the temptation to just hang out with her in bed for days and nights on end was enormous. He was coming to suspect her giving nature had caused her to be taken advantage of in the past, particularly by men, which might explain why she often seemed so skeptical of her own appeal. And yet he hadn't exaggerated what he'd said they'd shared was the hands-down most satisfying sex of his life.

But then sometimes you had to know bad in order to recognize good, make that *amazing*. Sex with Tiffany had been like an overly choreographed musical—the moves might come off as perfectly correct, even acrobatic, but there was no feeling in it, no emotional connection. It wasn't that he'd minded Tiffany telling him what felt good, that wasn't it at all. What had really worn on him was her attitude. She'd acted as though she was doing him some kind of favor, as though sex was a commodity she was doling out rather than an experience they shared. Toward the end, he'd felt like he was on the losing end of a competition with her vibrator, which she'd actually named "Dick" of all things. Looking back on the experience, it occurred to him that walking in on her with the lawn care kid had been a lucky break in a way, a reason for ending a relationship that had never worked all that well anyway.

Making love to Mandy was an entirely new, entirely fulfilling experience he hoped to repeat many, many times. Hell, he couldn't imagine getting enough of her—ever. He'd never before come close to losing himself in a woman the way he had done with her. Even teasing her with the toy had been playful and fun because of how receptive she was, how sensual, how entirely open and trusting. He wouldn't have thought watching something other than him glide inside her would be such an incredible turn-on, but it definitely had been if only because of the way she'd responded to him.

And yet despite the intimacy of the acts they'd shared, other than their coffee date, they hadn't been out as a couple. The very last thing he wanted her to think was that he was just using her for sex. Oh, he wanted to have sex with her all right, that was a given, but he wanted more than that, too. Mandy was what he'd come to think of as a total package, a quality woman. She deserved to be taken out on the town, not just taken to bed. If caring about a proper courtship made him come off as stuffy and old-fashioned, then so be it. It was important to him to do things the right way with her because… well, because Mandy was important to him. Though he still wasn't sure how or even if their lives might mesh, he didn't want her to look back on their time together and remember him as just another jerk who'd used her.

But it was next to impossible to think clearly or even at all with her touching him, so he reached down and gently disengaged her hand. Lacing her fingers through his, he brought her palm to his lips. "I really want to take you out on a real date. Is that so wrong?"

Meeting his eyes, she hesitated and then nodded. "No, of course it's not wrong. I'd love to go out on a date with you."

"Good, then it's settled." Pleased, he flashed a smile and slipped his arm out from under her head. Getting up, he headed toward the bathroom. "I'll go run the shower water. The pipes are old and it takes a while for the water to heat. Give me a minute and then join me, okay?"

She sat up in bed. "Okay."

Resting her chin atop her tented knees, she watched him head into the bathroom, marveling at how incredibly thoughtful and romantic he was, how unlike any man she'd ever been with before. Not only was he hot and smart and fun to be with and yes, a truly amazing lover, but he was so sweet to her, too, so thoughtful and tender. Until now she'd thought guys like that only existed between the covers of paperback romance novels. Even with the smell of his skin and the warmth of his body imprinted in the sheet beside her, she had trouble believing he was real. But Josh was real all right, the real thing. He'd already received all she had to give and yet he still insisted on taking her out on a date. The gentlemanliness of the gesture caught at her heart even as her fear factor spiked. Fells Point was where the murder, Josh's murder, had taken place. Wouldn't returning to the scene of the crime be tempting fate? On the other hand, maybe as long as they avoided Thames Street, and The Daily Grind and Recreation Pier specifically, they'd be all right? Either way, it was obvious he was determined to go out. If promising a rematch of the previous night's intense sexual pleasure couldn't convince him to stay safely inside, she didn't know what else she could possibly do. At least if they went together, she'd have a chance of protecting him.

The sounds of the shower running pulled her back to the present. She threw off the covers, slipped out of bed and headed for the bathroom. On the way, she pulled his Boston Red Sox T-shirt over her head and then off.

Shaking out her hair and enjoying the feel of it against her breasts and back, it occurred to her that just a few days before, strolling naked across a room, even an empty room, would have been an activity reserved for her thinner fantasy self but never acted out in real life. This time with Josh had changed a lot of things, including her image of herself. Based on the number of times they made love and the intensity of each encounter, her body obviously pleased him just as it was. With the pressure to be perfect removed, she found herself spending a lot less time and energy thinking and worrying about food. If she was hungry, she'd eat, if she wasn't, well, it wouldn't hurt her to miss a meal. After all these years of calorie counting and binge eating, could it really be as simple as that?

She had one hand on the bathroom doorknob when her cell phone sounded off to the tune of "Jingle Bells." She ran to catch it, managing to dig it out of her purse and pick up just before her voice mail kicked in. When she didn't recognize the local number at first glance, she decided she'd better err on the safe side and use her "work voice" to answer. "Delinski speaking."

"Hey, Mands, it's me, Mikey."

"Hey, Mikey, what's up?"

"Remember how you said I should call you if I was to come across any, uh…out-of-town customers?"

Heart ramping up for a full-on race, she said, "Yes."

"Well, I did, late last night in fact, and so I am."

Picking up on the nervous quaver in his voice, she decided her shower with Josh would have to wait. "Hold tight, Mikey. I can be down there in twenty minutes."

"Meeting here's no good, besides I'm working a double shift. There's no way I can get away today, but I'm off work tomorrow. Meet me at Duda's in Fells Point, say around noon. I'll buy you a crab-cake sandwich. They use all lump meat, you know, not like those schlock tourist traps at Harbor Place where they charge you an arm and a leg for a ball of breadcrumbs with a few crab flakes mixed in. Those chain restaurants, they'll rob you blind. And they call me the criminal."

Dialing down her impatience, Mandy said, "Okay, I'll be there, only lunch is on me, so screw the sandwich and go for the platter."

"Thanks, Mands, you're the best. See you then."

"Bye, Mikey."

She clicked off the cell just as Josh called out from the shower, "Are you coming in or do I have to turn into a prune all by myself?"

Her gaze darted to the closed bathroom door. The thought of Josh gloriously naked and glistening wet waiting behind it brought a warm tingle of anticipation building between her legs. "I'm on my way."

Though signing on to guard a hot hunk with a heart of gold was a rare comingling of duty and pleasure, duty still took precedence. Before joining him, she made a detour to the dresser and slipped her gun inside her purse.

BERTHA'S RESTAURANT AND BAR WAS located in an historic green-painted brick building on the corner of Lancaster and Broadway Streets. A Fells Point fixture since the early 1970s, it was famous for its steamed mussels served with crusty Italian bread and assorted sauces. Add a good bottle of crisp white wine and maybe a side salad and you had all the makings of a simple but satisfying meal.

Tucked into the wood-paneled dining room, the walls decked with maritime paintings, salvaged musical instruments, and sundry bric-a-brac, Mandy and Josh could hear the mellow sounds of the solo blues musician floating in from the sidebar. Swirling the last few sips of wine about her glass, Mandy looked across the table at her handsome and attentive date and admitted that if it weren't for the threat hanging over their heads, she would have been completely content and blissfully happy. As it was, they'd still shared a lovely day, starting with their chilly stroll about Harborplace, the city's horseshoe-shaped tourist venue of shops, restaurants and interactive museums. They'd walked from the National Aquarium to the Maryland Science Center and back again, taking in the outdoor Christmas decorations, periodically ducking into the pavilions to thaw themselves. It turned out Josh was even crazier about Christmas than she was, yet another thing they had in common.

The only thing that had held the day back from one hundred percent perfection was her anxiety about a possible attempt on his life. Scanning the areas for signs of trouble, by the end of the day she felt like she'd grown eyes in the back of her head. Fortunately the afternoon passed without event. Released from the pressures of holiday shopping, tourists and natives alike had flocked to the popular waterfront attraction, and Mandy maneuvered to make sure they were always in the thick of the crowd. When dusk set in, they'd braved the bluster and caught the water taxi over to Fells Point. The boat let them out on the other side of Thames Street, a short two-block walk to the restaurant where they'd sat down to an early dinner.

Even though circumstances fell far short of ideal, she was enjoying herself immensely. Josh was incredibly easy to be with, an even better dining companion than coffee date. A part of her had worried they might run out of conversation, that he might grow bored with her, but as the meal progressed, they only seemed to discover more topics to talk about. Coming from Boston, he loved seafood as much as she did, maybe more. They started out with cups of savory crab soup and then ordered a large bucket of steamed mussels with all eight sauces to share. Eating, talking, laughing over nothing and everything at once, the meal flew by. Never before had she felt anywhere close to this comfortable with a man in or out of bed.

"You've got to try this one. It's amazing." Josh pried the mussel from its opened shell, dunked it in one of the scampi dishes of sauce, and held the fork out for her to taste.

Mandy hesitated. Being on the receiving end of a lover's tender attention was a new and wonderful experience she was still getting used to. Leaning over, she opened for him and, smiling, he slipped the fork between her lips. The tender mussel doused in Bertha's garlic butter and capers was a sensual delight, but it paled in comparison to the thrill of him staring at her mouth as she chewed, then swallowed, licking butter from her bottom lip. Like her, was he thinking of all the ways she'd used her lips and tongue and even teeth to pleasure him? The prospect sent a telltale twinge of heat settling between her legs and she was suddenly glad they'd be making an early night of it and not just for safety's sake.

Touching her napkin to the corners of her mouth, she asked, "Are all shellfish supposed to be an aphrodisiac or is it only oysters?"

Setting the fork aside, he shook his head. "Don't know," he admitted, "though the last thing I need around you is an aphrodisiac. As it is, I may just have to resort to pouring that glass of ice water on my lap so I can get up from here without the waitress calling the police."

She smiled at that. "I am the police."

"That's right, you are, although you certainly don't look like any cop I've ever known." He reached across the table to take her hand.

"I don't?"

"No, you don't. For one thing, there's your skin."

"What about my skin?" She pulled back, resisting the urge to run to the lady's room and check her reflection for a zit or fever blister blooming.

Lifting his hand, he stroked a finger down the side of her face. "It's beautiful, porcelain perfect and silken soft. It's like you have this glow about you. I noticed it the first time I saw you."

She smiled into his eyes, a deep azure blue that made her think of foreign seas and exotic lands. He was so beautiful he could have passed for a male model, a movie star or a television news anchor…anything at all. What he saw in her, a working-class girl from East Baltimore, a street cop, she couldn't begin to say but whatever happened from here on she'd forever thank her lucky stars—make that her magical new moon—for the gift of this time together.

"Thanks. It's one of the benefits of being fat—the wrinkles stretch out like that lingerie you gave me."

His smile disappeared. "Why do you always do that?"

"Do what?"

He tossed her an exasperated look. "Turn a compliment into a put-down."

"I was just making a joke." She hesitated, and then admitted, "When you're as fat, as *heavy* as I am, you don't get all that many compliments."

"Ever think that maybe your weight doesn't have a damned thing to do with it? That if you're not getting compliments, maybe it's because of the way you react to hearing nice things about yourself?"

"That's not true, I—"

"Compliments make you uncomfortable, don't they?"

"A little… Okay, a lot."

He reached across the table and clasped her hand in his. Massaging her palm with his thumb, he said, "Then we'll just have to work on that, won't we?"

They were interrupted by the waitress returning to clear away their plates and bowl of shucked shells. Tucking a strand of pumpkin-orange hair behind one triple-pierced ear, she looked at Mandy and asked, "Would you like to hear about our dessert items?" Her smug "thin girl" smile said that bumping up their check total with at least one sweet treat was a given.

Ordinarily Mandy would have heard the chocolate chip pie or the pecan-butter tart calling her name, but the final water taxi was due in at six o'clock, and Josh's car was parked all the way back at the Inner Harbor's Pier Six parking lot. Glancing at her watch, she saw it was ten minutes to the hour. The very last thing she wanted was to put him in the vulnerable position of having to hang out on the street to flag down a cab.

She looked up at the waitress, nose stud twinkling in the dimmed light, and said, "No thanks, I'll pass."

Praying Josh wouldn't order anything, she released a breath of relief when he pulled his hand out of hers and reached for his wallet. "Just the check, then, thanks."

Once it arrived, her pleas for him to let her pay half at least were met with "your money's no good here" and a reminder that when it came to dating, he was unabashedly old school. "I asked you out, not the other way around," he said, refusing to even let her look at the bill.

Mindful of the time ticking away, she surrendered with a "Thank you" and a grateful smile. He helped her into her coat and, bundled against the cold, they stepped out onto the sidewalk. Standing beneath the green canopy, she scanned the near empty street, anxiety returning. The area above Broadway Market wasn't exactly deserted, but pedestrian traffic was a lot lighter than usual. Ordinarily the popular waterfront spot was hopping seven days a week, the sounds of live music and laughter spilling out from the bars lining both sides of Broadway and Thames Streets, the sidewalks packed with a potpourri of people ranging from suburbanites to panhandlers bold enough to venture beyond the marketplace boundary. But the week between Christmas and New Year's was notoriously slow, regular patrons worn out from the holiday party circuit or saving themselves for New Year's Eve.

Hooking her arm through Josh's, she said, "We'd better hurry if we're going to make that last water taxi, otherwise we'll have to catch a cab back to the car, and I don't see any."

Fortunately there was a small hub of people waiting at the landing point when they walked up. Under the guise of keeping as warm as was possible, Mandy suggested they move closer and join the group, which consisted of an elderly couple, their fortysomething daughter and a teenaged granddaughter.

Huddled together, it was easy enough to strike up a conversation. It turned out the elderly couple had flown in from Boston to visit their divorced daughter and granddaughter for the Christmas holiday.

The gentleman, a distinguished Sean Connery look-alike with a plaid cap and a dapper air, looked to Josh and said, "You sound like a native Bostonian yourself."

Glancing sideways at Josh, Mandy took note of his subtle withdrawal. He paused before answering. "Yes, I am."

"May I ask what part?"

Again there was that hint of hesitation that Mandy had

noted when they'd first met, only now she understood the reason for his reticence. "Oh, look, here comes the boat," she interjected, saving him from having to answer.

The pontoon docked, and Mandy and Josh held back for the family to board. They moved to take seats inside the enclosed blue awning, and Mandy surmised that joining them would mean continuing their friendly conversation, including more about Boston.

Turning to Josh, she said, "If you don't mind the cold, let's stand outside. The view coming into harbor will be better from the stern."

"No, I don't mind," he said all too readily and gestured for her to board first. Joining her at the rail, he opened his arms, motioning for her to step into them. "Come here, you, before you freeze to death."

Given their circumstances, Mandy didn't much care for his choice of words but otherwise it was a perfect moment. The boat pulled out, and leaning back against his solid warmth with her head tucked beneath his chin, she realized she felt happy or as close to it as she'd ever been.

Tipping her head back to look up at him, she made a silent pact with herself to savor the moment rather than spoil it by wishing it might be more. "By the way, thanks for being such a great date."

Mouth curving into a smile, he pressed a kiss to her forehead, a sweetly chaste tenderness that set her heart aflutter. "Thank you for going out with me. I had a great time, too, and the best part is I get to take you home with me."

Home. In just a few short days, she'd come to think of Josh's apartment as her home, too, which wasn't something she'd signed up for or expected. Try as she might, she'd yet to sort out the nature of the electrically charged connection between them—a fling, a framework for an actual relationship, or something in between? But that was a dilemma best left to puzzle out another day. For now, the immediate issue was keeping him alive.

"Hmm, that is the best part, isn't it?"

She snuggled closer, soaking up his warmth and sexy, shower-fresh scent. His skin always smelled like the beach to her, wholesome and fresh with just a hint of tang. The lights from the Inner Harbor were a distant twinkle and, barring the temperature, she could almost imagine they were in some exotic, romantic locale, freed from any danger and blissfully alone. But then again, as her mother was always pointing out, you had to take the good with the bad. If it weren't for the danger, Josh wouldn't have come to Baltimore in the first place. He wouldn't be with her now.

"I think so." He leaned in to nuzzle her neck.

A boom rang out. For a split second, you could almost believe it was an engine backfiring but then the bullet whizzed just above their heads, so close the movement stirred the hair at their crowns.

Swiveling around to the dock, Mandy spotted a red motorboat barreling toward them at full throttle. *Oh, shit.* She threw herself at Josh and screamed, "Everybody, hit the deck!"

She came down on top of him hard, popped open her purse, and pulled out her pistol and cell. She punched 911 into the cell, and then lifted her head to shout, "I'm a city police officer. Keep your heads down."

The 911 operator answered on the second ring just as Josh came up beside her, shifting position so that his body shielded hers. She tried pushing him back down, but he wouldn't budge. "Not a chance," he said, and reached up to cover a protective hand over her head.

Interrupting the operator's preamble, Mandy shouted into the phone receiver, "This is Officer Mandy Delinski, Baltimore City Police, and we have two men in a red motorboat firing into the Harbor Taxi. We're just a few yards from the Fells Point dock. Hurry."

"Officer, can you describe the assailants?"

Mandy managed to get out "ski masks and dark windbreakers" when they took the hit. Fast and hard, the motorboat rammed them in the rear, the impact setting the bones in her skull rattling and knocking the phone from her hand. She grabbed it back, but the call had gone dead. *Damn.* Another hit, and the pontoon upended, water rushing in, filling Mandy's nose and mouth. Lungs burning and sides splitting, she held her breath and struggled to swim out into the clear. Gasping, she surfaced amidst screaming passengers and the shrieking of the boat's SOS siren. Frantic, she grabbed hold of a piece of rail and searched the darkness for sign of Josh.

"Josh, Josh, where are you? Answer me. Oh, God, Josh…"

But he was nowhere to be seen in the inky water.

13

Number of near death experiences: one, but on bright side, hunky boyfriend finally entrusted me with his Big Secret. Feel like Luke Skywalker of *Star Wars* trilogy or Frodo, stalwart Hobbit of *Lord of the Rings* trilogy— Chosen One capable of rising to any challenge in service of good. Wish could reciprocate by confessing have known situation status all along but how to explain metaphysical New Year's Eve wish-come-true without appearing like nutcase on par with Joanne Woodward in *The Three Faces of Eve* (great movie, btw) or little boy in Bruce Willis paranormal flick, *The Sixth Sense,* who "sees dead people"? Either way, would never believe me, not in a million years.

JOSH HAD BEEN AROUND BOATS and water all his life. His family joked he'd learned to swim before he'd learned to walk. Still, even for the naturally amphibious, hypothermia was no trivial risk. The one thing that kept him pushing onward stroke after stroke was the drive to find Mandy. There was still so much he had left to learn about her, such as whether or not she could swim. If, make that *when,* they got out of this, he wanted to know more, a lot more. He wanted to know everything.

"Josh, Josh, where are you? Answer me."

It was Mandy, calling his name. Relief hit him like a tidal wave, bringing with it renewed resolve. "Hold tight, I'm coming," he shouted above the chaos and then swam toward her, numbed arms and leaden legs knifing through the icy water.

He surfaced at her side and wrapped an arm about her shuddering shoulders. Her teeth were clacking like castanets and he'd bet anything her nails were blue, but she was alive and so was he and for the moment that was all that mattered.

Sticking close, they managed to get a head count on the other passengers. Fortunately everyone could swim and all but one, the grandfather, had managed to grab hold of the side of the overturned boat. Knowing that older folks were particularly susceptible to hypothermia, Josh left Mandy with the others and went in search of him.

He found him a few feet from the capsized craft, a bird's-egg-sized bump on the side of his head and thin arms flailing. Vaguely aware of flashing strobe lights and screeching sirens coming from shore, Josh swam as fast as he could. He came up beside him and grabbed hold.

Treading water, he asked, "Are you okay, sir?"

The man managed a groggy nod. "My wife…not m-much of a…s-swimmer."

"Your wife is fine, and so is the rest of your family." Josh grabbed hold of one of his slack arms and slung it over his neck. "We're going to get all of you warm and dry in no time." Hoping that was indeed the case, he towed him back to the boat sidestroke-style just as rescue workers arrived on the scene.

Thanks to Mandy's quick thinking in calling 911, the fire department and police were already onsite, joined in short order by the nearby navy reservists whose divers managed to pull them all out of the water within minutes. Aside from the older couple taken to the hospital by ambulance to be treated for hypothermia, there were no injuries and, thankfully, no casualties.

Wrapped in thermal space blankets and seated on benches at the dock, they gave their statements to a homicide detective from Mandy's precinct. Seeing Mandy, he greeted her by name.

"Hey, Delinski, the 911 dispatcher said an officer made the call-in. I thought you were out on a family emergency."

Josh glanced to Mandy, wondering why she'd lied. She'd told him she had vacation time coming to her and that her boss had all but forced her to take it. Apparently that was less than the truth. "Er, I was. I mean, I am."

"I see." Pulling a notepad from the inside pocket of his polyester suit jacket, the detective continued, "Did you get a make or model on the craft?"

Mandy shook her head. Wet-haired and wide-eyed, she still managed to look beautiful, only younger, almost like a little girl rather than the fearless, grown-up woman whose quick thinking had likely saved all their lives. "It all happened so fast and well, I'm not really much of a sailing buff. I can tell you the color and give you a general description of the power boat, but that's about it."

Silent until now, Josh had no choice but to speak up. "I only got a quick glance myself, but it looked a lot like the new Fountain 47 Lightning. The Lightning packs two 1075 Mercury SCI engines that let it push upwards of 120 miles per hour. And it has a deep V-shaped hull with the steering console all the way in the rear. That would explain how the driver could hit us stern-side and still be intact to speed off."

The detective paused from scribbling to look up. "Wow, you really know your boats. Just out of curiosity, what does something like that run cost-wise?"

Josh hesitated. He knew the craft specs inside and out because he owned the previous year's model. Unfortunately he'd only got to take her out a couple of times before his life went to hell. The boat had been the real casualty in his faked death.

"Between 750 and 800 K, depending on what amenities you go for. The specialized paint job alone probably cost 50 K." Out of the corner of his eye, he caught Mandy looking at him and decided he'd better stop there.

The detective shook his head. "Wow, too rich for my blood."

The evidence so far suggested the attackers had lain in wait farther upriver, probably putting in at the Tidewater Fuel Dock and Yacht Service station until the water taxi had pulled out of the Fells Point slip. Unfortunately they'd taken advantage of the confusion to disappear. The police had issued an all points bulletin and were setting up checkpoints on all the ports and sundry put-in spots within a twenty-five mile radius. Still, without a tag number, they could be anywhere by now. As for the shooter and driver, "two men in ski masks and dark windbreakers" wasn't much of a description to go on.

As much as Josh wanted to believe the culprits were random snipers, his gut told him there was no way that could be. The shot fired had been meant for him alone. The shooter had missed the first time if only because he'd moved at the last minute to lean in and kiss Mandy. That impromptu embrace had probably saved his life.

But he couldn't count on his luck lasting forever. It was obvious the mob boys had tracked him down and now that they had, they'd be mounting a concerted campaign to take him out before the trial. He wasn't safe and no one near him was either, meaning Mandy. For her own good, he had to get her out of his apartment and out of his life.

In the midst of finishing up giving their statements, his pager went off. Glancing down, he saw the familiar number and stifled an "Oh, shit." Turning to Mandy and the detective, he said, "Excuse me, but I have to take this."

Mandy looked over at him. She opened her mouth as if to say something, but and then closed it again. Instead, she answered with a mute nod and returned to giving her statement.

When he phoned in, McKinney's voice crackled from the cell's waterlogged receiver. "What the fuck are you doing out in the open playing tourist on a goddamned water taxi, for

Christ's sake? Why not put a fucking bull's eye on your ass while you're at it?"

Holding the phone to his ear, Josh scanned the vicinity. "Where are you?"

"Don't worry about where we are. Worry about where you are. That was one close call. Next time you won't be so lucky—and you can bet that white-bread ass of yours there will be a next time."

Clenching the phone, Josh shot back, "I can't stay a prisoner in this rat hole of an apartment 24/7. Besides, you're the ones who set me up as a bartender for six months now. If that's not out in the open, I don't know what is."

"For chrissake, Thornton, it's less than a week to trial. Fuck bartending and lay low for a few more days. In fact, as of now, consider yourself on lockdown until the trial."

"I can't." Taking a deep breath, he admitted, "I've met someone."

"Yeah, the lady cop. We know all about your little fling. You've had your fun, but it's time to break it off."

"It's not a fling. I have...feelings for her."

If McKinney was a closet romantic, he hid it well. "The dead don't feel, Thornton. If you really care for this woman, you'll break it off for both your sakes. Continuing to see her endangers her life as well as yours as this little adventure goes to show."

That cinched it. Josh would sign up to take that risk, but he didn't have the right to make that choice for her. After the trial, he would call her and hope she'd understand—but would she still be willing to see him knowing he'd been lying to her all along?

"Okay, I'll tell her I'm going home for a few days to take care of a personal matter and that I'll get in touch afterward."

McKinney hesitated. "It's not that simple."

The agent's cryptic tone sent foreboding plowing into him like a fist in the gut. "But you said once I testified, I'd be in the clear."

"That was when Grady was still alive and on tap to testify, too. His death changed the whole landscape of the case. Now you're the sole federal witness."

"So?"

"A smart guy like you, you don't really think the Romero family is going to let you sail off into the sunset after you put one of their captains in the pen, do you?"

Not even narrowly avoiding a bullet in the head could come close to causing the visceral fear that hit him like a fist in the gut on hearing that not only was his life not his own, but apparently it never would be again. He'd put his ass on the line for more than six months now, exposed his family and friends to unimaginable grief, all in the service of justice. But as much as he wanted to see right done, he wasn't about to martyr himself so that some hotshot FBI special agent could get a promotion.

"What if I decide not to testify, call the whole thing off?"

"That's funk talk, Thornton, and you know it. Even if you bail on us, and I strongly recommend you do not, you know too much for them to let you live. But look, don't worry. We'll get you a new permanent identity. This time, you'll have your pick of locales. Hell, we might even be able to swing getting you a job that uses your business and technology skills."

Josh clicked off the cell without answering. The depth of the bad news penetrated his shock-fogged brain, sinking the sick feeling of foreboding deeper in his stomach. It seemed he was doomed to be on the run for the rest of his life. On the run—and away from Mandy.

JOSH RETURNED to the cordoned-off crime scene just as the detective tucked his notepad back inside his pocket. "I guess that about wraps it up. If you think of anything else, you know where I work."

A police squad car drove Mandy and Josh back to the Pier Six parking lot. Still wrapped in their emergency issue blankets, they climbed inside his car. It took three tries to get old Betsy started but once she revved to life, Josh turned the heat on full blast.

Turning out of the parking lot onto Pratt Street, he looked into his rearview mirror and saw a black sedan pull out of a parking space and make the turn behind them. Even though it was too dark to see through the windshield, he knew the driver would be Special Agent Walker and the passenger Special Agent McKinney. With the two federal agents just a car length behind, they would be safe, for the time being at least.

Relaxing marginally, he cast a sideways glance to Mandy. Sitting silent beside him, profile backlit by the headlights of passing cars, she hadn't said a word since they'd gotten in. Now that the first hard-hitting shock was ebbing, her brain was probably working overtime trying to process what had just happened, only unlike him she would be wondering why. He thought again of that terrifying handful of seconds before he heard her calling to him, when he hadn't known if she was dead or alive, and a fresh current of fear surged through him.

He tried for a joke to break the silence. "At least we'll always remember our first date."

She turned to him and in the dim light he saw her pretty mouth curve into a soft smile that didn't match the anxiety in her eyes. "If it's all the same to you, next time let's skip the water taxi part."

"It's a deal." He smiled back though it felt stiff, forced, and not just because his face like the rest of him felt as though he'd just emerged from a walk-in freezer, but because he'd been literally lying to her through his teeth.

Rule Number One: Don't give out personal information, no matter how innocuous, to anyone you meet—and that includes admitting you're a federally protected witness.

Fuck the rules. Mandy wasn't just *anyone*. She deserved to know what she was in for.

Turning right onto President Street, he couldn't stand it any longer. "Mandy, we need to talk."

"I thought we were talking."

"We need to talk about what just happened. The shooting, it was no random incident. That was a planned mob hit. A planned hit on me."

Rather than ask if he was prone to paranoia, a reasonable response under the circumstances, she said, "You're not really a bartender from Boston here for a change of scenery, are you?"

"No, I'm not." He turned onto Fleet Street and took a deep breath, bracing himself. "I've been in the federal witness protection program since last summer. Josh Thorner isn't even my real name, it's an alias. My real name is Joshua Thornton, and my family owns a telecommunications company based out of Boston. I came across some evidence that my brother-in-law, our VP for marketing, had been embezzling money from sales of WiFi networks and funneling it back to a Boston crime family, the Romeros. I didn't know what to do, so I went to the FBI with what we'd found so far. When another informant from my company turned up dead, they put me in the witness protection program. The feds staged my death as a sailing accident and relocated me here to wait out the trial date. My testimony is critical to not just indicting my brother-in-law but to bringing down the whole crime cartel, but only if I can stay alive until January second."

He'd expected her to freak out or at least ply him with questions, but instead she waited for him to wind down before asking, "Is that it?"

Of all the responses he'd expected from her, *is that it* wasn't among them. He couldn't believe how calmly she was taking the news, almost as if it wasn't news to her at all. Christ, he'd just told her he was a federal witness on the run from the mob and living under an assumed name. If that wasn't enough to shake her, he didn't know what would be.

"You do believe me, don't you?"

"Yes, I believe you. I just wish you'd trusted me enough to tell me before now."

"I thought about it, but keeping you in the dark seemed like the best way to keep you safe. And until the other day, I had myself convinced I'd given them the slip. But now they've found me, and it isn't fair of me to keep putting you in danger."

"You sound like you're breaking up with me." For the first time since he'd launched into his story, she looked alarmed.

"It's one thing if they get me. I signed up for this after all. But you, well, all you did was say yes to a cup of coffee with a stranger and look what's happened." He turned onto Boston Street and predictably the sedan did, too. "What I can't forgive myself for is putting you in danger. I haven't been fair to you and while I'm sorry about that, to be truthful, I can't say if I had it to do over again, I would do it any differently. The fact is these past days with you, they've been...well, magical, the best of my life, actually."

"Magical? You really mean that?"

He angled a look at her. Even with her hair plastering her head and mascara streaming her cheeks, she'd never been more beautiful to him—or more precious.

"Magical just like you."

She answered with a wobbly smile. "I want to spend the rest of this week with you. Whatever comes, we're in this together now, okay?"

If he hadn't been in traffic, he would have leaned over and kissed her. "You're sure about that?"

She turned to look at him, and her earnest eyes met his. "I've never been surer of anything in my life."

Glancing into his rearview mirror, he checked to make sure the black sedan still followed. Sure enough, it was there albeit at a discreet distance. The Men in Black were on the J.O.B. and taking no chances—and no prisoners, either, he suspected.

They'd make sure he and Mandy got inside his building. That was something at least.

Turning back to her, he saw a wicked smile light her eyes. The last time he'd seen that smile she'd been on top of him, straddling his hips. Its reappearance after what he'd just told her lifted his heart—and hardened his cock.

Reaching over the stick shift, she found his knee with her hand. Sliding it slowly upward to his thigh, she used her most sultry voice to say, "If it's okay with you, I'd like to place my dessert order in advance—a scalding shower and you in it making love to me."

Had that first bullet hit an inch or so lower, he might easily have ended the day dead, but it hadn't and for the moment, this moment, he was alive and so was she. "I think we can arrange that."

Her smile widened, and she moistened her lips in a way that had him forgetting all about being cold. "Good, I was hoping you might be hungry, too."

She settled her hand between his thighs, cupping his erection, and in spite of the threat hanging over his head, make that *their* heads, in addition to feeling aroused as hell, he felt almost happy. He *was* happy. Even dripping wet and pungent with dead fish and pollutants, not to mention packed into a car that ought to have been relegated to scrap metal long ago, it was good to be alive. *But for how long?* he asked himself. *How long?*

14

Calories consumed: may stop counting as realize body fat density gives Darwinian "survival of the fittest" (fattest) edge should ever find self dumped into hypothermic harbor waters again (God forbid!). Number of hunky hero boyfriends saved from speeding bullet and fished out of vile harbor waters to live and love another day: just one and will do anything, everything, in power to keep him alive.

THE BAR BENEATH Josh's apartment was a popular watering hole for Canton locals. Other than the fire escape ladder steps to be used in an emergency, the only way to access his second-storey apartment was to enter through the main door and then cut through the crowd to the back staircase. Fortunately it was a Sunday, the one day of the week when even the most intrepid pub crawler packed it in early. Mandy and Josh stepped inside, their bedraggled appearance drawing raised eyebrows from the few hangers-on. Even Smitty and Joe, two sixtysomethings sipping pints of Guinness and puffing dollar cigars, looked up from their game of dominoes to survey them with questioning eyes. From across the bar, Mandy spotted a slinky blond in a skin-tight cashmere turtleneck perched on a stool, her catlike gaze honing in on Josh.

He's a good-looking guy, so get used to it, she told herself. Even coated with harbor sludge, he looked amazing, ruggedly beautiful like a slightly mussed Indiana Jones.

Face lighting up like a Christmas tree, the blonde stubbed out her cigarette and sprang off her seat. Rounding the bar, she bounded toward them. Sensing Josh stiffen beside her, Mandy turned to ask if he knew the woman, but his shell-shocked expression answered that question loud and clear.

The woman hauled up in front of them. Ignoring Mandy, she threw her pencil-thin arms about Josh's neck. "Oh baby, it's you, it's really you. I've missed you so much."

Before he could answer, she rose up on the pointed toes of her Manolo Blahnik stilettos and planted an openmouthed kiss on his lips. Even looking through smoke-watery eyes, Mandy couldn't miss the rock-size diamond sparkling from her tiny left hand.

Staring over at them, Mandy felt a trickle run down her cheek and knew the extra moisture had nothing to do with the smoke. "Oh, Josh, you should have told me." Before she could humiliate herself anymore, she turned and ran for the door.

JOSH SLAMMED CLOSED the door to his apartment and swung around. Now that he'd gotten over the initial shock of encountering his former fiancée in a Baltimore bar, *his* Baltimore bar, anger was seeping in to take its place. "Brava, that was quite a performance you put on. I hope you're proud of yourself."

Tiffany actually had the nerve to look hurt. "I don't know what you mean?"

"The way you played the part of the loving fiancée, you almost had me believing it was true."

He thought of Mandy's stricken look when Tiffany threw herself into his arms and wished beyond anything he'd confessed his history with her when he'd come clean earlier about his status as a federal witness. The thing was, he'd written Tiffany off, considered her as being out of his life for good. Her surprise appearance had shocked him almost as much as it had Mandy.

"Oh, baby, I do love you, and I've been so afraid for you

these last months, I thought I'd lose my mind." Walking up to him, Tiffany wrapped her arms about his torso, taking advantage of the closeness to rub her breasts against his chest. "But it's going to be okay now, because I'm here for you. Aren't you happy to see me?"

Feeling disgusted instead of turned on, he reached down and disengaged her clinging hands from his waist. "You can drop the devotion crap, Tiffany. We're alone now."

And alone they were. White-faced and on the verge of tears, Mandy had run out of the bar while Tiffany still had him in a lip-lock. Setting firm hands on her shoulders, he'd pushed her away and gone after Mandy. Just his luck, he caught up with her on Boston Street just in time to see her flag down a passing city cab and get inside.

"Really, Joshie, is this any way to treat your fiancée?" Slanting her gaze up at him, Tiffany pulled her glossy lips into a pout. Once upon a time, that look would have driven him wild but now the affectation struck him as childish, the polar opposite of sexy.

"You're not my fiancée anymore or haven't you figured that out?" He glanced pointedly at the engagement ring sticking out from her bony finger, a three-carat monstrosity she'd bullied him into buying in lieu of the elegant family heirloom he'd planned on giving her. That much bling would look overdone on most women, but on someone as petite as Tiffany it bordered on grotesque.

Her mobile mouth formed a shocked circle. "Since when?"

"Pretty much since I walked in on you and the landscaper rocking like porn stars in our bed."

"I was hoping you might have forgiven me for that little misstep."

Little misstep. God, but the woman was a piece of work. It was funny how he'd never seen through her before, not completely, until now. "Well, Tiffany, they say hope springs eternal, but I wouldn't count on it if I were you."

"What happened wasn't entirely my fault, you know. You were working so much, all the time really. I hardly ever saw you."

As apologies went, it wasn't much, but then he'd learned not to expect much of anything from her, so in that sense it was all good. "Well, that would be because I was trying to get our London office open before the wedding and then there was the little complication of having my CFO murdered in cold blood and my life on the line."

"Well, I know all that *now,* but I didn't then. I was so lonesome and with you gone all the time and all the pressure of planning the wedding, I guess it all got to be too much."

"Are you saying you slept with the landscaper as some kind of...of tension release?"

He must be over her, *really* over her, because instead of reliving the shock and hurt of finding her in bed with another man, he found himself appreciating the absurdity of the situation. If it weren't for worrying about Mandy, where she'd gone and how upset she'd looked just before she ran out, he might find it not just absurd but laughably so.

She hesitated. Gaze demurely downcast, she nodded. "I know it was wrong of me, and that there's no excuse really, but it won't happen again, I promise. Can't we just let bygones be bygones and move forward with the future?"

Oh, he fully intended on moving forward with the future all right, only not with an ice princess like Tiffany. If he was fortunate enough to share his life with anyone, it would be with a warm-blooded woman with a generous, giving heart. A woman like Mandy.

He shook his head. "If you came all the way to Baltimore just to tell me you're sorry, then you could have saved yourself a trip because, sorry or not, it's over between us." He was about to turn away when a question occurred to him. "How did you find me, by the way?"

"With Grady turning up dead and everybody thinking

you were dead, too, and then Tony's trial coming up, I was afraid they'd come after me, too. I was frightened to stay in Boston."

Self-preservation, so now they were getting closer to the truth at least.

Her mouth twisted into an unbecoming snicker. "That woman you were with, the fat one with the dirty hair, I suppose she's the best you can do in a town like this."

The flash of anger struck him so fast and hard he had to force his hands down to his sides to keep from throwing her against the nearest wall. For the first time in his life, including the episode when he'd walked in on her in the act of cheating on him, he was tempted to lay violent hands on a woman.

For safety's sake—hers—he took a step back. "Well, Tiffany, as usual you've got only half of the story correct. Mandy is the best, the very best, I can hope to do but not just here in Baltimore. She's the best I could hope for anywhere, and it's about time I told her so."

IT WASN'T UNTIL Mandy stepped out onto the sidewalk in front of the bar that she remembered she didn't actually have a car. Josh had driven them home, a little logistical issue that had slipped her mind in the heat of the moment. Fortunately she only had to go down a block to Boston Street before a city cab pulled up to the curb. The rear passenger door opened and a family wearing assorted tourist paraphernalia piled out onto the sidewalk. Mandy didn't hesitate. She hopped inside.

From the front seat, the cabby asked, "Where to?"

Mandy thought for a second or two. As much as she might fantasize about throwing herself Anna Karenina style onto the tracks at Penn Station, such high drama was best saved for the pages of fiction. If the past week had taught her anything it was that life, even a lonely single's life, was very precious gift.

"Home. I want to go home."

He tapped the side of his temple with a grimy fingernail. "Look, lady, I'm not clairvoyant. I'm gonna need an address."

"Oh, sorry." She gave him her parents' address and settled back against the split upholstery.

Staring out the smeared window as they zipped along, she wondered what the hell her problem was. It wasn't as if she'd entered into any of this with blinders on. From the first she'd known that Josh wasn't exactly for real and certainly not for keeps. They'd shared a moment, a fling, or at least a beautiful affair. Whatever she chose to call it, it was officially over as of now. If she'd waited, he would have dumped her eventually. Better to cut the ties now while she was still in control than risk sustaining an even greater, more crippling wound down the road. Sitting back, she told herself it was a relief in a way. No more "I'll call you" followed by endless hours of frantic waiting for her cell to ring, no more fears about not measuring up, and most of all, no more anxiety about getting jilted. At least this time she'd been the proactive one, the one to initiate the breakup. Now that she had, getting jilted, getting hurt, was one major worry she could cross off her list—permanently. She should feel, if not exactly triumphant, empowered at least.

So why then was she crying in the back seat of a Baltimore City cab feeling more alone, more miserable, than she had in her whole life?

WHEN MANDY GOT BACK to her folks' house, she headed straight for her room. Barricaded behind the locked door, she dialed directory assistance and got the number for the FBI's Baltimore field office.

"This is Officer Amanda Delinski with the Southeast Precinct of Baltimore City Police, and I need to speak to either Special Agent Walker or Special Agent McKinney."

A monotonic female voice answered, "I'm sorry, but there's no one here by those names."

Mandy had never been a patient person but the near-death experience and dunking in the yucky harbor water topped off by the surprise appearance of the fiancée had dissipated what little patience she had left. Throwing caution, and professional decorum, to the wind, she shouted into the receiver, "The hell there isn't. Look, you tell them I'm calling about the Joshua Thornton case and have them call me back ASAP."

A long pause greeted her diatribe, followed by, "I'm not saying such persons are here, or even exist but if, hypothetically speaking, they did exist and were present in this office, at what number should I have them contact you?"

Shivering with nerves and cold, Mandy repeated her number and clicked off the call. Then she peeled off her waterlogged clothes, wrapped a bathrobe around herself, and sat down on the edge of the bed to wait.

Less than a minute later, the phone rang. She picked up on the second ring. "Delinski here."

"Who are you and why are you calling?" She recognized the clipped tones as belonging to the younger agent, McKinney.

Dragging a hand through her tangled hair, she said, "Look, let's cut to the chase. I know all about Josh being in the witness protection program just like you know all about me from watching him, which means you know we've been…" She paused. How to put their "relationship" if you could even call it that, into words? "We've been hanging out together since Christmas Eve."

McKinney hesitated, blowing a heavy breath into the receiver. "If you have information on the Thornton case, let's hear it."

"There's been a new er, *development,* and I'm not going to be able to babysit your boy any longer, so you'd better double up for 24/7 until the trial date, got it?"

"What kind of development?"

Mandy hesitated. God, this really hurt. "His fiancée just showed up and well, three's a crowd, especially in a studio apartment. Speaking strictly as an American taxpayer here, I wouldn't have minded you guys springing for a one-bedroom."

"His fiancée! He never said anything to me about having a fiancée."

Tears welling, Mandy shook her head. "Well, that makes two of us."

AFTER A VERY LONG, very hot shower, Mandy marched back down the short hallway to her room, and did what someone in her position, someone who was *real* detective material, would have thought to do from the very start. She fired up her laptop, dialed into the Internet, and ran a Google search on Joshua Thornton.

The search engine yielded slightly fewer than 2,000 hits, pretty impressive for a guy still in his early thirties. The most recent items were news clips detailing the tragic boating accident that had resulted in his alleged death. She scrolled farther down the list, stopping when she got to a *Boston Globe* clip in the paper's wedding announcements section: Heir to Telecommunications Empire to Wed. She clicked on the article link, hands shaking so badly she could barely muster the computer mouse. She only had a dial-up modem and the article, including the black-and-white photo of the happy couple, took several minutes to load. Watching Tiffany's lovely, smiling face take slow shape on her computer screen was a special kind of torture. She focused on the text of the article instead.

Joshua Sedgewick Thornton the Third to Wed Miss Tiffany Ann Clarence. Thornton serves as president of the Boston office of Thornton Enterprises, a national tele-communications corporation that last year announced plans to go global, opening offices in London and Tokyo. Thornton holds bachelor's degrees in Computer Science

*and Finance from Harvard University and a MBA degree
from the Harvard Business School.*

*Miss Clarence, who earned a bachelor of fine arts from
Vassar College in 2003, is also employed at Thornton Enterprises as an analyst. The couple plans a September
wedding with private reception to be held at The Plaza
Hotel in New York. A Paris honeymoon will follow.*

Feeling sick inside, Mandy turned away from the screen.
As if being born blond, beautiful and thin wasn't enough,
Tiffany also boasted an Ivy League education, white-collar
career, and engagement to a fabulous man. The woman
seemed to have it all going on. In comparison, Mandy felt like
a slacker—make that a loser.

As for Josh, while she'd known he wasn't a bartender,
reading the litany of degrees and corporate credentials in bold,
black newsprint was pretty damned daunting. Even without the
petite and perfect Tiffany in the picture, Mandy could see she'd
never had a hope of holding his interest beyond a few days.

But the hardest part of all was facing up to the fact that Josh
had been lying to her all along. Okay, maybe not exactly lying
but not exactly being truthful, either. She'd given him any
number of opportunities and not once had he mentioned
having a fiancée waiting for him back home. She'd almost
started believing he thought of her as The One, too. And yet
she couldn't ignore the facts, not now when the evidence in
the form of a model-thin blonde had stared her straight in the
face. All along, he'd been planning to go back to his life in
Boston, his life with Tiffany. He'd been stringing Mandy
along, using her for sex on the side. She supposed it served
her right for settling for crumbs instead of cake, as her pop
would say, and yet she still couldn't shake the sense that underlying all that fabulous sex had been some genuine feelings.

To be fair, she reminded herself she hadn't asked for any

promises. And yet, though she considered herself to be a modern woman in many ways, there were some traditional values worth keeping—and sleeping with an almost-married man violated every one of them.

Settling on the side of the floral-patterned bedspread, she dragged a hand through her damp hair and took a good look around. Whether the walls were green or pink didn't really matter because they weren't her walls, not really. No matter how she dressed it up, this would always be her childhood bedroom in her parents' house—and contrary to Virginia Woolf, a room of one's own wasn't nearly enough. What she needed was a true haven, a place that was all hers where she could pick out colors and fabrics and furnishings, leave dishes in the sink overnight if she felt like it, keep a cat or maybe two.

By moving back with her folks and filling up their empty nest with the clutter of her problems, she hadn't done anyone any favors, including herself. With or without a man in her life, it was high time she stepped out on her own again. Sure, paying monthly rent would set her back buying a place, but then again home ownership no longer seemed the magic-bullet solution it had just the week before. Like losing weight, buying a house would be something nice to do for herself, an investment in her future, but it wasn't a panacea for happiness.

Oh, Josh, I guess I've known all along that what we had was for now, not forever. I just wished it had lasted a little longer, a lot longer.

I wish it had lasted forever.

15

Thursday, December 28 (again!)

Quasi-adulterous affairs broken off: one but went south in manner of film, Escape from New York—frantic exodus with no time to lose. Times mother looked up at velvet painting of Virgin Mary and Baby Jesus and asked when will marry and have babies like a good Catholic girl: don't know and don't plan on finding out as am officially swearing off men. If must face future of enforced celibacy, might as well get credit for God-like life and join convent as self-styled Pistol Packing Nun, morphing edgy, crusader-for-justice vibe of Clint Eastwood's *Dirty Harry* with dimple-faced perkiness of Sally Field's *Flying Nun* surfer girl turned novice. Who am I kidding? No order will take Mary Magdalene-like fallen woman into its fold, especially if find out Sodom and Gomorrah-esque destination headed later in week. Too bad, really, as basic black and navy always so classically chic and slimming...

EVER SINCE MANDY'S FLIGHT from the bar, Josh had felt like the lone tiger he'd seen at the Boston Zoo as a kid and never forgotten. All the other animals had been exhibited in pairs or packs except for the tiger whose mate had been transferred to another facility. Even as a kid, he'd thought that was all wrong, had sensed the animal's sadness in his restless pacing and searching eyes. Trapped in a life that no longer made any sense, more than ever he understood how the animal had felt— caged, desperate, and very much alone.

Only he wasn't alone, because Tiffany was still there. Thanks to the Men in Black, it looked as though they'd be roommates for the rest of the week. He'd just finished up his argument with her when Walker called on the cell.

"Look, we know about your fiancée showing up and well, it couldn't have happened at a worse time."

Josh thought again of the wounded look on Mandy's face and fought back a groan. "Tell me about it."

"She's seen you. She's identified you. That means you'll both have to stay inside and out of sight until we pick you up for transport back to Boston on the first."

"Are you telling me I have to put her up here, in my apartment, for the rest of the week?"

"Yes, that's exactly what I'm saying. Turn her loose, and you'll be jeopardizing not only your life but hers. If she wouldn't talk, they'd find ways to make her, and then as soon as they got your location, they'd get rid of her."

Oh, Tiffany would talk all right, no doubt about that. Any illusions he'd harbored about her loyalty had washed away in the landslide of shock he'd felt when he'd walked in on her humping the landscaper. Now that he looked back on their two years together, though, he realized he shouldn't have been so shocked. There'd been signs aplenty along the way that they were a less than perfect match—her insistence he buy her the biggest, flashiest diamond for sale at her retail namesake's, Tiffany & Co., her complaints about the attention he'd lavished on his ailing golden retriever, Samson, just before the poor old guy had to be put down, her habit of treating his administrative assistant, Jennifer, as though she was her personal gopher.

Still, as much as he despised spending his remaining few days in Baltimore living cheek-to-jowl with the woman who'd betrayed him in the most flagrant and hurtful of ways, he couldn't exactly throw her out on the killing streets.

But worse than the repercussions to his personal life was the prospect that the Mafia men who'd tried to kill him must also know about Mandy. He didn't need Grady's ghost to tell him what happened to informants left unprotected. The incident on the water had shown him how brave she was, but sometimes bravery wasn't enough. The thought of what the mob might do to her to get at him made him crazy with fear. The safest place for her at this point was right beside him— only he'd let her get away.

His latest circuit about the room brought him back over to the bed where Tiffany lay sleeping, a baby-doll-pink eyeshade covering the top portion of her face. In typical Tiffany fashion, she'd taken over his bed and dresser drawers as though she owned the place. Though she'd offered him a seductive smile and the mattress space beside her, he'd opted for lower-rent real estate without strings. Grabbing a blanket, he'd camped out on the kitchen floor. With the hard surface beneath his back and his own racing thoughts to keep him awake, he'd found plenty of time for analyzing the situation.

He realized with a sort of relief that the strongest emotion Tiffany aroused in him now was annoyance. The memory of finding her in bed with someone else no longer brought about the sharp stab of pain it once had. The hurt had faded to a barely noticeable twinge. If anything, on looking back, he considered that in a strange way by cheating on him she'd done him a favor.

Knowing Mandy had caused his perspective on his past relationship to shift. The short but entirely wonderful time he'd spent with her so far showed just how lacking his and Tiffany's relationship had been in all areas, including the bedroom.

But the great sex he and Mandy shared was only a part of the equation. Mandy was everything Tiffany wasn't—and so very much more. Along with being intuitive and funny, kind and smart, she listened, really *listened* to people, including him. He loved the wind-chime sound of her laughter, and the way she looked when she first woke up in the morning, all doe-eyed and warm and sexily rumpled. He even loved that she ate oranges in bed, peeling off sections and popping them into her luscious mouth, then licking the juice from her fingers.

The thing was, he loved her. Not just liked, not just lusted after, but loved. Big screen Hollywood love, cross-your-heart-and-hope-to-die kind of love.

If only he could find a way to get her to give up the self-deprecating comments she made with the same ease he'd gotten her to give up her initial sexual inhibitions, their relationship, as he was coming to think of it, would be ideal. How to get her to see that as long as she was healthy, he didn't care if she shed a single pound? That he adored every soft, curvy inch of her just the way she was?

He spotted a scrap of black peeking out from beneath the pillow next to Tiffany and realized it must belong to Mandy. Carefully peeling it out so as not to awaken Tiffany, he saw it was Mandy's teddy, the one he'd bought her as a belated Christmas gift from Victoria's Secret. The lacy black lingerie had showcased her gorgeous breasts and generous curves to perfection, but it was the image of her first stepping out of the bathroom to model it, shy-eyed and hesitant, that stuck with him like a splinter in his heart.

Balling the lingerie into a fist, he told himself it was high time he stopped running, stopped blindly following orders, and reclaimed his life, for his sake as well as Mandy's. As long as the FBI was invested in keeping him alive, they would just have to keep her safe, too. Decided, he dug his cell out of his jeans pocket, walked into the bathroom, and punched in the FBI's local number on speed dial.

McKinney answered on the third ring. Rather than waste time on pleasantries, Josh came straight to the point. "I know you told me to stay put, but I need to go out. I am going out."

"No way, Thornton. Your going out in public is no longer feasible."

Sick of being told what he could and couldn't do, Josh snapped back, "Feasible or not, I'm leaving this goddamned apartment. You can cover me or not, the choice is yours."

McKinney's exhaled breath echoed in the phone's receiver. "All right, all right, don't get your boxers in a twist. Give me five minutes, and we'll be right over. Where do you want to go?"

"Highland Town."

"Highland Town? What the hell's in Highland Town other than some Formstone row houses and a handful of German bakeries?"

The woman of my dreams. The love of my life. Rather than answer, Josh said, "I'll wait exactly five minutes, but if you don't show, I'm still out of here."

Without hanging on for the agent's reply, he clicked off the call. He tucked the phone back into his pocket and walked over to his closet. Casting a glance over his shoulder to make sure Tiffany still slept, he pulled off his T-shirt and buttoned on a fresh shirt. Tamping down his impatience, he tried to look on the bright side of the situation. If he made it through this little adventure, it would be something to tell his grandchildren. Certainly it wasn't every guy who got a FBI escort to see his girlfriend.

His girlfriend. At what point had he started thinking of Mandy in that way? From the moment they'd locked eyes at the museum gala or during their coffee date when they'd all but finished one another's sentences? Either way, girlfriend, he liked the sound of it, he liked it a lot. Hopefully, after he explained things to Mandy, she'd like it, too.

IN ALL THE EXCITEMENT, Mandy had almost forgotten about her lunch with Mikey. The fact that Josh had if not lied to her outright, omitted some pretty important details of his personal life, namely his engagement status, didn't change that she was still a law enforcement officer with a sacred duty to defend and protect. Even with the fiancée in the picture, she was still one hundred percent committed to pursuing her plan to smoke out the hit man, make that, hit *men,* before they could strike again. Though running on too little sleep and too many tears, she pulled herself together and headed down to Fells Point for the meeting with her cousin.

Duda's Tavern was on the corner of Thames and Bond Streets, a pocket-sized pub-style restaurant that served some of the most bodacious crab cakes of any establishment in the area. Entering the narrow, dark-paneled room, Mandy spotted Mikey sitting at the sidebar munching on the free hard pretzels and mustard. Tall and lanky, her cousin had inherited the Delinski appetite without the accompanying metabolism.

He beckoned her over to the empty brass-backed stool beside him. "Hey, Mands, have a seat. Pretzel?" He pushed the glass canister toward her.

Taking a seat on the brass-backed stool beside him, she shook her head. "No thanks, I'm good." Since meeting Josh, food definitely had taken a back seat on her list of priorities.

Squeezing a ribbon of French's Mustard on a pretzel, he said. "How 'bout what went down on the water taxi last night? That was some weird shit, huh? Fucking city's chockfull of nuts these days."

Mandy wasn't surprised Mikey knew all about the water taxi incident. The supposedly whacko sniper duo had made front-page headlines in all the local newspapers, including *The Baltimore Sun.* "I was there, a passenger actually, and the snipers were no random crazies. It was a botched hit."

He paused from sucking mustard from his thumb to stare over at her. "No shit? But Jesus, Mands, you could have been killed."

"Tell me about it." She glanced over to the bartender. Busy drawing drafts for a group congregating at the far end of the bar, he hadn't yet registered her presence. Still, you could never be too careful. Lowering her voice, she asked, "So what do you have for me?"

Expression thoughtful, he took a swig of his beer. "Okay, so late the other night this suit by the name of Tommy walks in and reserves a private room. I figure he wants a lap dance or...somethin', but it turns out he wants it for a meeting. Seems like a real class act, and definitely from out of town, so I say, 'Sure thing, I just need the money up front.'"

"Out of town? You sure about that?"

He nodded and reached for another pretzel. "With that accent, he sounded like a fucking Kennedy." Crunching, he went on, "I put my best waitress, Janice, on the table. 'Bout ten minutes later, two other guys show up, both locals."

"You get a good look at them?"

"Yeah, I did. The one was a big guy—dark hair, dark eyes, really in shape. Maybe I seen him once or twice before, but he's not a regular. The other guy comes in every now and again, usually on a weekend."

"What's he look like?"

"Scrawny rat-faced little weasel. Always gives the waitresses a hard time and then tips like shit."

"Speaking of waitresses, did Janice catch any of their conversation?"

He shrugged. "Bits and pieces here and there. Somethin' about a 'big job' that would be going down between now and January second and how any 'local support' would be appreciated—and rewarded."

Excitement mounting, Mandy asked, "You get any names? Anybody use a credit card we could trace?"

He shook his head. "Sorry, Mands, you know how it is. Those types, they always pay in cash."

She'd thought as much, but it never hurt to hope. Contrary to television portrayals, not all criminals were brilliant masterminds. Face it, if you had half a brain, wouldn't you figure out a way to make a lucrative living without risking prison?

"Any chance you'll be seeing them again soon?"

He broke into a broad grin. "That's the best part. They've booked the room for tomorrow night."

"Tomorrow night, huh?"

Feeling hopeful for the first time since before Josh's blond bombshell of a fiancée had exploded into her life, she reached for a pretzel. Biting off a piece, she chewed, the wheels of her mind turning over a possible plan. It was far-fetched if not downright crazy but then again who knew, it just might be crazy enough to work.

Dusting salt crystals from her fingers, she said, "In that case, Mikey, I need another favor and brace yourself, because this one's a whopper."

CAMPED OUT IN A PARKED CAR across the street, Tommy the Terminator punched the "send" button on his cell. As soon as the other party picked up, he said, "Hey, it's me. I thought you'd wanna know Delinski just exited the restaurant."

"You sure it's her?"

"Hey, it's not like Thornton's been any kind of Don Juan for the past six months. Long red hair, boobs like a centerfold, great ass—it's her all right, the lady cop. You want her taken out, too. 'Cause if you do, I'll expect double my fee."

"No, not yet anyway. I'll keep you posted on that. For now, just follow her and see where she goes, who she talks to. And don't fuck it up like you did last night."

"Hey, that wasn't my fault. It was that bozo Baltimoron you hooked me up with who botched it. And how was I to know a swell would hit the fucking boat just when I got ready to take the shot?"

"I don't want excuses, I want results."

"Okay, okay, I'm on it."

16

Near-death experiences: none so far, though day still young. Calories consumed: crab-cake sandwich with tartar sauce and fries (very, very bad as fried food modern-day equivalent of Satan's forbidden fruit—then again, when in Rome…). Also hard pretzels but as is fat-free snack food, no need to count. Times mother looked up at velvet painting of Virgin Mary and Baby Jesus and asked when would settle down and have babies like a good Catholic girl: am beginning to think maternal unit may be a lot cooler than she lets on.

Number of hunky boyfriends saved from speeding bullet and reclaimed from vile harbor waters only to be lost to viperous blue-blooded model thin blonde: one— but how much heartbreak can a girl take?

WHEN MANDY GOT BACK from her lunch with Mikey, her mother was camped out in the living room waiting for her. "Amanda, come in here please. We need to talk."

One foot on the stair landing, Mandy stifled a groan. Now that she knew about Josh having a fiancée, continuing to have an intimate relationship with him was out of the question. Between coming to terms with that heartbreaking reality and working out the details of putting her plan into play to trap the hit men, she felt as though her head might fly off her shoulders. What she needed was a Motrin, a nap and a pint of Ben & Jerry's

Chocolate Fudge Brownie ice cream—and not necessarily in that order. What she most definitely did *not* need was a lecture from her mother, no matter how well-intentioned.

"Later, Ma. I'm in no mood."

"So get in the mood and get your butt in here." Tone softening, she added, "Please, Amanda, it's important."

"Okay, but for just a few minutes." Surrendering to the situation, she headed for the living room.

She couldn't expect to avoid her parents indefinitely. Though last night she'd promised herself to start apartment hunting the moment Josh was safely back in Boston, for the present she was still living under their roof.

Her mother sat perched on the edge of the vinyl-covered sofa wearing a powder-pink checkerboard apron and a look of determination. A plate of chocolate chip cookies, freshly baked judging from the aroma, was set out on the coffee table.

Predictably, her mother pushed the cookies toward her the moment her butt hit the sofa cushion, but she shook her head. "No thanks, I just had lunch. What's, uh…what's on your mind?"

Her mother sat back, causing the vinyl cover to squeak. "Your father and I are worried about you, Amanda. You go off with this young man. For two days—and two *nights*—we don't hear so much as a word from you, and then all of a sudden here you are, back again only you stay in your room with the door closed like some kind of hermit. You don't talk to nobody. You don't even go to work."

"I'm fine, Ma. I'm just taking some time off. I had vacation coming to me, and I didn't want to lose it." It fell far short of being the whole truth but there was truth at its core, so she wasn't lying, not exactly.

Her mother looked at her and shook her head. Her expression was the same all-knowing look she'd used to coax out a confession when, as a four-year-old, Mandy had crayoned on the walls and then tried blaming it on the dog. Like that day, it was clear her mother was neither satisfied nor fooled. "You think I don't hear you crying at night? I hear you in there, and I know your heart is breaking. It's this young man, this Josh person, isn't it?" Mandy started to protest, but her mother held up a broad-palmed hand, cutting her off. "You think I didn't see how you looked at him Christmas Day or know that you never came home Christmas Eve night. You don't really think I bought that cock-and-bull story your pop came up with to cover for you, do you?"

Busted, I am so busted. If anyone in the Delinski family was detective material, it was her mother, not her.

Mandy hadn't realized how tightly wound she was until that moment. Like a jack-in-the-box, she sprang off the seat. "Okay, Ma, you win. I spent Christmas Eve and most of Christmas morning in his bed making love with him. I slept with him without benefit of marriage and if that makes me a disappointment in your eyes, a Magdalene, well, I'm sorry about that, but it's just the way it is. I'm thirty years old and until now, until Josh, I never felt like that before. I didn't even know it could be like that between two people but now that I do, even though it's not going to work out, I'm really, really glad I got to experience it even for a little while. There, you have it, my confession. Throw stones or throw me out of the house, whatever you want."

Expression softening, her mother shook her head. "Oh, Amanda, you're not a disappointment, and I don't think you're bad. I just don't like to see you hurting is all." She hesitated and then asked, "But what makes you so sure it won't work out between you two?"

This wasn't turning out to be the fire-and-brimstone lecture she'd anticipated. Feeling the knot of tension at the back of her neck begin to unwind, Mandy stopped pacing and sat back down. "Let me get this straight, you know I slept with Josh, and you're not mad at me?"

For the first time Mandy could remember, her mother actually hesitated. "Well, I'm not going to give you no trophy, that's for sure, but no, I'm not mad. For those who'd care to count, your oldest brother, Bobby, came a good two months early and still he weighed almost ten pounds. How you figure that happened, huh?"

Oh my God. All her life, she'd thought of her parents as so straight-laced, almost asexual. That they'd apparently engaged in premarital sex was enough to send her sliding off the sofa's slippery cover.

Dreamy-eyed, her mother stared off into the distance and for once her gaze was nowhere in the vicinity of the velvet painting of the Virgin Mother and Child. "I know it may be hard to believe, but your father was quite the Don Juan in his day." She pronounced the *J* in Juan as a hard *G*, but it wasn't Mandy's place to correct her. "When I first met him, he was going to join the Peace Corps and go overseas to Africa with this skinny hippie girl named Frances who made us all call her Free. Can you imagine?"

Picturing her pop with his outdated sideburns, love handles and Mr. Rogers' button-down sweaters, Mandy couldn't imagine any of it. Then again, how well did we really know anyone, including ourselves?

"It's not that simple, Ma. He's, uh…got someone waiting for him back in Boston." She didn't have the heart to use the word, *fiancée* or to add that the certain someone apparently had gotten tired of waiting and come to Baltimore instead.

Her mother reached for a cookie and broke off a piece. "This woman, does he love her?"

Did Josh love Tiffany? Funny how until now Mandy had never stopped to ask herself that all-important question. Replaying the painful reunion scene in her mind, she remembered him looking shocked but not really happy, certainly not like a man who hadn't seen the woman he loved in six long months. Now that she thought of it, it had been the blonde who'd kissed him, not the other way around. He hadn't taken so much as a step toward her or even made the effort to lift his arms to embrace her—details Mandy had been too shocked and upset to process at the time but which now jumped out at her as telling indeed.

Feeling foolish, she admitted, "I don't know. I, uh…never asked him. I saw them together and I just…I just bolted."

Her mother looked up from the cookie she was busy crumbling. Holding Mandy's gaze with the force of her own, she said, "The only reason your pop isn't living in some grass hut fighting off malaria and pooping parasites is because I fought for him. I fought hard, Amanda. If you want something or someone bad enough, you fight for it. You fight because fighting for it is the same as fighting for your future."

Feeling tears prick her eyes, Mandy looked away. "I don't know. I'll think about it."

"If your heart is telling you this is the man for you, the one, then don't think too long, Amanda. Don't think but do."

The doorbell rang. Taking advantage of the intrusion to mull things over, Mandy got up. "I'll get it."

Distracted, she crossed the carpet to the doorway. Her parents' street was generally pretty safe but it paid to be cautious. Looking out the peephole, she saw a set of broad shoulders encased in a familiar-looking black leather jacket. The caller stepped back, and a crop of thick blond hair, high brow and bedroom-blue eyes came into view.

Heart pounding, Mandy threw open the door and blurted out the first thing she could think of to say. "What the hell are you doing here?"

"I MISSED YOU, TOO." Taking advantage of Mandy's stunned state, Josh shouldered his way inside. He glanced over at her stern-faced mother, standing behind her in the small entrance foyer. "Hello, Mrs. Delinski." Receiving only a gruff nod in response, he leaned in to Mandy and added, "We need to talk. Is there somewhere we can go in private?"

Mandy hesitated and then gestured to the stairs behind them. "That would be my room." Turning around to her mother, she said, "Relax, Ma, we're just going to talk."

She led the way up the narrow stairs to her room. Once inside, Josh pulled the door closed behind them. "Nice woman, your mother, though I don't think she likes me very much right now."

"That makes two of us." Turning to face him, she regarded him with folded arms. "You lied to me."

"I did not lie to you. I didn't get a chance to say much of anything. You ran out before I had the chance to explain."

"What's there to explain?" she said with a shrug as though she couldn't care less but looking closer he thought her eyes seemed unusually bright like she might be holding back tears. "That woman in the bar, she's your fiancée isn't she?" He hesitated, searching for the right words to win back her trust, to win back her. When he didn't immediately find them, she added, "Okay, I'll make this really simple for you. Did you or did you not give her that engagement ring she's wearing?"

He took a step toward her, the soles of his boots sinking into the out-of-date shag carpet. "I did, but I don't have any intention of marrying her, not now and not ever."

"Do you always give rock-sized diamond engagement rings to women you're *not* intending to marry?"

He'd never seen this side of her before, but he sensed the lashing out was a defense to keep him from seeing just how much she was hurting. Reaching for his patience, he took another step toward her. "Okay, yes, I asked her to marry me a year ago and gave her the ring but no, I am not marrying her, not now and not ever."

Mandy stepped away an equal measure, bumping the backs of her knees against the side of the bed. For a second she teetered, and he thought she might fall back on the mattress—or maybe he was just willing that to happen so he could join her there. Balancing herself, she said, "If you called off the engagement, then why is she still wearing your ring?"

He took note of her firm tone, matched by the firm set of her jaw, and admitted this wasn't looking good, not good at all. "I never exactly called it off, not officially anyway."

"Not exactly or not at all?"

"Look, my CFO had just been found murdered and it was looking like I might be next. I couldn't exactly stick around town to have the big breakup heart-to-heart with Tiffany. Hell, Mandy, I'm in the witness protection program, in case you've forgotten. My life isn't my own and hasn't been for more than six months. I couldn't contact anyone back home—not work, not family and certainly not my so-called fiancée."

He hadn't meant to speak to her so sharply, but Tiffany's turning up had rattled him more than he cared to admit. Ever since her melodramatic reentry into his life the other day, he'd asked himself what had ever attracted him to her in the first place and for the life of him, he simply couldn't see it. Thin to the point of angularity, sharp-eyed and as perfectly coiffed as a department store mannequin, she reminded him of the Madame Alexander china doll his sister had kept on display in her bedroom but rarely ever took down from the shelf—brittle, stiff and prone to breakage.

But what really set Mandy apart from his former fiancée wasn't any physical attribute such as her hair color or fuller figure but rather her giving nature, her amazing generosity. She was generous in her relationships, generous at work and, to his great delight, generous in bed. Even in the midst of their arguing, he couldn't quite forget they were alone together in a bedroom, couldn't seem to stop replaying in his mind the last time they'd made love. She'd gone down on him, pleasuring him with her amazing mouth, her hair sliding like a silk scarf over his thighs. The memory prompted an urgent ache in the vicinity of his groin.

"Yet you apparently made time to acquire a fiancée, to plan a September wedding and a Paris honeymoon." Her hurt tone sliced through the sensual, perfect memory, bringing him back to the far from perfect present.

"That was before."

"Before you entered the witness protection program?"

He hesitated. Even though Tiffany was the last woman on the planet he was interested in marrying, admitting she'd cheated on him in his own home, his own bed, amounted to ingesting a pretty hefty slice of humble pie. But if swallowing his pride was what it took to win Mandy back, then so be it.

"No, before I walked in on her doing the landscaper in our bed."

That got her attention. Her pretty mouth dropped open and her big doe-like eyes looked poised to pop. "Are you saying she cheated on you?"

He nodded. "Yes, that's exactly what I'm saying. Before I left Boston to come here, I stopped by the house to let her know what was going on. It was a risk, a stupid risk, but I couldn't bring myself to just go off and leave her thinking I was dead. I put my life in danger because I didn't want her worrying about me when the truth was she couldn't have cared less if I was alive or dead. Can you believe that? Pretty stupid, huh?"

"Nuh-uh." She shook her head, eyes searching his face. "Pretty wonderful, actually. Too bad Tiffany obviously didn't come close to appreciating what she had in you."

He hesitated, more moved than he cared to admit. "Thanks."

"What…what did she say when you caught her?"

"She didn't say anything or at least if she did, I didn't stick around to hear it. I ran out just like you did the other day. Until she showed up in the bar last night, I honestly thought she knew it was over between us. Then suddenly there she was acting like nothing ever happened and for a minute, I guess I froze. I thought she was out of my life for good, but it turns out we're roommates."

"Roommates?"

He nodded, feeling his frustration well up all over again. The one saving grace of being under 24/7 lockdown was he would have gotten to spend all that one-on-one time with Mandy. If that were still the case, he wouldn't have traded his crappy one-room apartment for a suite at the Ritz Carlton, but now Tiffany had come along and spoiled even that, their last few days together.

"Until they take me back to Boston for the trial, I'm stuck with her though not by choice. Believe me when I say I'd like nothing better than to kick her out, but I can't. Now that she's made contact, letting her loose is just too dangerous. Whoever is after me knows who she is but they probably don't know we're broken up. They could use her to try and get to me. Whatever she has coming to her, no one deserves that." Feeling as uncertain suddenly as a teenager about to knock on his prom date's front door, he shoved his hands into his jacket pockets. "See what comes of accepting invitations to coffee from strangers—nothing good apparently."

"Nothing good, is that what you really think?" She looked up at him, smile tender. "Is that what you call making love to me like I've never been made love to in my whole life, making me feel things I didn't even know I was capable of?" She crossed the remaining few feet of carpet toward him, stride catlike and subtly sexy. "Only it wasn't just any old coffee, it was café mocha, as I recall, with extra whipped cream. I also seem to recall that it was entirely satisfying and definitely delicious, surpassing my highest expectations." Coming up to him, she stood on tiptoe and brushed her mouth over his, a light closed-mouth kiss that set his heart pounding and other portions of his anatomy stirring to hot, hard life. "Hmm, definitely delicious." Licking her lips, she stepped back. "In fact, I'd have to say it's even better than I remembered."

Feeling his erection rocket to full hard-on, he ventured his first real look around the room. High school trophies, stuffed animals and a doll with a faded yellow dress shared shelf space with plaques, framed photos and a community service award. Turning back to Mandy, he said, "Ever fooled around in here before?"

She looked over his shoulder and shook her head. "Um, not exactly."

"What does 'not exactly' mean?" He had a pretty good idea, but he wanted to hear her say it.

"Not with another person anyway."

The smile she sent him was both sexy and shy, making him want to throw her down on the bed to fuck her fast and hard and hold her gently against him and make tender love to her all at the same time. Either way, he wanted her so very badly.

He found her waist with his hands and pulled her against him. Shifting his hips, he rubbed his pelvis against her, letting her feel just how much he desired her, needed her. "As they say, there's a first time for everything." He leaned in to kiss her.

From downstairs, a maternal voice rang out, "Amanda, would you and your *guest* like some apple strudel? I just took it out of the oven."

Like guilty teenagers, they broke apart. Mandy turned her head and called down, "No thanks, Ma, we're good." Sending Josh an apologetic look, she said, "Sorry. That would be one of the many joys of living home with the folks. By the way, this is a temporary situation. My New Year's resolution is to start apartment hunting ASAP."

"You don't have to explain yourself to me."

"Well, I don't want you thinking I'm some kind of perpetual parental freeloader like Matthew McConaughey's character in *Failure to Launch* or something."

He shook his head, smiling in spite of the seriousness of

their situation. But that was the magic of Mandy. No matter how dire things were, she could always get him to smile.

"I don't think of you that way at all. I know you lost your life savings a couple of years ago and that you're working on rebuilding." Hands on her shoulders, he held her at arm's length, thinking how natural she looked and smelled, appreciating that she didn't wear cloying perfumes or heavy makeup to mask the essence of the beautiful being she was. "For now, what I'd really like is for you to come back to my apartment with me. You're not safe, either."

Her eyes widened. "Josh, we just can't stroll out the front door. The hitter could be out there now, waiting." Casting her gaze away, she added, "Besides, won't your apartment be a little crowded, with um…the three of us?"

Cupping her chin in his hand, he coaxed her into looking back up at him. "There's a decent-sized closet where Tiffany can hang out with the other coat rack—sorry, just joking—sort of." He winked, feeling lighter now that he'd unburdened himself to her. "As for getting out of here and back safely, don't worry, we're covered."

"We are?"

"Uh-huh." He let her go and walked over to the window. Pulling back the lacy curtain, he looked down onto the street, checking that the black sedan was still parked out front. It was. Being a "valuable commodity" to one's government was a pain in the ass, but the status of federally protected witness did carry certain privileges. Gesturing for her to join him, he said, "Meet Special Agent Walker and Special Agent McKinney, my own personal Men in Black."

Mandy stepped up to the window. Standing beside him, she followed the downward direction of his pointed finger. Biting at her bottom lip, she said, "It occurs to me your FBI buddies might be extremely useful in helping to put a little plan of mine into play."

For the first time since they'd cleared up the fiancée issue, he felt anxiety tighten his gut. He turned away from the window to look at her. "What kind of plan exactly?"

"As they say, sometimes the best defense is a good offense, so I figure the best way to keep the hitter from striking again is to find him first. I have it on very good authority that a suit with a Boston accent has rented a private room in a downtown club for tomorrow night, and I'm signed on to be the new cocktail waitress."

He shook his head. "No way am I letting you put yourself in any more danger for me than you already are."

The water taxi episode more than illustrated how brave she was. Every time he thought of how she'd selflessly thrown herself atop him, a chill ran down his back.

Placing a gentle hand on either side of his face, she lifted her long-lashed eyes to his. "Josh, you said yourself whoever attacked the water taxi knows all about me, about…us. I meant what I said the other day in the car. We're in this together."

"But you've said yourself what a small town Baltimore is. If you know the criminals by face, then the reverse must hold true."

She dismissed his objections with a toss of her red curls. "It's no big deal—really. With the right wig and makeup, my own mother wouldn't recognize me. Okay, maybe my mother would but nobody else. The thing is, since I'm not assigned to the case, not even supposed to know it exists, right now I'd be going in without departmental support. What do you think the chances are of your two friends helping us out, making sure we get the backup I need if…well, if I need it?"

Us—there it was again, a simple two letter word but fraught with meaning. It was too early to tell whether or not he'd like her plan but he definitely liked the sound of *us*. For the first time since the attempted hit the day before, Josh found his smile. "I'd say that if they want a certain federal witness to go through with testifying, the chances fall somewhere between good and excellent."

17

At last, time to put "Operation Smoke Out…the hit men before they kill my hunky boyfriend" into play. Thank God! Butterflies in stomach have expanded to vampire bats but at least have G-men on the J.O.B. in parked van nearby, multitasking by covering lush ass of Yours Truly and guarding hunky boyfriend turned federal witness at same time. (On sunny side, can no longer say personal life is boring.)

Now, if can survive next hours without spilling drinks or falling flat on make-up masked face, all should be over soon. Likelihood of needing orthopedic surgery afterward to correct damage to arches imposed by instrument-of-torture fuck-me pumps: high. Number of bikini waxings, make that full-body waxings, required to pull off skimpy cocktail waitress outfit without looking like cast member from *Planet of the Apes*: one but unfortunately no time to make appointment.

Number of bitchy blond ex-fiancées (with emphasis on ex) stashed away in hole-in-wall apartment: only one but can't put her on a plane back to Boston fast enough.

TEETERING IN FOUR-INCH fuck-me pumps and balancing a blond wig that definitely constituted Big Hair, Mandy pushed through the haze of tobacco smoke over to the club's main bar. Going undercover as a cocktail waitress might not be the most novel approach, but it was tried-and-true. She felt like Gloria Steinem infiltrating Hugh Hefner's Playboy Club in the sixties *sans* the bunny tail and ears, only her motive wasn't journalistic exposé in the service of feminism but a much more basic instinct: preserving a life.

Though not yet eight o'clock, the club was packed in preparation for the early show, the stage side tables occupied by regulars and those who'd paid extra for the privilege of watching the dancers up close. Though her scanty cocktail waitress's outfit covered about the same amount of skin as the Victoria's Secret lingerie Josh had given her, she was the most clothed woman in the room especially as she was wearing a wire, the apparatus hidden beneath the baby-pink satin change apron at her waist.

It had been a busy twenty-four hours for everyone involved: her, Josh and the two FBI agents, Walker and McKinney, who'd finally come onboard. Only Tiffany had been left out of the loop. When they'd returned to Josh's apartment the day before, they'd found her soaking in the clawfoot bathtub, overflowing bubbles onto the floor and singing at the top of her lungs as though she hadn't a care in the world. After the first hour or so, most of Mandy's feelings of inadequacy melted away like leftover winter snow hit by spring sunshine. The woman might be a dead ringer for Jessica Simpson, but she was also one of the most self-absorbed people Mandy had ever met. In the fewer than twenty-four hours she'd known her, and it certainly seemed longer, Tiffany had managed to find anything and everything to complain about from there being no Evian in the refrigerator to the absence of cable TV. But the worst part of the whole setup was that Mandy and Josh didn't have the privacy to make love. Being in such close proximity and being able to do little more than hold hands had turned out to be more sensual torture than tease. The time they'd shared so far had seemed to fly by. Who knew how many more opportunities they'd have before he left town.

The one saving grace of their situation was that working out the details of putting their plan into play had provided them both with plenty else to think about. Winning over Walker and McKinney had certainly taken some doing. Holding firm, Mandy had assured them she fully intended to carry out the operation with or without their help. Not even their threats to file a complaint with her department head could dissuade her. But it took Josh's threat to rescind his agreement to testify should they fail to cover her back that proved the tipping point in getting them to agree.

As for Josh, despite the fact that he had two FBI agents guarding him, she still had misgivings about leaving him in the van parked in the alley out back. Normally mob hits followed a pattern: abduction, removal of the intended victim to some remote location, and then execution. But the water taxi episode made it clear that the hitter was desperate and determined enough to take a potshot out in plain view. They'd been lucky the other day, but with the clock ticking like a bomb set to explode before January second, they couldn't expect that luck to hold out indefinitely or even much longer. The best, the only, way to foil another strike was to make sure there wasn't one. That required taking a proactive approach, namely turning the tables so that the hunter became the hunted. As long as she kept the hit man and his cronies under her eye, Josh should be safe enough, for the time being at least. Still, she didn't want overconfidence to lead any of them to take unnecessary risks.

A tall blonde wearing only bikini bottoms, fishnet hose and a smile passed her by, and Mandy couldn't help staring.

Size D boobs topped the blonde's reed-thin body, the nipples pointed north. *No way are those real,* Mandy thought, and kept going when the woman did a double-take and retraced her steps, coming to stand at the servers' station beside her.

Cracking gum, she looked Mandy up and down. "Hey, you must be the new girl Mikey hired." She held out a hand capped with three-inch nail tips. Each nail sported a delicately painted tongue. Amazing.

"Yes, that's right. My name's Amy."

"Hi, Amy, I'm Janice." Janice followed up on the welcome with a broad smile of red lips and tobacco-stained teeth. "I guess Mikey told you you'll be training with me tonight."

Mandy nodded. Between savory bites of Duda's crab cakes the other day, she and her cousin had put together the basics of the undercover operation. To make sure things were still on track, she asked, "We're working that private party, right?"

"Yeah, it's a small group, just a few guys, so it should be a lot less crazy than out here on the main floor. I waited on them once before earlier in the week. The big Italian from New England goes by Tommy the Terminator."

"Tommy the Terminator?"

Janice shrugged. "I dunno, maybe it was his wrestling name or something. By the size of him, he mighta been in the ring at one time. Anyway, he's a little demanding but if you serve him right, he's a big tipper."

Afraid to ask what *serving him right* might involve, Mandy said, "Good to know. I'll try not to slow you down."

Janice laid a friendly hand on Mandy's shoulder. "Hey, try not to be nervous. Everybody's gotta have a first night. Stick with me, hon, and you'll be a pro in no time." She ran her heavily lined eyes over Mandy, gaze stalling at chest level. "Awesome boobs, by the way. Those real?"

Mandy looked down to where her pink nipples poked

through the gauzy lace of her flesh-colored top, and felt a blush burn its way up from her throat to the roots of her beneath the wig. "Yep, that's all me, with the gut and hips to prove it."

"You're lucky. No, seriously, I'd kill for those curves. I'm always trying to put on weight, but the diabetes makes it tough." Janice settled a hand over one hat-rack hip and made a face.

Until now, it had never occurred to Mandy that a thin woman might covet a fuller figure. "Really, sorry to hear that. You have such a beautiful slender figure, I never would have guessed."

"Yeah, well." Janice lifted her breasts for Mandy's inspection. "These I had to pay for, but they were worth every dime. The first day back to work from the surgery, my tips more than doubled even with the scars still showing."

"Wow, good to know."

Janice leaned closer, nudging her in the side. "Just a word to the wise, you'll do a lot better tonight if you lose the top."

"What…oh, I don't know if that would be such a good idea. I'm, uh…just getting over a chest cold."

Janice shot her a knowing glance. "Shy, huh? Well, hon, all I can say is get over it and fast, otherwise this sure as shit ain't the gig for you. With the wad of bills you'll walk out of here with tonight, you can buy yourself all the Vicki's Secret bras you want."

HUNKERED DOWN in the back of the FBI van with Walker and McKinney and thousands of dollars of surveillance equipment, Josh looked between the two agents and asked, "Are you sure one of you shouldn't make contact? It's been a while since she checked in." He glanced at the monitor where the infrared dot that was Mandy was positioned in the club's lower left quadrant, otherwise known as the service bar.

"Relax, Thornton, she's still making small talk with the other cocktail waitress. It's just after eight o'clock."

As if on cue, Mandy's low whisper came through the receiver. "I'm about to head into the private room to help set up."

Sitting up straight, Walker asked, "Any sign of the suspect?"

"Not yet. Oh, wait, he just showed. He's at the door talking to my cousin, the bouncer."

"What's he look like?"

She hesitated. "Beefy guy in a dark suit. I'd say about six feet tall. Wavy dark hair slicked back. He must use some product to give it that wet look. Wait, he's coming closer. Face scarred like maybe he had bad acne as a kid. Nose's definitely been broken. Okay, hold tight, he's stopping to say something to Janice. I can't hear what he's saying but the accent's got to be New England. Boston, I'd bet money on it."

McKinney chimed in. "What about his buddies, the two locals?"

"No sign of them yet."

They waited for her to say more but when she didn't, the silence brought Josh to the edge of his seat. If anything happened to Mandy, he'd never forgive himself.

Her voice filtered through the audio once more, and Josh released the breath he hadn't realized he'd been holding. "Okay, Janice just sent me to grab the drink and snack setups. I've got to sign off for now."

McKinney answered, "Okay, Delinski, but keep us posted. Just remember, we're bending all kinds of rules here. Don't do anything stupid and don't be a hero."

"Right, got it. Over and out."

MANDY TURNED AROUND in time to see Mikey, dressed in pin-striped suit and pink silk tie, striding toward her. "I thought you'd wanna know, the suit's two buddies just walked in."

Pulse pounding, Mandy reached up to make sure her wig was in place. Pretending interest in straightening the stack of cocktail napkins, she asked, "Where?"

"Six o'clock and coming toward us, one skinny as a rail, the other pumped up like Arnold Schwarzenegger."

Mandy turned away from the bar and cast her gaze out onto the floor. Her heart caught in her throat. Walking her way were two very familiar faces: her ex, Lenny, and the bodybuilder she'd met at Suz's New Year's Eve party, Danny Somebody.

She turned back to Mikey. "You sure those are his buddies? The same guys he met with the other night?"

"Yep. Slipped me a fifty to keep a lookout for them and show them inside. Speaking of which, I gotta get back to the door. You need me, you call me, okay?" He squeezed her shoulder and then pushed off to greet the mismatched pair.

Loading up her tray with bowls of snack mix and drink setups, Mandy asked herself what business a down-on-his-luck investment broker and an iron man would have with a Mafia hit man unless somehow they were in on the deal.

Suz's voice as she led her toward the kitchen. *See the Italian hunk standing by the beer cooler talking to my brother? His name's Danny Romero, and he owns a gym downtown.*

Romero as in Romero crime family. It was a fairly common Italian surname, and so Mandy hadn't given it much, make that *any* thought at the time, but suddenly it all made a crazy kind of sense. The gym probably served as a Mafia front business, hence Danny's bragging about his expansion plans as though he'd just come into a windfall of cash. Cash she'd bet anything he'd been paid for helping to take Josh out.

As for Lenny, she didn't know his angle just yet, but given his background, it figured he might be helping to cook the books. Given her personal experience of being on the receiving end of his "financial expertise," if the Romeros were counting on him to be their money guy, they might be in for a rude awakening.

Tray in hand, she cut around the curved where stage a top-heavy brunette dressed in what supposedly passed for a Native American costume gyrated to the Cher tune, "Half-Breed."

She was stripping off her first Velcro layer as Mandy passed by on her way to the private room.

The three men were sitting down to a game of poker when she entered, a canopy of cigar smoke hanging over them like an atomic mushroom cloud.

Janice was already inside, pouring out pink champagne from a magnum-size bottle. Addressing herself to the suit, she said, "Mikey wanted you to know this is on the house."

The beefy guy in the suit looked up from the cards he was shuffling and smiled, the expression making his squinted eyes all but disappear in his fleshy face. "Thanks, doll. You tell Mikey for me that I appreciate his hospitality. If he ever gets to Boston, he should look me up." He reached into his inside suit pocket and tossed a twenty-dollar bill onto the table.

Great, fabulous, just what her cousin needed now that he was trying to turn his life around—a best buddy who was a Mafia hit man. Hoping her cousin's new "friend" would be behind bars before too much longer, she let her gaze flicker to the other two men seated at the round table.

"Thanks, Mr. Tommy, you're the best," Janice purred. Leaning over him, she slid the bill into her change apron, letting her hand linger before slowly drawing it back out.

Oh, pull-eeze, don't tell me men actually fall for that? But sneaking a peek at the three rapt males, Lenny all but drooling onto the table, she saw apparently they did—hook, line and sinker.

Beckoning Mandy closer, Janice said, "Gentlemen, I'd like to introduce Amy. She'll be helping out tonight. Amy, this is Tommy, Danny and Lenny."

"Pleased to meet you."

Praying they wouldn't recognize her beneath the wig and caked-on makeup, Mandy advanced, mindful of the heavy tray balanced on the fingertips of her left hand. She'd done a stint as a waitress years ago, one in a long line of dead-end and short-lived jobs she'd tried before she'd found her calling as a cop. Balancing a tray was a lot like riding a bike—you might never forget how but you were bound to be wobbly at first.

Speaking to the suit Tommy, Janice said, "You let me know when you're ready for that lap dance, okay?"

"Nothing personal, doll face, but it's her I'd really like to do the tango with if you know I mean."

Mandy froze. She looked up from the gin and tonic she'd just set down in front of Lenny and into Tommy's eyes fixed on her breasts. "I'm not, uh…I'm not really much of a dancer."

He frowned. "You think you're too good for me, is that it?"

Janice intervened. Laying a hand on his shoulder, she gently nudged him back into his chair. "Easy, big guy, it's Amy's first night on the job. She's just shy. She'll warm up, you'll see."

"Well, she'd better get her ass un-shy and warmed up here pretty fast. I paid good money for this room."

"Don't worry, I'll show her the ropes."

Janice leaned over him, a deliberate move, and he reached for her breasts. "These milk jugs of yours real?" He rolled one rouged nipple between his thumb and forefinger while the two other men looked on with hungry eyes.

Mandy swallowed hard, her face so hot she hoped her makeup wouldn't melt. Modesty aside, if Tommy tried feeling her up like he was doing to Janice, he'd discover she was wearing a wire. That would spell the end of her sting operation and, more than likely, the end of her.

Janice shrugged. "What's real? Reality's overrated anyhow. Tonight's all about fantasy."

"You got a point there. Come back in a half hour, and we'll talk about that lap dance." He slapped her on the butt.

"You got it." Sending Mandy a look that all but screamed, "Don't fuck up," Janice turned to leave.

Mandy started to follow her out, but Tommy's beefy hand

closed about her wrist. "Not you. You stay here and serve us. I think we're going to need a lot of service before this night's over, don't you, gentlemen?" He glanced over to his two companions who nodded, grinning.

Knocking back his drink, Danny spoke up. "If it's all the same to you, I'll wait for the tall, thin one with the fake boobs to come back."

Lenny shook his pin head. "Not me. I like 'em with some meat on their bones and real tits, not fake ones." Beckoning Mandy over, he said, "Come here, hon. I'll bet anything that rack of yours is real."

You ought to know, asshole, you certainly never lost out on an opportunity to feel me up when we were dating—even after you lost my money in the market.

Stepping out of reach, Mandy glanced to his highball glass, already two-thirds empty. "How about I make you another drink first?"

If Lenny was anything close to the lightweight she remembered from their dating days, he'd be out cold in another hour.

She caught Tommy the hit man staring at her again and looked quickly away. *Another hour, if only I can last that long, if only I can last.*

HEARING THE BYPLAY coming out of the bugged room, Josh gritted his teeth. "Maybe this isn't such a good idea after all. I think we should get her out of there."

McKinney lifted the minimike out of his ear. "Relax, Thornton, Delinski obviously knows what she's doing. She's a real professional. I don't say this often but frankly I'm impressed."

Even in the midst of his fear for her, Josh felt a surge of pride. "She's trying to make detective, you know."

Taking a sip from his bottle of Evian, Walker said, "Well, she certainly has all the makings of an A-list one."

Josh divided his gaze between the two federal agents. "Maybe after this is over, you two could pass on those comments to her supervisor?"

Walker didn't hesitate. "You got it, Thornton. Actually I'd planned on commending her in my report." He turned back to the monitor as a new stream of audio filtered through. "For now, though, let's focus on accomplishing the mission— including getting Officer Delinski out of there alive."

DEALING THE CARDS, Tommy the Terminator took control of the meeting. "The reason I asked you two back here is we need to come up with a backup plan and fast. January second is D-Day, and the boss ain't any too pleased with the level of local support you've given me so far."

Standing like a sentinel inside the closed door in case anyone needed any "servicing," Mandy's ears perked up at the mention of "local support." *Now, we're getting somewhere,* she thought, pretending interest in picking at the polish on her nails.

Danny reached for the bowl of peanuts parked at his elbow. Tossing back a fistful, he said, "It's not our fault he's holed up 24/7 in that shit apartment ever since that water taxi episode went south. As far as I can tell, the only way to get him to budge is to smoke him out."

Earlier, they'd disguised Josh as one of the cooks, complete with chef's puffy white cap and apron, and had snuck him out the restaurant's back door. They'd even given him a full garbage bag to carry as though he was headed with it to the Dumpster and not the FBI van parked in the gravel lot behind. Relieved to hear the ruse had worked, Mandy told herself that for the time being Josh was safe. As much as possible, she needed to stop worrying about him and focus on getting the job done.

Tommy snickered. "It's the cop girlfriend he's doing. He's too busy banging her to get out of bed."

Lenny, silent until now, tossed down his cards with a look of disgust. "Another shit hand, just my luck. I fold." Sucking an ice cube from his drink, he said, "I used to date her, you know. She was about as warm as this fucking ice cube."

Under the screen of her fake eyelashes, Mandy glared at him. *That's because you treated me like crap and then lost all my money, you asshole.*

"No shit, imagine that." Picking up his cards, Tommy rolled his eyes. "Well, judging from all the moaning and groaning coming from that apartment, she ain't cold with him, that's for sure."

Oh my God! Somehow they'd gotten in and bugged Josh's apartment. For however long, these jerks had been getting their jollies listening to her and Josh making love. Ears burning, she reminded herself that after tonight, she'd probably never have to see any of them ever again. Thank God because apparently she was a little more old-fashioned than she thought.

Lenny's jaw hardened. "Good-looking rich guys like Thornton get all the action. She's just too infatuated to know a solid guy when she sees one."

Danny stared down at the cards in his hand. Dropping them, he said, "I'm out, too. Another hand?"

Tommy shook his head. "Fuck poker, let's get back to brainstorming our little problem, making sure a certain troublesome telecommunications mogul gets what's coming to him."

Lenny cast a nervous glance to Mandy. "Maybe we should send the bimbo away while we talk shop."

Danny rolled his overly developed shoulders in a shrug. "She must hear this shit all the time. Besides, if Mikey says she's okay, then she must be."

Lenny glanced to his watch. "Okay, so what's the new plan going to be?"

Tapping a thick finger to the side of his jaw, Tommy thought a moment. "Lenny, you said you used to date Delinski, right?"

"Yeah, what about it?"

"Why don't you call her up and invite her to lunch or something? Once we have her, smoking out Thornton should be a cakewalk. You can tell by the way he looks at her, all melty-eyed, he's crazy about the broad."

Josh is crazy about me, really? Heart warming, Mandy swung her gaze back to Lenny. He hesitated and then admitted, "We didn't exactly end things on the best of terms."

It was all Mandy could do to keep from marching across the stained carpet to deck him. *Best of terms, my ass. And we didn't end anything, I ended it*

Tommy shifted his gaze to the bodybuilder. "What about you, Romeo? Feel like putting that muscle of yours to use pumping somethin' else besides iron?"

"Yeah, sure, why not? It's worth a try. So I guess this means we'll be taking her out, too, along with Thornton, huh?"

Tommy tossed a look to the door, and Mandy dropped her gaze to her feet. Out of the corner of her eye, she caught him assessing her and hoped her "dumb and dumber" routine was still working. Turning back to the table, he reached for the bottle of sparkling wine and refilled his glass. Under his breath, he warned, "Watch your mouth, asshole. She may be dumb, but she's not deaf."

Danny nodded. "Sorry. That's what eating this junk-food crap does to me. It's loaded with fat."

Tommy snorted. "I guess that explains that fat head of yours, huh?" He dug a fist into the salted peanuts, spilling them over the sides of the bowl. "I'd order up some fucking power bars if I thought they'd help improve your brain power, but they don't have any, so shut the fuck up."

The reference to "offing" her and Josh should give them enough verbal evidence to get an arrest warrant. She'd been lucky so far but no one's luck could be expected to hold out indefinitely. Besides, her gut instinct was telling her to get the hell out of that room now and in five years in the field, her gut had never once lied.

Strolling over to the table, she turned to Danny. Poking out her chest, she gave her best imitation of Janice's seductively husky tone. "How about I use my, uh…*influence* and get the kitchen to make you something healthy, say a nice fruit and cheese plate?"

"You'd do that for me?" At her nod, he turned to the table. "What a sweetheart. Is this broad a class act or what?"

Tommy lifted his eyes to her, the lids looking heavier than when she'd first come into the room. She couldn't be sure but she thought he might be getting a little drunk on all that pink champagne he was quaffing.

Gaze dropping to her breasts, his mouth curved into a silly grin. "I don't need any fucking fruit plate, but I'd sure as hell like to get a closer look at those melons you're carting around, maybe even give 'em a nice little squeeze to make sure they're fresh—and firm."

Before she could react, he wrapped his hands around her waist and pulled her down on top of him. She tried to get up but it was no use, he had her pinned on his lap, a boner of an erection pressing against her bottom. Ugh! In the struggle to avoid his touch, she bumped her head against his massive chest, knocking her wig askew.

He pulled the wig off and tossed it across the table. "Looks like we got a redhead, my very favorite, but first I'd better make sure she's a natural one." Ducking her flailing hands, he slid a hand down her middle and squeezed her crotch. Predictably, his smile dissolved. "Hey, what's this?" He stared at her face for a long, terrifying moment before shouting to the table at large, "It's Delinski and she's wearing a wire."

SWEAT BREAKING OUT ON HIS BROW, Walker pulled the mike out his ear. "Damn, we were almost home free."

Josh went into instant alert. "What is it? What's happened?"

The fed pulled the revolver from his side and reached for the van's door handle. "Delinski's cover's been blown. We're going in." Turning to his partner, he said, "Call for backup—now!"

"KILLING ME WON'T SOLVE ANYTHING, you know. We already have the audio." Standing with her back up against the stained flocked wallpaper, Mandy stared down the pistol pointed at the space between her eyes.

On the other end of the weapon, Tommy the Terminator cocked the hammer with the calm matter-of-factness of an assassin accustomed to killing in cold blood. "Okay, I'll do you for pleasure then, how's that?"

Flanking Tommy's right, Lenny and Danny exchanged worried looks. Two weak men who'd gotten in over their heads trying to make a fast buck, they were losers but not career criminals.

Lenny was the first to voice the fear written all over both their faces. "Right now all they've got on us is maybe racketeering and accessory to *attempted* murder. But if he kills her now, we're accomplices to an actual murder."

Danny hesitated, and then nodded. "You're right." To Tommy, he said, "I'm out of here."

"Me, too." Lenny grabbed his jacket to go.

"Hold up." Tommy swung around to them. "You two aren't going nowhere. This is all your faults anyway. If you hadn't botched the boat deal, I'd be sitting down to pasta primavera in the North End of Boston about now."

Mandy might not be much of a whiz in PT when it came to sit-ups and push-ups, but she was pretty good about recognizing an opportunity when one came knocking and this was certainly one of those times. The hit man, Tommy, had shifted his stance, the gun he held no longer trained on her. What was it her martial arts instructor at the academy was always saying? Oh yeah—*the bigger they are, the harder they fall.*

Kicking out, she slammed the spike of her high heel into the back of Tommy's right knee.

With a cry of pain, he folded to the floor, the gun falling from his hand just as the door burst open. The Men in Black, Walker and McKinney, stood framed in the open doorway, guns drawn. "Freeze—FBI. Put your hands up in the air—now."

18

Bad guys hauled off to lockup: three, not a bad score for one night. Glasses of celebratory (pink) champagne imbibed: zero as am a) on duty, well sort of and b) still recovering from New Year's Eve that technically hasn't happened yet.

Hunky boyfriends saved from Darth Vader–like menace to live and love—and testify—another day: one but won't have as boyfriend for much longer now. Not much longer now...

JOSH STOOD out on the sidewalk, searching the cast of characters and police pouring out the club's main door for any sign of Mandy, when his cell phone went off. Thinking it must be her calling him from inside, he took the call without bothering to glance down. "Hey you, how much longer before you can wrap this up so we can celebrate?"

Instead of Mandy, Tiffany, voice trembling, answered him back, "Josh, it's me. They've got me and unless you do what they say, they're going to kill me."

Gripping the phone more tightly, he glanced over to McKinney, busy talking into his own cell. Lowering his voice, he asked, "Hold up, who's got you? Where are you?"

"I'm at the Recreation Pier Building on Thames Street. They say if you don't come in the next half hour, and alone, they're going to kill me. Alone, Josh, that part's really, *really* important."

"Tiffany, I don't know. I—"

"Please, Josh, hurry…"

The call clicked off. Stunned, Josh took a minute to process what he'd just heard. Tiffany had been taken hostage just as McKinney had warned him might happen. Whoever had her wouldn't hesitate to use her as a means to get at him. Whatever he'd once felt for her couldn't begin to touch the feelings Mandy brought out in him, but that didn't change the facts— he'd cared for Tiffany once, cared enough to ask her to marry him. She wouldn't be in this position if it weren't for him.

McKinney stood next to him, his cell plastered to his ear. Heart pounding, Josh mouthed the words, "Be right back," and turned to walk away.

"Hold up, Thornton." McKinney's voice stopped him in his tracks. "Where are you off to?"

Heart kicking into overdrive, Josh concentrated on at least giving the appearance of calm. Turning back around, he said, "Relax, I've got to go relieve myself. I'll be back in a minute."

McKinney hesitated. "Just let me finish up this call, and I'll go with you."

Shit. Shaking his head, he said, "Thanks, but I don't need you holding my hand, or anything else for that matter. Besides, you've got the hitter and his two cronies in custody, and the area's crawling with cops."

A stream of conversation poured out from McKinney's cell. Distracted, the agent waived Josh off. "Okay, I guess it'll be all right. Just come back as soon as you're done."

"You got it." Josh nodded and headed for the alley.

The stakeout team had cordoned off the entire city block, which meant he'd have to cut through the back and then circle around to a main street. He turned the corner and darted down the alley, the reek of rotting garbage and urine filling his nostrils. Looking over his shoulder to make sure no one followed, he climbed up on a dumpster and used it as leverage to get his footing atop the chain link fence. Straddling the post, he jumped over the side. He landed hard, the soles of his feet stinging from the contact with cement, the jolt making him aware of the knee he'd hurt in high school football that had never been quite right since. Limping slightly, he made his way past the flashing neon. Unfortunately, his car was parked back at the apartment in Canton, so public transportation was the only option. Lifting his jacket collar to obscure the side of his face, he headed for the queue of cabs parked in front of the apparently very popular Circus Bar fronting East Baltimore Street.

He pulled open the door of the first cab in the line and got in. "I need to go to Fells Point, the Recreation Pier Building on Thames Street."

Shifting around to look back at him, the driver shook his head. "Building's been dark since *Homicide* wrapped its final episode. The show used it as a stand-in for their police station, you know. Couple of years ago some developer wanted to turn it into a hotel, but the way things move in this city, who knows when that'll ever happen."

Dragging a hand through his hair, Josh snapped, "Just drive me there, okay."

The driver held up his palm. "Geez, buddy, relax. I'll take you wherever you want to go. But for your own good, you'd better dial it down. Stress will kill ya."

A TAN TRENCH COAT covering her skimpy costume, Mandy emerged from the club. Ahead of her, two Baltimore City police officers led a cuffed Tommy the Terminator toward a waiting squad car.

Twisting his head around to look at her, he said, "You'll never get away with this, you bitch. This is entrapment pure and simple. My lawyer will have me out in no time."

She shook her head, lighter now that she'd gotten rid of the wig. "Yeah, well, we'll see about that. For your sake, you better hope you're in for a nice long incarceration. Personally, I wouldn't want to be you when the Romeros find out you fucked up. I'd say your career is definitely over and maybe your life, too."

A second police car pulled off and she caught Lenny's eye from the caged back seat. Earlier she'd had the satisfaction of reading him his rights and slapping the bracelets on him personally. The glare he shot her as the squad car sped by had her hugging her coat more tightly around her, but she reminded herself he would very likely be the governor's "guest" for a good long while.

As for her, it had been a long night filled with some of the most stressful moments of her career. Now that the adrenaline rush was running out, fatigue was settling in. What she really wanted was to find Josh and go back to his apartment, or better yet, splurge and check them both into a luxury downtown hotel, thaw in a long, scalding shower, and then slide naked beneath the hundred percent Egyptian cotton sheets for some rest and recreation—with emphasis on the recreation part.

She turned to McKinney as the agent was finishing up a phone call. "Where's Josh?"

"He went off to take a leak." He nodded to the alley.

"Why would he go to the bathroom in an alley when there are plenty of men's rooms inside the club?"

McKinney shrugged. "Who knows, maybe he thought the alley would be cleaner or maybe that cell phone call scared the piss out of him."

All at once, Mandy's adrenaline started to spike "Someone called him on his cell?"

"It was you calling from inside…wasn't it?"

"No." She shook her head, her lulled senses coming back to full alert. "But he's still a federal witness, right? Other than you, me and Walker, who would be calling him on his cell at this time of night?"

Before he could answer, Special Agent Walker materialized from the front of the building wearing a dark overcoat identical to McKinney's. Walking briskly toward them he said, "I just spotted someone who could pass for Joshua Thornton's identical twin climbing into a cab a few blocks down."

"Fuck, he told me he was going to take a piss." McKinney punched a fist into the air.

Walker shook his head. "That's the oldest trick in the book. Any ideas why he'd want to give us the slip now?"

Mandy shook her head. Gut instinct told her Josh wouldn't run off without good reason and yet once again he'd chosen not to confide in her. A part of her couldn't help feeling shut out, abandoned even. But now was the time for taking action, not nursing hurt feelings. There would be plenty of time for asking questions *after* they tracked him down.

Thinking out loud, she said, "There aren't all that many downtown cab companies willing to service this area." Addressing herself to Walker, she asked, "What did the vehicle look like?"

He didn't hesitate. "It was solid yellow, taxi-cab yellow as they say."

The cop part of her brain kicking in, she said, "That would be Yellow Cab Company. They're on Lombard Street, right downtown. If he just left, we should be able to call and get his destination from their dispatcher."

McKinney graced her with a grudging nod. "Good thinking, Delinski." He grabbed his cell phone off his belt clip and punched 411 for information. "I need the number for Yellow Cab on Lombard—and hurry!"

RIDING INSIDE THE CAB, Josh was trying to focus on how he would handle things once he got to the drop-off point when his cell went off a second time. He wasn't really surprised to see Mandy's number show up on the display window. What did surprise him was how much discipline it took for him not to pick up. In the short but intense time he'd known her, he'd gotten so used to sharing things with her, the good as well as the bad.

But for her sake, he made himself let the thing ring. She'd put her life on the line for him two times already, and he'd be damned if he'd let her risk herself again. No one's luck could hold out indefinitely, not even that of a plucky lady cop with Polish moxie and street-smart charm.

From the front seat, the cabbie called back, "Hey, mister, can you switch that thing over to vibrate or somethin'? I'm trying to drive up here."

The call ended and bell-like prompt told him a voice message waited. Not trusting himself to listen to it, Josh settled back against the cracked leather seat. *Sorry, baby, I can't let you take any more risks for me. I can't and I won't. This time, I have to go it alone.*

"COME ON, JOSH, pick up. Pick up."

Riding in the backseat of the FBI van as they sped toward Fells Point with Walker at the wheel and McKinney riding shotgun in the front seat, Mandy felt like a jack-in-the-box poised to pop—out of her skin. It had taken her about ten minutes, but they'd managed to get Josh's destination from the cab company's dispatcher: the Recreation Pier Building on Thames Street. Hearing the address chilled her to the bone even though the van's heater was at full blast. Recreation Pier was where his body, his *dead* body, had been found on Christmas morning the week before. Whether his murder had taken place last week or in some parallel universe no longer mattered to her. All she cared about was keeping him alive in whatever time construct "the present" existed.

Josh's voice mail picked up on the sixth ring. "This is Josh. Sorry I missed your call but leave me a message."

Mandy had no choice but to do just that. "Josh, it's me. I'm on my way to you now with Walker and McKinney. I don't know why you walked away or why you're headed to Recreation Pier but whatever the reason is, don't go there, baby. Don't go inside."

THE CAB PULLED UP in front of the Recreation Pier Building. The driver glanced at Josh in the rearview mirror. "You sure this is where you want me to let you out?"

"Positive." Josh tossed a twenty-dollar bill over the front seat back, flung open the door, and stepped out.

The shuttered brick building was dark as he'd known it would be. Ducking inside the arched entrance used for ground-level parking, he made his way through the building.

"Tiffany. Tiffany, can you hear me? Tiffany…"

"I'm up here, Josh."

She sounded scared but he told himself that if she could talk, they must not have hurt her. Senses on alert, he came to a doorway marked Stairwell. Fortunately it wasn't locked. He turned the gummy knob and entered, the smell of urine hitting him in the face like a fist. Finding the metal rail post, he climbed upward to the top. He opened the door to step outside, and a gust of wind hit him full force, the pressure so intense he had to keep his shoulder to the door so it didn't fall back in his face.

Though the pier was unlit, there was enough ambient light for him to find his way to the cordoned-off entrance. He swung a leg over the chain and started down, feeling like the condemned walking the plank on a pirate ship, an apt analogy in his case.

Gaze darting about, he called out, "Let her go, it's me you want."

A muffled cry drew his attention to an open archway running along the building's side. Peering through the shadows, he spotted Tiffany. Dressed all in black, her long blond hair pulled into a ponytail, she appeared to be alone.

Drawing closer, he saw the swatch of duct tape covering her mouth and surmised the kidnapper had muzzled her in response to her crying out.

If so, he must be close by indeed. Treading carefully, he advanced and came up beside her. "Are you okay?" At her tearful nod, he reached out to tear off the tape.

Predictably she let out a squeal. Swiping the back of her hand over her reddened mouth, she said, "It's fucking freezing out here. What took you so long?"

In the midst of his crazy mixed-up life, it was good to know there were still some constants in the universe, in this case his ex showing herself to be just as ungrateful and bitchy as ever. "I got here as fast as I could. What's going on? Where is—"

The hard metal jabbing into his abdomen caused him to leave the sentence unfinished. Staring down, he saw her slender hand holding the pistol, the barrel digging into his gut. "What the hell?" He jerked back up to look at her.

She shook her head, blond ponytail catching on the wind. "Sorry, Joshy, I really am. You're a good guy and an amazing fuck, and frankly I'm going to miss you. If only you and Grady hadn't gone sticking your noses into my business, we all might have been one big happy Thornton Enterprises family."

"What are you talking about?"

"Grady got too close. I didn't have any choice but to have him…eliminated. He was a nice guy, too, but frankly he was a bore. Having him taken out didn't really bother me all that much. But you, Josh, I resisted getting rid of you for a long time. I tried to save you from yourself, really, I did. I thought if I could keep you busy enough in bed and then with the wedding plans, you'd leave well enough alone at the office. But that New England work ethic of yours kept getting in the way. You wouldn't leave well enough alone, and when I found out you went to the FBI and snitched, well, I didn't have any choice."

"Are you saying you're in league with the Romeros?" At

this point, he supposed the details didn't matter a whole hell of a lot, but the longer he kept her talking, the longer he had to stay alive. And life had never seemed as precious as it did at this very moment when it was about to end.

She shook her head. "I am a Romero, on my mother's side. Tony is my first cousin. We thought we had a pretty good plan, he and I. Marry into the firm, get control of the stock, and then corner the WiFi market for the entire East Coast for starters."

He shook his head, amazed he'd ever missed the ugliness simmering beneath all that surface beauty. "I never would have gone along with that. Sooner or later I would have found out and shut you down."

"That's too bad because we could have been so good together, you and I. We were good together, a power couple, at least until that thin WASP blood of yours got in the way. What do you say to a farewell kiss for old time's sake?" Lips parting, she leaned in.

He jerked back. "You disgust me."

Her face hardened, making her look older than her twenty-six years but then again maybe her age was a lie, too. "Okay, then, we'll get straight to business." Stepping back from him, she raised the pistol, pointing it at his head. "Turn around, get down on your knees, and put your hands behind your back."

Josh shook his head. He was going to die, that was a given, but he'd be damned if he'd make it easy for her. "Not a chance. You're going to have to look me in the eye when you pull that trigger."

She shrugged. "Suit yourself." There was a clicking sound as she pulled back on the hammer.

"Noooooooo!"

Josh swung around in time to see a female figure flying toward them, her long hair billowing out behind her like a curtain of red silk.

"Mandy, no, stay back. Stay back!"

Tiffany shifted position, the pistol no longer pointed at him but at Mandy. Taking advantage of her turning away, Josh launched forward, grabbing hold of her legs and taking her down on the deck just as she squeezed the trigger.

A shot rang out, and then…silence.

19

Given breakneck pace of life over past two days, consider it okay to combine two diary entries in one, especially as days and nights all seem to run together. Hunky boyfriend saved from grizzly homicide: one, and thank God got there in proverbial nick of time. Bad-ass guys (and gals) arrested and hauled off to lockup: count officially at four, including blond ex-fiancée. Am happy to stop there especially as final arrest involved taking out Mafia captain and romantic competition in single move—talk about multitasking! Bullets taken in line of duty and service of True Love: one and is more than enough. More than enough...

PACING THE FOUR CORNERS of the hospital's emergency waiting room at 2:00 a.m., Josh struggled to wrap his mind around the events of the past few hours. Every time he replayed the episode on the pier, which he'd done repeatedly on the ambulance ride over holding Mandy's cold hand in his, he was torn between gratitude to the powers that be for saving her and a terrible fear that he would awaken and find that this was all a dream, that she was dead after all. Thankfully the physical damage was minor. The bullet had grazed her shoulder, missing the bone and leaving a flesh wound that would heal with time. Because of the bruising and stitches, they'd be sending her home with a sling and a prescription for antibiotics to prevent infection, but otherwise she was good to go.

It could have been so very much worse. Every time he thought of the spectrum of possible outcomes, one or both of them shot dead or at least badly injured, he wanted to go back to that moment on the pier if only to wring Tiffany's slender neck.

That she'd apparently masterminded the whole Mafia operation on Thornton Enterprises still astounded him. To give the devil his—in this case *her*—due, she was a hell of a lot smarter than he'd imagined as well as a consummate actress. Her debutante act had fooled him, indeed everyone, from the very beginning. Aside from getting caught screwing the landscaper, she'd played out the game to perfection almost to the very end. And an ambitious game it had been, with the goal being not just to embezzle funds but to hijack the entire firm. Even though she'd confessed it all to his face, he still had difficulty wrapping his mind around that level of deception. The whole scenario seemed straight out of an overplotted fiction novel rather than something that would occur in real life, his life anyway. If they'd succeeded, Thornton Enterprises, founded by his great-grandfather back when technology was synonymous with Bell's invention of the telephone, would have been a pawn of organized crime. The prospect sent chills sliding down his spine.

A nurse with tired eyes and a friendly smile shuffled in. "You can see her now if you like."

"Great. Thanks."

He followed her back to the treatment area. Pulling back on the divider curtain, she said, "We're going to keep her overnight, but she should be able to go home tomorrow morning."

"That's great news, thanks."

Mandy was lying on the narrow hospital gurney when he stepped inside, pulling the curtain closed behind him. Even with mascara smudges beneath her eyes and her hair a wind-whipped tangle, she'd never looked more beautiful to him.

"Hey, you." He came up to the side of the narrow bed. Leaning over the raised metal rail, he asked, "How are you feeling?"

Eyelids heavy, she smiled up at him. "A little groggy. They gave me something for the pain."

"That's good. I hear they're going to release you tomorrow morning. I'll be here when they do."

Her smile dimmed. "Don't you, uh…have to get back to Boston now?"

Sidestepping the touchy subject of his leaving, he said, "I'm not flying back until the first, but in the meantime, I told the Men in Black I'm done with that apartment. I think we've both earned finishing out the week at a luxury hotel, say a Ritz-Carlton or a Four Seasons."

"Sounds really nice, but I don't think Baltimore has either. But according to my friend, Suz, the Renaissance Harbor-place has amazing beds, a sky-top cocktail lounge, and a covered walkway over to the Inner Harbor."

For the first time since he'd picked up Mandy's limp body from the pier's planked decking, Josh found his smile. "As long as we don't have to take any water taxis to get there, I'm sold."

THE NEXT EVENING, Mandy lay propped up in the hotel's king size bed. To her, the executive suite at the Renaissance seemed like something out of a fairy tale or at least the Julia Roberts-Richard Gere blockbuster movie, *Pretty Woman*. To Josh, though, their luxurious surroundings were obviously standard fare. He never asked how much anything cost, never hesitated to make use of the minibar or order from the room service menu. But then again, he'd grown up surrounded by wealth, yet another of the differences between them.

And yet in so many ways, on so many levels, they clicked perfectly. He'd just finished making gentle love to her and though her shoulder was sore, otherwise she felt wonderful. It was only his leaving early the next morning that put a damper on her bliss. But they still had eight solid hours of awake time together. If recent events had taught her anything, it was to live in the moment.

Turning over on her good side, she reached up and brushed a lock of blond hair back from his brow. "Penny for your thoughts."

Like her, he was naked beneath the covers, and she ran her gaze over the terrain of strong neck and sleek broad chest, caressing him with her eyes as she'd recently done with her hands and lips and tongue, feeling her body filling but her heart filling, too. Knowing this was the last night they'd be together, she wanted to grab hold of each precious minute and stretch it out like the fabric of lacy lingerie to make it last as long as possible—forever.

Reaching out to capture her hand, he pressed a kiss to her palm. "I was just thinking how much I'm going to miss you."

She swallowed against the lump building at the back of her throat. Funny how it hurt a lot more than her shoulder. "I know. I'm going to miss you, too."

From the very beginning, she'd known this moment was coming and yet it hit her like a sucker punch all the same. The whole situation had a funky, surreal sense like reading *Romeo and Juliet* or watching the DVD of *Gone with the Wind* and expecting the happy ending you knew would never come and yet wanting it so badly, you couldn't help hoping all the same. It defied reason but then again rational thought and matters of the heart didn't exactly go hand-in-hand, not in her experience anyway.

"Hey you, what gives with the long face? I live in Boston, not Bosnia. It's not that far. We can still see each other."

She shrugged, wincing when the movement brought the pain in her shoulder back to burning life. "Long-distance relationships never work out."

"Then let's not make it long distance."

She hesitated. "What are you saying?"

His gaze locked on hers. "You could move to Boston. You could move in with me."

"But what would I do there?"

He smiled. "That's the best part. Whatever you wanted or nothing at all—it'd be your call."

"But I'd need to support myself."

Smoothing her hair back from her face, he said, "You wouldn't have to worry about money. The fact is I'm pretty well off, rich actually. I'd take care of you, give you whatever cash you needed, use of the credit card, a car, you name it."

"You mean like a mistress?"

His smile dimmed. "It wouldn't be like that, Mandy."

A short while ago what he was offering would have looked like a pretty sweet deal but a lot of things had changed for her recently, and now she couldn't sign up to be in a relationship where she was so essentially powerless. What she wanted was to be his girlfriend, his lover, his full partner, but she couldn't be any of those things, not fully, if she settled for the arrangement he was offering.

"That's very generous of you, but I couldn't possibly accept."

He looked puzzled. "Why not? It's only money, a means to an end. If the fact that I have it lets us be together, then why not take advantage of the situation and just be happy?"

But it wasn't only money, not to her anyway. In this case, money was a symbol for so many things—for pride and self-sufficiency and finally finding the guts to strike out on her own again. If she moved out of her parents' house and moved in with a boyfriend, with Josh, she'd only be trading one dependency for another.

"The fact is I'd be a kept woman, someone you fit into your schedule between meetings and business trips. I couldn't live like that or at least I won't."

Frowning, he pulled himself up on one elbow and stared down at her. "So instead you'd rather we just go our separate ways?"

"Listen, I know what we had here was a fling." Had— amazing how she was already speaking of them in the past tense. "And we've had a good time, no doubt about it. But that good time is winding down, and it's probably best if we just say goodbye now and end things on the upswing." Holding her shoulder, she started up from the pillow, hoping she could make it to the bathroom before the tears started.

Josh looked as stricken as she felt. "Are you telling me you don't want to see me anymore?"

Reaching for her complimentary fluffy white robe, she threaded her good arm through the sleeve. "What I might want and what will work are two very different things." That was certainly true. Wincing, she pulled the other side of the robe over her bandaged shoulder and then reached inside her handbag for her wallet. Pulling out a twenty, she tossed the bill on the night table.

Staring at her, Josh said, "What the hell is that, my tip?"

"This should cover my part of our room service order." The feds were covering the cost of the hotel, and using her tax dollars as well as his to do so, so at least she didn't have to feel beholden about that.

Shaking his head, he leapt up from the bed. "Mandy, I don't want your money."

Setting her purse down, she shook her head. "Sorry, Josh, but I'm a Delinski. We always pay our own way."

20

Two Weeks Later

Have fallen off diary wagon as move has made life too hectic for finding regular time to write, hence new diary mostly blank pages so far, but here goes… Apartments leased in own name: one, a studio, but all mine, thank you very much and compact size plenty of space for one woman with no time to clean and one very fat cat. Calories consumed: no longer bother to count as have finally mastered Zen of eating when hungry and stopping when full. Now if can only find some way to impart this ancient wisdom to food-obsessed cat.

Hunky boyfriends saved from grisly homicide and sent off to live and love another day (in Boston): one— and will cherish the memory of our time together for the rest of my life.

MANDY WAS STEPPING OUT of the shower when her apartment buzzer rang. *Damn, that was fast.* The delivery guy with her carry-out Chinese must have set some kind of all-time record.

The buzzer blared again. "Okay, okay, I'm coming."

She pulled on her robe and hurried through the walk-through closet into the living room, which also happened to be the dining room and the bedroom, too. Her studio apartment in Charles Village was certainly compact, but it was all the space she needed right now. One of the best things about it was its animal-friendly policy permitting residents to keep small pets. The same day she'd signed the lease, she'd driven out to the humane society shelter and adopted a cat. Adorable kittens were in plentiful supply, but it was the sad, soulful eyes of a three-year-old silver Bengal mix that snagged her heartstrings. A compulsive eater from his years of fending off starvation on the streets, "Sweeney" sat curled up in the middle of her fold-out futon, front paws tucked into a perfect meat loaf.

Bypassing the stack of still-to-be-unpacked boxes, she punched the intercom button by her apartment door. "Sorry, I was in the—"

"Mandy, it's me. Buzz me in, we need to talk." Instead of the delivery man's accented English, Josh's voice emerged amidst the speaker's static.

She reached out a shaking hand and punched the buzzer, emotions seesawing between shock and elation. Josh. What was he doing here? Other than a one-line e-mail to let her know he'd gotten back safely, she hadn't heard from him since the trial where he'd testified, effectively linking his brother-in-law's embezzlement activities back to the mob. With Tony the Terminator's testimony added to his—the hit man had accepted a plea bargain and sang like a bird—Tiffany would be going away for a long, long time. As for the Romeros, while not exactly out of business, with the feds monitoring their every move and the high-profile trial putting organized crime back in the national spotlight, their crime cartel would be operating with wings clipped from now on. It would likely be a good long while before they tried to hijack any more major U.S. corporations.

Heart pounding, she waited for the imminent knock on her door. Even though she'd been the one to break things off, she couldn't help wishing there'd been time to dry her hair and dust on some makeup. As it was, she must look like a drowned rat, not that she cared of course. Yeah, right.

A light rap sounded and taking a deep breath, she opened the door. Josh stood in the hallway wearing a Burberry trench coat and a hesitant smile and looking even more gorgeous than she remembered.

Taking in his closely cropped hair and polished wing tips, she said, "You look very...corporate."

He shrugged. "After my last meeting, I headed straight for the airport and caught the next flight into BWI. I didn't have time to change. May I come in?"

"Oh, right. Sorry." Feeling like a fool—so what else was new—she stepped back for him to enter.

She closed the door and turned to face him. "Can I uh...take your coat?"

"Sure." He shrugged it off and handed it to her.

Oh my God. If she'd thought he looked amazing in a worn leather jacket and jeans, the sight of him in a charcoal-colored Armani suit and knotted silk tie all but knocked the breath from her lungs.

Hanging the coat up on the hook, she said, "I've been following the trial in the newspapers and TV." She turned back around and their gazes locked, reminding her of that first electrically charged encounter at the museum gala. "You did good, Josh. I'm really proud of you."

"It was a team effort as I recall, but thanks."

His gaze raked over her, making her mindful that she was naked beneath the terry-cloth robe. Backing up a step, she said, "I'd invite you to sit down but the only furniture I have so far is a futon." A futon she'd just folded down into a bed for the night.

He glanced beyond her to the bed where Sweeney had taken up residence. "I see you got a cat. Does she mind sharing?"

"He's a he actually and given that last week this time his home was a cage in the shelter, I guess he can deal with sharing his space."

He walked over to the foldout and sat down on the edge.

Stretching his long legs out in front of him, the cuffed trousers falling into a perfect crease, he patted the space beside him. "Join me?"

Mandy swallowed hard and shook her head. The last time they'd been on a bed together, they'd made nonstop love all night and into the next morning, a sweet memory that, under the circumstances, it would be foolish to repeat. "I'm waiting on some Chinese carry-out. It should be here any time, so I'll just hang here by the door."

"That's too bad because I was hoping I'd get to take you out to dinner."

"You flew all the way from Boston to take me out to dinner?"

He nodded. "No water taxis this time, I promise."

She smiled in spite of her aching heart. Why did he have to be so damned charming? "Oh, Josh, as much as I love seeing you, we can't keep doing this. I thought we said our goodbyes two weeks ago."

He surged to his feet and crossed the few steps of carpet to reach her. "What if I don't want to say goodbye to you— ever? What then?"

"We've been through this all before. It would never work out between us."

He tilted his head to the side, studying her with intense eyes. "What makes you so sure about that?"

She hesitated, struggling to frame her answer so that she didn't sound like a snob-in-reverse. "As clichéd as this sounds, we're from two separate worlds. If you really were a bartender, things would be different. But you're not just some hot guy with an amazing body who's rolled into town for a change of scenery. You're from this old money family of New England moguls, and not just anywhere in New England but Boston of all places. My grandparents were immigrants in the thirties. Your ancestors probably stepped off the *Mayflower*."

"The *Mayflower* landed at Plymouth actually, some fifty

miles from Boston, so I doubt it. Do you really think I have an amazing body?"

She nodded, feeling a blush burn its way upwards from her throat. "Uh-huh."

His mouth formed a wry smile, but his eyes looked so sad it was all she could do to keep from reaching out to touch him. "Look, Mandy, whether I'm a bartender or a business executive, whether my net income is six figures or six dollars, it really doesn't matter. I'm still the same man who asked you out for coffee on Christmas Eve, the same man who's held your head while you slept and watched your face while you came, and the bottom line is I want you in my life. Whatever changes I need to make for that to happen, I'm ready to make them."

She shook her head. "I don't know. Our backgrounds, we're so different."

"Mandy, it can work out. It will work out. Actually, if you think about it, it already has."

"It has?"

He nodded. Reaching for her hand, he laced his fingers through hers and looked deeply into her eyes. "I don't know about you, but I've never felt this good, this *right,* with anyone before. Look, if you want a guarantee, a play-by-play on how it's all going to work between now and the rest of our lives, I can't give you that because I don't know, either. I'm pretty much figuring this out one day at a time myself, but you know what, I'm coming to think that's the way life goes. So let's talk about what I do know. I know that three hours in bed with you flies by like three minutes, and I'm not just talking about the sex though that's pretty amazing, by the way. I love holding you afterward, I love the way you hold me back and trace slow circles between my shoulders with your fingernails. I love looking at you just after you've climaxed, seeing you all rumpled and relaxed and well, glowing. Christ, Mandy, I even love that you eat oranges in my bed. My goddamned sheets smelled like oranges the whole time we were together and though that ought to have annoyed the hell out of me, it didn't. Instead when I think of oranges I think of you wrapped up in my bedsheets and now every time I walk down some grocery store's produce aisle and smell citrus, I get a hard-on."

She couldn't help it, she smiled. "You don't...really?"

He wiggled his eyebrows. "Want to test it out sometime?"

She hesitated, and then shook her head. "Nuh-uh. On second thought...maybe."

He lifted her chin on the heel of his hand. "The bottom line is I love every goddamned thing about you because I love you." He settled a hand on her good shoulder, drawing her against him. "I love you, Mandy Delinkski. I love you, and I want to spend the rest of my life finding new ways to make you happy in and out of bed, so, what do you say? Do you feel lucky because if you agree to give this a try, to give us a try, I know I'll feel like the luckiest man on the planet?"

Mandy looked up at Josh, his handsome features drawn taut with tension and his blue eyes shadowed with uncertainty, and admitted that happiness in the form of a six-foot-four-inch hunk with a heart of gold was literally staring her in the face. So just what was holding her back? On the surface, the answer was a no-brainer—fear. But fear of what exactly? Fear of not measuring up to some ideal female size or shape that didn't exist beyond the pages of a fashion magazine? Fear of being happy, of loving and being loved back by an extraordinarily special man? *If that was the case, she'd better work on getting over being afraid starting right now.*

Her mother's wise words came back to her with crystal clarity, urging her not to be afraid. *If you want something or someone bad enough, you fight for it. You fight because fighting for it is the same as fighting for your future.*

And that was exactly what Josh was doing in coming back,

she suddenly saw. He was fighting not just for her but for them, for the chance at a future together. Could she do any less?

"I do feel lucky, lucky to have met you and made love with you, lucky to have you in my life for however long whether that means forever or just this moment." She drew a deep breath, gathering her courage to take the proverbial plunge. "If you really think you can be happy with a brassy Polish cop from East Baltimore, then be warned you're probably going to end up stuck with me because the thing is, I'm crazy, head-over-heels in love with you."

Sliding his hands on her hips, Josh looked at her, eyes sparkling with light and love. "In that case, instead of dinner out, how would you feel about Chinese carry out in bed?"

Rather than answer in words, Mandy wrapped her arms about his neck and lifted her mouth to his for the silver-screen-era kiss she'd fantasized about ever since he'd left.

Against her lips, Josh said, "God, baby, I've missed you so much." His hands went to the sash of her robe. Untying it, he pulled the robe open and then off, baring her body, still damp from the shower.

Following his downward gaze, Mandy had to admit there was something undeniably erotic about standing stark naked against a man who was fully and formally clothed, the worsted wool of his suit coat abrading her nipples, the crease of his pants leg chafing her inner leg—especially when he slid his hand down her belly to the warm, aching portal between her thighs.

Kissing him back, she said, "I've missed you, too, so much. Every time I touched myself, I couldn't help it, I pretended it was you."

"Well, you won't have to pretend any longer because I'm here. I'm here for you for as long as you'll have me." He leaned forward and kissed the raw, red scar topping her right shoulder. Drawing back, he shook his head. "God, when I think how close I came to losing you, not once but twice…"

"Shush." She laid a finger across his lips. He had the hands-down sexiest mouth she'd ever seen on a man, and remembering all the ways he'd used it to pleasure her had the warm wetness spurting between her thighs. "It's over, in the past. It's only the future we have to think about though right now the present feels like a pretty great place to be."

Only there was a big chunk of the past, *his* past, missing from his memory. Even though he'd likely write her off as crazy after she told him, she couldn't get past the need to fill him in on just how badly things could have turned out or rather just how lucky he—they—really were.

"Believe me, the present, this moment, is the only place I want to be." Smiling against her throat, he added, "God, baby, I want you so bad. Do you mind waiting on that dinner?"

Mandy thrust against his hand, willing his seeking finger to slide all the way inside. "Mind? You must be kidding. Only, Josh…"

"Yes, Mandy?"

Taking a deep breath, she held her hips still. "Before we go any farther, I really need to tell you just how very lucky we are."

Epilogue

Citations for bravery: one. Promotions awarded: one, to police detective, finally! Hunky boyfriends turned fiancé—and totally alive, thank you very much—one. Orgasms reached with aforementioned hunky fiancé: one so far today, before breakfast…actually *was* breakfast. Times mother asked when will settle down and start having babies like a good Catholic girl: don't know as live on own now, but given new status as engaged woman, would guess is zero, fucking zero!

Romantic sunsets walked off into hand-in-hand with Mr. Right: one—but then how many happy endings, make that Happy Beginnings, *does a girl need?*

AWARD PLAQUE IN HAND, Mandy slipped away from the office party in her honor to steal a moment alone at her desk. It had been an amazing afternoon, with the mayor himself turning out to award her citation for bravery as well as to personally pin on her detective's badge. Her parents, sister Sharon, Mikey and Suz had all stayed for the reception afterward and were eating cake and congregating at the conference table in the squad room next door.

But the icing on the proverbial cake was that Josh had flown back from Boston the night before to surprise her.

Looking across the room, she saw him cutting down the aisle between cubicles and coming toward her, heart-stoppingly handsome in a dark suit and burgundy silk tie.

Taking the paper cup of punch from her hand, he leaned over to kiss her. "Congratulations, detective." His warm breath hit her ear, drawing her shiver. "I have a gift for you, but I left it back at the apartment on your pillow."

"You already gave me the best gift I could ever ask for." She glanced down to her left hand where the tasteful diamond engagement ring sparkled from its Art Deco setting. The ring had belonged to Josh's grandmother, which only made it all the more special.

Dropping his voice, he said, "Well, think of this as more of a...novelty item."

"A novelty item, huh?" Smiling, she turned her head and whispered back, "Is it...naughty?"

He wiggled his eyebrows. "Do you even need to ask?"

Meeting the head-on heat of his gaze, she felt warmth rolling over her face and throat, part embarrassment but part desire, too. Definitely desire. "Is it for private time or would it be all right to enlist the help of an assistant?"

"As long as you promise to be very selective, I think an assistant would be a great idea. Got anyone in mind?"

She pretended to hesitate. "Well, the fact is there's a certain telecommunications executive who's a whiz with electronics. The only problem is I'm feeling the need to open my gift soon, very soon, and I'm not sure he's free for, um...lunch."

Ever since he'd opened a satellite office of Thornton Enterprises in downtown Baltimore, she'd gotten spoiled with seeing him for "meals" and just about everything else in between. It wasn't quite the perfect setup—for a while at least, he still had to fly back and forth to Boston once or twice a week—but on balance it worked, *they* worked, and Mandy couldn't imagine being happier.

"Why, detective, it must be your lucky day, because it so happens the executive in question has cleared his schedule for the rest of the afternoon, which means he's free not only for lunch, but also for dinner and any snack breaks in between."

"Really?"

He grinned. "Really. So what do you say to us trading in this punch for the bottle of Dom chilling in the fridge at home? After all, you only live once—more or less." He ended the statement with a wink.

Mandy looked up at him, the heat pooling in her panties matched by the warm glow enveloping her heart. She wanted him so much, she loved him so much, she couldn't wait to get him home alone, and her eagerness had nothing to do with opening her gift. The real gift was standing right in front of her and if there was any unwrapping to be done, it would involve getting him out of that pressed designer suit and into her bedsheets as quickly as possible.

Overwhelmed with happiness, she reached out and took his hand in hers. "Well, Mr. Joshua Sedgewick Thornton the Third, I guess I'd have to say that sounds like a plan—and to add that every day feels like Christmas Day, and my very luckiest day, because I get to spend it with you."

* * * * *

Ambience is everything. Imagine eating a foie gras at a luncheonette counter or a side of coleslaw at Le Cirque. It's not a matter of food but one of atmosphere. Remember that when planning your dining room design.
—Tips from *Teddi.com*

"Now that's the kind of man you should be looking for," my mother, the self-appointed keeper of my shelf-life stamp, says. She points with her fork at a man in the corner of the Steak-Out Restaurant, a dive I've just been hired to redecorate. Making this restaurant look four-star will be hard, but not half as hard as getting through lunch without strangling the woman across the table from me. "*He* would make a good husband."

"Oh, you can tell that from across the room?" I ask, wondering how it is she can forget that when we had trouble getting rid of my last husband, she shot him. "Besides being ten minutes away from death if he actually eats all that steak, he's twenty years too old for me and—shallow woman that I am—twenty pounds too heavy. Besides, I am *so* not looking for another husband here. I'm looking to design a new image for this place, looking for some sense of ambience, some feeling, something I can build a proposal on for them."

My mother studies the man in the corner, tilting her head, the better to gauge his age, I suppose. I think she's grimacing, but with all the Botox and Restylane injected into that face, it's hard to tell. She takes another bite of her steak, chews slowly so that I don't miss the fact that the steak is a poor cut and tougher than it should be. "You're concentrating on the wrong kind of proposal," she says finally. "Just look at this place, Teddi. It's a dive. There are hardly any other diners. What does *that* tell you about the food?"

"That they cater to a dinner crowd and it's lunchtime," I tell her.

I don't know what I was thinking bringing her here with me. I suppose I thought it would be better than eating alone. There really are days when my common sense goes on vacation. Clearly, this is one of them. I mean, really, did I not resolve less than three weeks ago that I would not let my mother get to me anymore?

What good are New Year's resolutions, anyway?

Mario approaches the man's table and my mother studies him while they converse. Eventually Mario leaves the table with a huff, after which the diner glances up and meets my mother's gaze. I think she's smiling at him. That or she's got indigestion. They size each other up.

I concentrate on making sketches in my notebook and try to ignore the fact that my mother is flirting. At nearly seventy, she's developed an unhealthy interest in members of the opposite sex to whom she isn't married.

According to my father, who has broken the TMI rule and given me Too Much Information, she has no interest in sex with him. Better, I suppose, to be clued in on what they aren't doing in the bedroom than have to hear what they might be doing.

"He's not so old," my mother says, noticing that I have

barely touched the Chinese chicken salad she warned me not to get. "He's got about as many years on you as you have on your little cop friend."

She does this to make me crazy. I know it, but it works all the same. "Drew Scoones is not my little 'friend.' He's a detective with whom I—"

"Screwed around," my mother says. I must look shocked, because my mother laughs at me and asks if I think she doesn't know the "lingo."

What I thought she didn't know was that Drew and I actually tangled in the sheets. And, since it's possible she's just fishing, I sidestep the issue and tell her that Drew is just a couple of years younger than me and that I don't need reminding. I dig into my salad with renewed vigor, determined to show my mother that Chinese chicken salad in a steak place was not the stupid choice it's proving to be.

After a few more minutes of my picking at the wilted leaves on my plate, the man my mother has me nearly engaged to pays his bill and heads past us toward the back of the restaurant. I watch my mother take in his shoes, his suit and the diamond pinkie ring that seems to be cutting off the circulation in his little finger.

"Such nice hands," she says after the man is out of sight. "Manicured." She and I both stare at my hands. I have two popped acrylics that are being held on at weird angles by bandages. My cuticles are ragged and there's marker decorating my right hand from measuring carelessly when I did a drawing for a customer.

Twenty minutes later she's disappointed that he managed to leave the restaurant without our noticing. He will join the list of the ones I let get away. I will hear about him twenty years from now when—according to my mother—my children will be grown and I will still be single, living pathetically alone with several dogs and cats.

After my ex, that sounds good to me.

The waitress tells us that our meal has been taken care of by the management and, after thanking Mario, the owner, complimenting him on the wonderful meal and assuring him that once I have redecorated his place people will be flocking here in droves (I actually use those words and ignore my mother when she rolls her eyes), my mother and I head for the restroom.

My father—unfortunately not with us today—has the patience of a saint. He got it over the years of living with my mother. She, perhaps as a result, figures he has the patience for both of them, and feels justified having none. For her, no rules apply, and a little thing like a picture of a man on the door to a public restroom is certainly no barrier to using the john. In all fairness, it does seem silly to stand and wait for the ladies' room if no one is using the men's room.

Still, it's the idea that rules don't apply to her, signs don't apply to her, conventions don't apply to her. She knocks on the door to the men's room. When no one answers she gestures to me to go in ahead. I tell her that I can certainly wait for the ladies' room to be free and she shrugs and goes in herself.

Not a minute later there is a bloodcurdling scream from behind the men's room door.

"Mom!" I yell. "Are you all right?"

Mario comes running over, the waitress on his heels. Two customers head our way while my mother continues to scream.

I try the door, but it is locked. I yell for her to open it and she fumbles with the knob. When she finally manages to unlock and open it, she is white behind her two streaks of blush, but she is on her feet and appears shaken but not stirred.

"What happened?" I ask her. So do Mario and the waitress and the few customers who have migrated to the back of the place.

She points toward the bathroom and I go in, thinking

it serves her right for using the men's room. But I see nothing amiss.

She gestures toward the stall, and, like any self-respecting and suspicious woman, I poke the door open with one finger, expecting the worst.

What I find is worse than the worst.

The husband my mother picked out for me is sitting on the toilet. His pants are puddled around his ankles, his hands are hanging at his sides. Pinned to his chest is some sort of Health Department certificate.

Oh, and there is a large, round, bloodless bullet hole between his eyes.

Four Nassau County police officers are securing the area, waiting for the detectives and crime scene personnel to show up. They are trying, though not very hard, to comfort my mother, who in another era would be considered to be suffering from the vapors. Less tactful in the twenty-first century, I'd say she was losing it. That is, if I didn't know her better, know she was milking it for everything it was worth.

My mother loves attention. As it begins to flag, she swoons and claims to feel faint. Despite four No Smoking signs, my mother insists it's all right for her to light up because, after all, she's in shock. Not to mention that signs, as we know, don't apply to her.

When asked not to smoke, she collapses mournfully in a chair and lets her head loll to the side, all without mussing her hair.

Eventually, the detectives show up to find the four patrolmen all circled around her, debating whether to administer CPR, smelling salts or simply call the paramedics. I, however, know just what will snap her to attention.

"Detective Scoones," I say loudly. My mother parts the sea of cops.

"We have to stop meeting like this," he says lightly to me, but I can feel him checking me over with his eyes, making sure I'm all right while pretending not to care.

"What have you got in those pants?" my mother asks him, coming to her feet and staring at his crotch accusingly. "*Baydar?* Everywhere we Bayers are, you turn up. You don't expect me to buy that this is a coincidence, I hope."

Drew tells my mother that it's nice to see her, too, and asks if it's his fault that her daughter seems to attract disasters.

Charming to be made to feel like the bearer of a plague.

He asks how I am.

"Just peachy," I tell him. "I seem to be making a habit of finding dead bodies, my mother is driving me crazy and the catering hall I booked two freakin' years ago for Dana's bat mitzvah has just been shut down by the Board of Health!"

"Glad to see your luck's finally changing," he says, giving me a quick squeeze around the shoulders before turning his attention to the patrolmen, asking what they've got, whether they've taken any statements, moved anything, all the sort of stuff you see on TV, without any of the drama. That is, if you don't count my mother's threats to faint every few minutes when she senses no one's paying attention to her.

Mario tells his waitstaff to bring everyone espresso, which I decline because I'm wired enough. Drew pulls him aside and a minute later I'm handed a cup of coffee that smells divinely of Kahlúa.

The man knows me well. Too well.

His partner, whom I've met once or twice, says he'll interview the kitchen staff. Drew asks Mario if he minds if he takes statements from the patrons first and gets to him and the waitstaff afterward.

"No, no," Mario tells him. "Do the patrons first." Drew raises his eyebrow at me like he wants to know if I get the double entendre. I try to look bored.

"What is it with you and murder victims?" he asks me when we sit down at a table in the corner.

I search them out so that I can see you again, I almost say, but I'm afraid it will sound desperate instead of sarcastic.

My mother, lighting up and daring him with a look to tell her not to, reminds him that *she* was the one to find the body.

Drew asks what happened *this time.* My mother tells him how the man in the john was "taken" with me, couldn't take his eyes off me and blatantly flirted with both of us. To his credit, Drew doesn't laugh, but his smirk is undeniable to the trained eye. And I've had my eye trained on him for nearly a year now.

"While he was noticing you," he asks me, "did *you* notice anything about him? Was he waiting for anyone? Watching for anything?"

I tell him that he didn't appear to be waiting or watching. That he made no phone calls, was fairly intent on eating and did, indeed, flirt with my mother. This last bit Drew takes with a grain of salt, which was the way it was intended.

"And he had a short conversation with Mario," I tell him. "I think he might have been unhappy with the food, though he didn't send it back."

Drew asks what makes me think he was dissatisfied, and I tell him that the discussion seemed acrimonious and that Mario looked distressed when he left the table. Drew makes a note and says he'll look into it and asks about anyone else in the restaurant. Did I see anyone who didn't seem to belong, anyone who was watching the victim, anyone looking suspicious?

"Besides my mother?" I ask him, and Mom huffs and blows her cigarette smoke in my direction.

I tell him that there were several deliveries, the kitchen staff going in and out the back door to grab a smoke. He stops me and asks what I was doing checking out the back door of the restaurant.

Proudly—because, while he was off forgetting me, dropping by only once in a while to say hi to Jesse, my son, or drop something by for one of my daughters that he thought they might like, I was getting on with my life—I tell him that I'm decorating the place.

He looks genuinely impressed. "Commercial customers? That's great," he says. Okay, that's what he *ought* to say. What he actually says is "Whatever pays the bills."

"Howard Rosen, the famous restaurant critic, got her the job," my mother says. "You met him—the good-looking, distinguished gentleman with the *real* job, something to be proud of. I guess you've never read his reviews in *Newsday*."

Drew, without missing a beat, tells her that Howard's reviews are on the top of his list, as soon as he learns how to read.

"I only meant—" my mother starts, but both of us assure her that we know just what she meant.

"So," Drew says. "Deliveries?"

I tell him that Mario would know better than I, but that I saw vegetables come in, maybe fish and linens.

"This is the second restaurant job Howard's got her," my mother tells Drew.

"At least she's getting *something* out of the relationship," he says.

"If he were here," my mother says, ignoring the insinuation, "he'd be comforting her instead of interrogating her. He'd be making sure we're both all right after such an ordeal."

"I'm sure he would," Drew agrees, then looks me in the eyes as if he's measuring my tolerance for shock. Quietly he adds, "But then maybe he doesn't know just what strong stuff your daughter's made of."

It's the closest thing to a tender moment I can expect from Drew Scoones. My mother breaks the spell. "She gets that from me," she says.

Both Drew and I take a minute, probably to pray that's all I inherited from her.

"I'm just trying to save you some time and effort," my mother tells him. "My money's on Howard."

Drew withers her with a look and mutters something that sounds suspiciously like "fool's gold." Then he excuses himself to go back to work.

I catch his sleeve and ask if it's all right for us to leave. He says sure, he knows where we live. I say goodbye to Mario. I assure him that I will have some sketches for him in a few days, all the while hoping that this murder doesn't cancel his redecorating plans. I need the money desperately, the alternative being borrowing from my parents and being strangled by the strings.

My mother is strangely quiet all the way to her house. She doesn't tell me what a loser Drew Scoones is—despite his good looks—and how I was obviously drooling over him. She doesn't ask me where Howard is taking me tonight or warn me not to tell my father about what happened because he will worry about us both and no doubt insist we see our respective psychiatrists.

She fidgets nervously, opening and closing her purse over and over again.

"You okay?" I ask her. After all, she's just found a dead man on the toilet, and tough as she is that's got to be upsetting.

When she doesn't answer me I pull over to the side of the road.

"Mom?" She refuses to meet my eyes. "You want me to take you to see Dr. Cohen?"

She looks out the window as if she's just realized we're on Broadway in Woodmere. "Aren't we near Marvin's Jewelers?" she asks, pulling something out of her purse.

"What have you got, Mother?" I ask, prying open her fingers to find the murdered man's ring.

"It was on the sink," she says in answer to my dropped jaw. "I was going to get his name and address and have you return it to him so that he could ask you out. I thought it was a sign that the two of you were meant to be together."

"He's dead, Mom. You understand that, right?" I ask. You never can tell when my mother is fine and when she's in la-la land.

"Well, I didn't know that," she shouts at me. "Not at the time."

I ask why she didn't give it to Drew, realize that she wouldn't give Drew the time in a clock shop and add, "...or one of the other policemen?"

"For heaven's sake," she tells me. "The man is dead, Teddi, and I took his ring. How would that look?"

Before I can tell her it looks just the way it is, she pulls out a cigarette and threatens to light it.

"I mean, really," she says, shaking her head like it's my brains that are loose. "What does he need with it now?"

nocturne™

**WAS HE HER SAVIOR
OR HER NIGHTMARE?**

HAUNTED
LISA CHILDS

Years ago, Ariel and her sisters were separated for
their own protection. Now the man who vowed
revenge on her family has resumed the hunt, and
Ariel must warn her sisters before it's too late.
The closer she comes to finding them, the more
secretive her fiancé becomes. Can she trust the man
she plans to spend eternity with? Or has he been
waiting for the perfect moment to destroy her?

On sale December 2006.

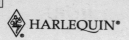

HARLEQUIN®

Happily Ever After Is Just the Beginning…

Harlequin Books brings you stories of love that stand the test of time. Find books by some of your favorite series authors and by exciting new authors who'll soon become favorites, too. Each story spans years and will take you on an emotional journey that starts with falling in love.

If you're a romantic at heart, you'll definitely want to read this new series!

Every great love has a story to tell.™

Two new titles every month
LAUNCHING FEBRUARY 2007

Available wherever series books are sold.

HEIBC

In February, expect *MORE* from

HARLEQUIN® Romance®

as it increases to six titles per month.

What's to come...

Rancher and Protector

Part of the
Western Weddings
miniseries

BY JUDY CHRISTENBERRY

The Boss's Pregnancy Proposal

BY RAYE MORGAN

Don't miss February's
incredible line up of authors!

REQUEST YOUR FREE BOOKS!

2 FREE NOVELS PLUS 2 FREE GIFTS!

HARLEQUIN®

Blaze®

Red-hot reads!